THE POLICEMAN

By

M. K. Jones

Cover Design: www.alicat-design.co.uk
Cover Image: Alamy Stock Photos

Chapter 1

1878

The man can run. He is fit and strong, I must concede on that point. But I am stronger and I will catch him. After all, his burden is heavy. I am panting a little. It is not easy to run in your Sunday best. My mouth is salivating with the thrill, not just of the chase but what will come at the end of it, which gives my legs impetus. I am closing on him. He will soon cease be the bearer of my secrets. In any sense.

He has reached the trees. Hmm. More difficult to follow than across this beautifully manicured lawn. Richard is so proud of his lawn, I swear by God he trims it every night before dark with his nail scissors. The landscape here is luscious. How droll, given its name.

He must be trying to reach the road at the far edge of this small wood. I wonder if he has transport waiting. It is of no concern. He will not reach it before I reach him.

He is slowing. I hear footsteps crashing through the undergrowth ahead. My pistol is ready. I will soon be upon him.

Ah, he has fallen. He has damaged his leg. He is crying. He looks up at me, eyes begging. He fears I will not heed his begging eyes. I move the burden to one side with great care. I cannot afford to have it impaired. Its profitability is in its flawlessness.

He is begging for his life, for his wife and children. I smile and nod. For an instant, his body sags with relief. I raise my arm. His eyes shoot upward, following my pistol, his lips move as tears run down his face. I understand this. He is begging his final forgiveness, of his God, of his wife, of his children.

I pull the trigger. I am a good shot. Through the forehead – dead centre.

Now I must return my precious burden, make sure it is safe.

Then I will come back and bury him. Deeply.

Chapter 2

Funerals

In an armchair in front of a blazing log fire, Maggie Gilbert looked up at the aggressive snow blasting itself against the windows, hoping it might force its way in and envelope her. She closed her eyes again and tried to block out the horror of the past two weeks.

Her partner Inspector Bob Pugh, who had been sitting close by got up, knelt in front of her and put his arms around her shoulders.

"It is not your fault," he said, hoping soon he would be able to prove it for her. "We're convinced it was a random hit-and-run."

He had not been allowed near the case, officially, given his almost-family connection, although he had kept himself informed of every piece of information coming in, every day. They were getting closer, he knew it. As a detective inspector with South Wales Police, he saw a pattern emerging in the discovery of each nugget of information. A man had been killed. They would not rest until the culprit was collared.

He stood up. "I'll make tea."

Maggie shivered, despite the excessive warmth in the room from the combination of central heating and wood fire and her outside coat which she hadn't taken off since they returned from the funeral. This was shock, she knew. She had been feeling cold since New Year's Day, when the phone call came.

Her son Jack had taken the call. She had been in the kitchen, enjoying a lazy morning. Earlier she had dropped her daughter Alice at the house of her former

5

schoolmate Janine. They were going to have a catch-up gossip on what had happened in the months since Alice's departure to the boarding school for gifted children who did not fit into mainstream education.

Maggie heard screaming coming down the phone as Jack held it away from his ear, his expression of panic, enough to tell her something terrible had happened.

She identified the voice as she got closer. Her sister, Fiona. She and Fiona had not seen or spoken to each other for months, which suited both. Now her stomach muscles tightened and clenched as she grabbed the phone from Jack and ordered her sister to calm down and tell her what had happened. She would never, ever forget what came next.

"He's dead. Graeme is dead. It's your fault." The phone clicked and hummed.

Maggie dropped the handset, picked up her bag and coat, told Jack to stay put and ran to her car. Throughout the thirty-minute journey to Fiona's house she had one thought. *Kennet Quinn.* Bob had organised some security for Fiona's family, which Fiona had not appreciated. She had blamed Maggie and her 'stupid job' for getting them into a situation where they had to be protected against implied threats from the Quinn family. Nothing had happened in the months since they had denied Rufus Quinn his longed-for statue of his ancestor, Councillor Adolphus Quinn. They had thought the security was overkill and it had been eased back but now...

Worse was waiting when she arrived at Fiona's house. The eldest of her three nieces, Jade, answered the door, wrapped in a heavy overcoat, her eyes red raw. Instead of letting Maggie in the girl walked out and hugged her aunt, resting her head on Maggie's shoulder, speaking in sobs and whispers.

"Dad was walking home from the pub on New Year's Eve, about eleven thirty. He was planning to get back in time to see in the New Year with us. He was laughing and chatting to his friend Mike when a car came straight at them, veered across the road and hit him." She paused for a moment and dug her fingers into the back of Maggie's coat.

"It... it tossed him into the air, then drove over him on the ground before it sped off."

"Did his friend see who was in the car?"

"No. The police are on it now." Jade raised her head and wiped her nose on her sleeve. "The ambulance came soon enough and rushed him to hospital but he was dead by the time they arrived. The doctors said he had never had a chance; his injuries were too great." She paused again, looking over Maggie's shoulder. "Mum thinks it was that man who's giving you the trouble."

Maggie stood back. "Can I come in and talk to her?"

She turned towards the front door but before she could take a step it flew open and her sister Fiona charged up to them, pulled Jade away and spat, "This is down to you. You've killed him. You and your vile job. I will never speak to you again. Now get out of my garden. Get away from my family." Holding onto her daughter by the shoulder, Fiona stumbled back in and slammed the door.

Maggie didn't move, her brain numb. She didn't know whether to bang on the door, demand to be let in, or do what Fiona said and leave. No-one appeared again. After a few minutes she turned away.

At home Bob, summoned by a panicking Jack, had arrived. He had already talked to the local police who gave him as much detail as they had so far. When Maggie returned, pale, trembling and silent, he sat her down in the kitchen with Jack.

"All they know at the moment is it was hit-and-run. They've identified the make of the car and the colour and they're checking CCTV in the area. I've told them I'm associated with the family and I want to be kept involved. How's Fiona?"

Maggie told him.

"Right. I'm not going to give you any platitudes like 'she's grieving', which she is, or 'she'll come round' because you and she haven't been close lately. Give it time, will you. Give her a chance, at least."

Maggie sniffed and nodded.

Jack jumped up from the table. "I'm going to message Jade."

"Wait," Maggie called him back. "She's grieving, too. Don't be hard on her, Jack. She's not her mother."

"I lost my dad, too, in a terrible accident," he said and walked away.

"Oh my God, I've forgotten about Alice," Maggie said. "I must tell her."

"Wait. Remind me, what time are you due to pick her up from Janine's house?"

"At three. You're supposed to come with me."

"Well, it's almost two. Nothing is going to happen to her in the meantime. Let's think this through."

"I can only think about Graeme. How could this have happened, Bob? He is... he was the nicest, most innocuous, fair-minded, decent person. It's so wrong."

He moved into the seat next to her and put his arm around her. "It's always wrong," he murmured.

* * *

After picking Alice up and delivering her safely to the house, Maggie had called her colleagues Zelah and Nick and told them what had happened.

"How is Alice taking it?" Nick asked.

"It's hard for her and Jack," Maggie replied. "Too many memories. Jack contacted his cousin Jade earlier. They have something in common, now."

"Are you going to contact your sister again?" Zelah's question.

"I don't know," Maggie replied. "Not right away. I want to hear more about what's happening. Bob has explained how the investigation takes place. There's a lot of work for the police to do."

"What does he think about... you know?"

"He isn't saying. He thinks it sounds like a random hit-and-run, too. He's going to keep close to the investigation. He'll keep me informed."

"Will you go to the funeral?"

"Of course. Whether she'll let me into the chapel is something else."

* * *

Bob reappeared with a mug of tea and put it into her hands. Maggie hadn't worn gloves to the chapel, which was as cold inside as out and her hands were still tingling. Bob and Jack had accompanied her. Alice had declined.

Blowing gently on the tea, Maggie thought through events they had just experienced at Graeme's funeral.

As the coffin entered, from her position at the far end of a bench at the back of the packed congregation, she saw her sister following with her head down, her hands grasping a daughter on each side with Jade walking in front of her. Fiona didn't see Maggie. At the end of the emotional service, as Fiona walked past again, glancing at the people on either side, she caught sight of Maggie and was in the process of raising an arm in anger when Jade and Lucy stopped her, pulled her arm back and drew her forward towards the vestry.

Maggie's little group had waited until the chapel was empty. They had tried to leave without being noticed, but were waylaid in the doorway by Graeme's brother. Expecting an onslaught, Maggie steeled herself not to respond, but he put out a conciliatory hand and without hesitation she took it.

"It wasn't your fault," Dennis Morgan said, chiefly to Maggie but loudly enough for Bob and Jack to hear. Turning to Bob, he added, "We appreciate your lot are doing everything you can. Any progress?"

"Some," Bob replied, "but it's not my case." He glanced around. "But there might be news in a day or two."

Maggie's head whipped around towards Bob, to ask the question, but his expression shut her down. They left shortly afterwards. Fiona had kept away from her.

* * *

Bob sat back alongside her as she cradled the cup in both hands and the pain increased as the heat thawed out the numbness.

"You said back at the chapel there was news. What news?" she asked.

"There's a lead," he replied. "All I can say for now. And before you ask, no."

"No, it wasn't them or no, you aren't going to tell me?"

He stood and walked towards the door. "I can't. Don't push me."

As she sat grasping the mug, her mind wandered like a speeded-up film across various scenarios, watching but not touching. She was roused by a noise close by, a persistent tapping. A few taps, then a few seconds silence, then a few more. She looked up. At first she couldn't make out where it was coming from and it annoyed her. It seemed to be somewhere at the back of the room, at the bottom of the French window leading out onto the garden. Looking down, she saw sitting on the sill and tapping away with his beak a robin redbreast. Maggie had been leaving seeds and nuts out for him over the past few days, since it began to snow, but today she had forgotten. She smiled.

"Somebody appreciates me."

She called out to Bob to bring in a handful of seed, then opened the door and threw it onto the snow-covered patio. The bird bobbed his head from side to side for a moment, then hopped over to the food. She watched him for a few minutes until he stopped, gave her one last beady stare and flew off.

"See you tomorrow," she murmured and made her way across the hall to the office, the former dining room of her Cwmbran home that she had turned over to Maze Investigations when she, Zelah and Nick set up the company five years previously.

* * *

It wasn't as if there was a lot of work to distract her. The usual post-Christmas slump gave Maze breathing space, to catch up on filing, reply to posts and comments, to organise a get-together about what they thought the coming year would bring and any special new ideas. Maggie had an idea and she walked across the hall into the office to pick up on what work she could find.

Although she enjoyed her work, had been immersed in it in a way she had never been in a previous career, what had gripped her in the past twelve months was finding she was a particularly dogged investigator who could not resist a brick wall. As soon as she found herself up against one, her inner warrior, or terrier, had risen up and not just seized the challenge, but treated it as a personal duty to bring the wall down. She found the sweetness of success the most satisfying thing she had experienced in her time as a family history researcher. So much so, she was planning to put this to Zelah and Nick as a separate, dedicated arm of their business. Maze Investigations: Brick Walls No Bother. Or something like that, in better marketing language.

Lunchtime passed. The tea Bob made for her had gone cold as she continued to think on the rudiments of her plan and how to pitch it to Nick and Zelah – where were they? The memory came as a gut punch. Graeme's wasn't the only funeral today.

Rufus Quinn was being buried this afternoon. Where Graeme's funeral was quiet and dignified, Maggie knew Rufus' funeral would be a magnificent show of the great and the good, suited and booted.

Rufus had died in his bed, of a massive heart attack. Given how much the man drank, Maggie wasn't surprised at his death at the age of sixty-eight. The last time she had seen him, in the Council Chamber where the approval for the statue of his revered ancestor, Adolphus Quinn, was passed but would never materialise thanks to Maze, she thought he looked... what? Old, saggy, hunched? After the meeting, she had seen him red-faced and puffing as he climbed the stairs, pausing for breath halfway up like a mountaineer gulping down precious oxygen.

Would Kennet Quinn blame Maze for his father's death? Yes. Their thwarting of his father's plan had annoyed him and he had subtly threatened them all, so much so they had been under the watchful eye of the police for months, although this had recently eased off.

Kennet appeared to be concentrating his efforts on his property empire, which had lately been encountering difficulties, courtesy of Zelah. Was Graeme's death a consequence of Zelah's relentless efforts to bring Kennet down? Kennet Quinn was capable of it. He had beaten his own daughter close to death in front of Rufus – who had done nothing to stop it. In Kennet's psychopathic brain his daughter Mischa had betrayed him, so he was justified in taking revenge. He would know by now Zelah was taking care of Mischa, had arranged for somewhere for her to live and would support her through university. Maze had taken one of his family, he would take one of theirs. This had been on Maggie's mind since Graeme's death. Nick and Zelah had probably thought it too, and Bob, but no-one said anything. A sure sign they saw it as a possibility.

Bob was in the kitchen on the phone and she caught a few words that made her sit up. "Bloody great news, thanks," and went to see what he was talking about. What could possibly be great today?

"Colleague in Abergavenny on the phone," he said. "They've got something." He took her hands in his. "I'll tell you, but you can't tell anyone, you understand, not yet."

"She wouldn't take a call from me anyway," she replied, snuggling into his chest. "What news?"

"They've got him."

Chapter 3

She jumped back. Bob nodded. "Little bastard. Seventeen years old, from Ebbw Vale. Nicked the car with his mates. We knew it was nicked, earlier on New Year's Eve. He was high and showing off. They aren't sure he even saw Graeme, just heard a thump. Didn't bother stopping to look. His mate told him he'd hit someone, but he just drove off."

Maggie screwed up her eyes, wanting to howl in anger. "How did you... they find him?"

"The mate gave him up. Found out the man they hit was dead and couldn't live with it. He walked into the station yesterday and gave it all up, told us where the car was. Forensics are on it since yesterday."

"What next?"

They sat down. "The driver's been interviewed. Broke down, didn't he. Tried to tough it out, but the evidence was too great, with his mate's confession. There's still a lot more to be done, but he's been charged."

"With murder?"

"No. For now they believe he didn't set out to kill Graeme. That's no excuse, but time being it'll be causing death by dangerous driving whilst under the influence. I'm expecting he doesn't have a licence and has previous. The maximum sentence is fourteen years, under the usual terms of seven in prison, seven out on licence."

She sat down. "You hear about it, but it's so different when it's your family. So if he doesn't get the maximum sentence, he could be out earlier?"

"Depends on whether he shows any remorse. Likely he'll get a brief who persuades him to plead guilty; but he never gave himself up. That should count towards a longer sentence."

He reached out across the table and took her hand in his. "I'm so sorry, love."

She frowned. "And was there a suggestion anyone put him up to it?"

"No. He's been asked the question. Didn't know what they were talking about. From what I can gather he's too stupid to act that well. If someone did put him up to it, it would have been for money for his habit. They're going to check it out but the feeling right now is no, no-one did."

"When will Fiona find out?"

"I understand it'll be tomorrow. You can't speak about it before it's official."

"I won't. I promise." She stood up. "As much as I'd like to say it's a relief Kennet Quinn isn't involved, I can't. Will the boy be let out now he's been charged?"

"No. It's too serious. He'll be on remand."

"I was starting to do some work. Distract myself."

"Good idea. I need to phone my sergeant."

"Need?" she replied, grinning, as he left the room, phone in hand.

Since Bob told her the replacement for his old sergeant was a newly promoted detective constable, thirty-five years old, single, fit and attractive, she had been teasing him, which he had taken in good humour. Then she met Sergeant Sherry Martin. There was something about her Maggie didn't quite take to.

Bob's description was accurate. Sherry was blond, intensely blue-eyed and tall. Judging from her physique she was someone who spent her non-working hours in a gym, or running up a mountain. She was a skilled kickboxer and practised karate. She was polite and keen to make a good impression. But regarding the latter, Maggie got the sense, from her body language, tone and expression, the woman had an agenda. Nothing she said or did had, so far, given anything more interesting away, so for the time being Maggie decided to take Sherry at face value. Zelah hadn't liked her either, but that didn't necessarily mean anything. Disliking people was Zelah's first base. Then Nick said Sherry flashed more intense energy when she was face-to-face with Maggie which confirmed there was something else going on. She wondered if it was Bob. Sherry's lips and eyes widened ever so slightly when she looked at him. Perhaps this was admiration for his skills, but Maggie suspected it was more than learning his skills Sherry might be wanting. Enough of that. More important things to think about.

An hour later she had read, replied to and filed her emails. There was always background and admin work to do. The team had built a shared log of research items on each of their projects, so if one of them had spare time they could pick up an item, put time in and record the results. She went to it, but half-heartedly and couldn't see anything that woke sufficient enthusiasm to get started on. She had just decided to call it a day when the sound of the front door opening and voices in the hall caught her attention. Zelah and Nick were arguing. She couldn't make out many of their words as Nick rarely raised his voice but his inflection was curt.

She leaned over to open the door wider. "Is this a private argument or can anyone join in?"

"Zelah attended Rufus Quinn's funeral," Nick said as he walked into the office and put his briefcase on his desk. "I was saying she shouldn't have gone. Anyway, how are you? How was it this morning?"

Zelah followed him in. "Did she make it difficult for you?"

"No," Maggie replied. "But she might have, as they were leaving, if the girls hadn't pinned her arms down. Outside we kept away from her. Graeme's brother Dennis came over to speak, though. He doesn't hold me responsible."

"Does he know about Kennet Quinn?" Zelah asked.

Maggie started to speak, but remembered she couldn't. "I'm not aware of how much Graeme or Fiona said outside of the family. Knowing Fiona it's probable she told everyone, even though she wasn't supposed to. Graeme? I'm not sure. I never got chance to ask him." Her voice wobbled at the end of the sentence and Nick jumped in with, "The police will find out, soon enough."

Maggie nodded, hoping it wouldn't be too long before Bob's news became public.

Bob finished another call and came in pulling his coat on. "Sorry, must go. News on a case." He raised his eyebrows at Maggie and she nodded. "See you later?"

"Yeh, I think so."

"What was that about?"

"What?" Maggie replied, looking away from Zelah.

"I saw that look."

"Personal stuff," Maggie said. "Not for public consumption."

Zelah leaned forward to retort, but a touch on her arm and a shake of the head from Nick stopped her.

"Well, do you want to hear about the funeral rites of the great and the good, or not?"

"Well, you want to tell us, so crack on."

"Kennet adopted a suitably sad expression. Interesting news – the lovely Helen Redland was with him. And she's pregnant, looks as if it might be due any day."

18

"Wow, that was quick," Maggie said. "I wonder if she was already having an affair with him when brother Tim died?"

"Wouldn't put it past her," Zelah replied. "She struck me as being a girl not to miss an opportunity, when we met her at the Quinn house. She's probably as evil as her maniacal brother was, so well-suited to pair up with Kennet. I pity the baby."

"Indeed. What else?"

"Talking about Kennet's offspring, Gerard looked uncomfortable. He spotted me but against my expectation he didn't tell his father I was there. I suspect young Gerry is having private thoughts about his absent mother. He sort of snarled at me, though I did wonder if it might have been a smile. Anyway, it was a fine turnout by the Council. Speeches praising Rufus' good works and charming character etcetera, etcetera. The mayor saw me, gave me a quick nod. I recognised some councillors and some Arts Committee members. There were other smart suits. That's about it. They toddled off to the cemetery, then on to a sumptuous feast, to which I was neither invited nor welcome. I didn't see any people who looked like his tenants."

"Not surprising," Maggie replied. "I expect they're glad to see the back of him."

"But he hadn't been at the forefront of the housing and tenancy business for some time, had he?" Nick interjected. "Kennet took it over a good while ago."

"And God help them now," Zelah said.

"Maggie, is there anything you want us to do especially, this afternoon?" Nick asked. "Why don't you take a break, have a nap, whatever. You seem tired."

"Nothing specific," she replied. "I've been looking at the research items, but I can't see anything there in need

19

of urgent attention. If you don't mind, I'll just sit here. I need the company. I have this new book about marriage customs I've been meaning to read since Christmas. By the way, any news on your son?"

"No," he replied, turning to his computer. "I thought he might be back in the country, but that was a false hope."

"I'm sorry, Nick," she replied. He shrugged. Ever since Nick had dropped the bombshell back in the summer that he had a grown-up son, he had been more open about his efforts to find the boy, who would now be around eighteen.

"Something will break, soon. You're making enough effort." When he didn't reply she put her feet on the settee, adjusted her glasses and opened the book. Nick and Zelah began to read emails and messages.

Before Maggie reached halfway through the first chapter she was distracted by an "oh" from Nick.

"What's up?"

"A news item," he replied. "And an email. They seem to match. Weird."

Zelah stopped what she was doing. "What does that mean?"

"My old, closed case, of the missing Liverpool policeman, William McRoberts, you remember? I thought this was going to be the ultimate brick wall." He stopped and returned to the screen.

"Hello, earth to Nick, what's the story?"

"Sorry, Zelah. Just thinking. Right. You remember your visit back last summer to the medium, what was she called?"

"Claire. Claire Lewis, and she talked about McRoberts, and something about him lying on fallow ground?"

"That's right. Well he's not lying on fallow ground."

"It was a hillside," Maggie said.

"Exactly," Nick replied. "Well, not exactly."

"Just tell us, will you," Zelah said with a sigh.

"It's not a hillside and it's not fallow in the sense of uncultivated wasteland. That could have been anywhere. It's Fallough Hill. It's on Anglesey. This news report," he pointed at the screen, "says developers were preparing the ground to turn what has been an old, ruined mansion into a resort and golf club. They were digging out a trench for utilities when they found a skeleton, on the edge of the grounds close to the old roadway. It dates from around the 1870s."

"Not a police matter, then," Maggie added.

"No, more than seventy years ago, so it's archaeological. They got the dating from a coin."

"Why would it be him? And if it's him," Zelah said, "what would he have been doing there?"

"It's not far from Liverpool," Nick replied. "He could have been on a case. He was a detective."

"What's the second thing, Nick? You said there was an email."

He looked back from the screen. "It's from the descendant who asked me to look into William's disappearance. I'd told him a few months ago we got the information – I didn't tell him at first where from – that William was supposed to be lying on a fallow hillside, but I had no more information. Of course, he asked where it came from then, so I told him about the medium. He thought it was a bit 'out there'. Anyway, I said to keep in touch, because you never know when something new comes up, which it has, on his side. I'll read the email."

He picked up the laptop and turned around. "He says, *Hi Nick, you said to get back in touch if anything new came up, regarding William McRoberts. Well, it has. My uncle just moved house. He's in his late eighties and needs care so he's going into a home. He was born in the family home and never left. When we moved him out just after the New Year I found a couple of old suitcases full of stuff in his bedroom. Inside one were photographs and letters and other papers. One of them tells a strange story, about William McRoberts' disappearance and explains why you haven't been able to find a death record for him. Can you call me or even better, get to Liverpool to see me? Regards, John McRoberts."*

"Interesting," Maggie said. "But this doesn't give any clue the skeleton is William McRoberts."

"No, that's true. However, what's more than interesting is the skeleton has a bullet hole in the front of its skull."

"OK, worth following up. What are you going to do?"

"Not sure," Nick replied. "I think I'll go to Liverpool, if that works for you both. I can meet with John. If there's anything in his uncle's documents connecting to this place in North Wales, I'll get hold of the people at Fallough Hill, tell them we might be able to provide a potential identity for their skeleton."

"Yes to both," Zelah replied. "I have a case to write up. What about you, Maggie? Do you want to work this week?"

"Most definitely. Not today, but from Monday I'll get back to business. Jack's a bit less stressed now his mock exams are done and Alice is coming home tomorrow for the weekend. We'll have a quiet family weekend."

"Good luck with that," Zelah muttered. "I'm going away this weekend, too. I'm joining Mischa and the boys in Alpbach. They're skiing. I'm going to watch and encourage."

"When are you back?"

"Monday morning. I'll be here around lunchtime."

"So you'll go to Liverpool?" Maggie said to Nick.

"I'll seize the day and see if John McRoberts can meet tomorrow. I might ask Stella if she's free and we'll stay the weekend."

"Just a moment, are we still dealing formally with this client? Is he going to pay for this additional work?" Zelah asked. "Because, interesting though it is, we are not a charity."

"We weren't a charity on the Quinn case either, Zelah. We took it on because of your medium friend Madame Ramona, who turned out to have lied to us. We don't have a lot of work, but that will change soon, but—" Maggie didn't get any further.

"Ex-friend. And I paid for the hours we spent on the Quinn case."

"You didn't tell us that," Nick replied. "I'll pay for the trip to Liverpool this weekend. I sense this is going to be an important case, and one which could bring us a lot of publicity. I won't pursue it, though, if you don't want me to."

"I want you to pursue it. I want Maze to pursue it. He's right," Maggie said to Zelah.

Zelah shrugged. "I agree, it's interesting, but we can't prioritise it over our paying clients, Maggie."

"I wasn't suggesting we should, Zelah," Maggie retorted, turning away.

"How about I go to Liverpool tomorrow, speak to the client, and report back to you both on Monday. Then we can decide about what to do next."

Zelah turned back to her laptop with a grunt, which Maggie presumed meant agreement.

She nodded at Nick, sat back on the sofa and picked up her book, thinking, with any luck, Bob's news would be out by Monday and they could relax, just a little. Because the tension level in the room needed serious dialling down.

Chapter 4

Kennet Quinn paced around his living room for the third time, slapping his hand against the back of chairs as he passed them.

Helen sat in silence in front of the fire, knowing better than to interrupt when Kennet was in a rage. He was normally a controlled man. She had no idea what happened to make him this angry on the day after his father's funeral. She had expected a quiet few days whilst he made plans. Something, however, had not worked out and Kennet was waiting for his son Gerard to arrive. There was going to be trouble. Whatever Gerry had done, Kennet was not in a forgiving mood.

He ceased his pacing to pause for a moment in front of her, putting his fingers on the baby bump; he smiled at it, then paced again. Helen smiled back at him, supressing the shudder whenever he touched the squirming, agitated thing growing inside her. She didn't think she could stand it much longer. She had been secretly looking at ways of inducing it out, but they seemed to come with an element of risk she couldn't afford. This baby was her meal ticket. Once it was out, there would be a nanny; she would insist. Her mind shrank away from the conversation with Kennet during which he told her how important it was for her to feed it herself. Disgusting thought though it was, it would have to be endured, for a short while. She flicked back her long auburn hair, stood up, stretched and strolled over to warm her hands in front of the fire. A squeezing pain bent her over and she grasped her stomach and winced.

Kennet ambled to her side. "Is everything alright, my dear?"

"It's fine, Kennet. Just practice contractions. Please, don't fuss. Here." She took his hand and placed it on the bump. "Squirming around nicely. He's looking forward to meeting us in person."

"Let's hope this one has brains." He walked to the window, looked up and down the street, muttering, "Where the hell is the idiot boy?"

"He'll be on his way, Kennet."

"I told him 'now'. I expect him to run. Ah, at last."

He went to stand with his back to the fire, nodded to Helen to sit and she scooted into the armchair. He stood feet slightly apart, arms by his sides. The stance and the expression didn't change as his son flung the door open. Gerry paused on the carpet. He knew the stance.

"Explain yourself."

"What, um, what do you mean, Pa?" The boy shuffled towards the fire, hands in pockets, eyes wide, going for nonchalant.

"Sit." Kennet nodded to the expensive leather chesterfield couch, against the back of which Gerry was now leaning, keeping himself propped upright, hoping his father couldn't see his shaking hands.

"I said sit."

The boy pulled his hands free and scurried around the settee, falling into its deep centre. Kennet took slow steps across the room, stood in front of the settee and looked down, piercing his son with his unblinking black eyes.

"You have messed up."

Gerry's heel was tapping uncontrolled on the carpet. "I'm sorry, Pa. I did what you said."

"No," Kennet growled. "If you had done what I said we would not be in this position. You were not supposed to be in the car. Total deniability."

"I used my initiative, Pa. It was going to go wrong."

Kennet closed his eyes for a few seconds.

"You think it hasn't?"

"It's... It's going to be OK. They think my name is Jack Quincey. I never told them about you, honest." His muscled arms and neck twitched but he attempted to display his usual inane grin.

Kennet put his hands up to his face, covered it for a second, and, before Gerry could react, reached down and pulled his son out of the chair, holding him inches away.

"You believe Inspector Pugh won't recognise you from the description the others will give? Where is the money?"

"I told Malky to hide it. Look, Pa, he was high. You told me to get him high so if he did get caught, he could say it was the drugs. He was supposed to knock the guy over, but he was out of control. He took something else as well as what I gave him. I got into the car after I seen the bloke leave the pub, didn't I, to stop it being, I dunno, to stop it being too much, but Malky was crazy. Soon as I'd pointed the bloke out Malky drove straight at him. He was laughing and screeching. I took over the driving and got us out of there pronto. I had gloves on all the time so there's no fingerprints. We put the car in the lock-up I'd arranged, but Jez decided to take it out again and set fire to it. I'm sorry, OK, Pa. I did my best."

"You chose your tool badly. You have let me down. I cannot now use the threat of injury." He sighed. "I have made arrangements. Your tool will be removed. You will go away for a while. There will be evidence showing you left the country before the accident took place."

The boy's cheeks drained of colour. "Away? By myself? Where?"

Kennet sighed again and let go of Gerry's collar. "You will be accompanied. Probably Mr Kostov, not Mr Dawes, he has work for me here. Now go to your room and pack. Do not come out until I call for you."

Gerry's eyes, filling with tears, turned to Helen for support. She turned away from them, raised a hand, examined her nails. He slunk out and made his way up the stairs. As soon as he was gone Kennet nodded to Helen. "I have arrangements to make." She gave him her sweetest loving smile, which disappeared as soon as his back was turned.

Chapter 5

Liverpool 1878

Lizzy McRoberts could not take any more. Willie had been gone the best part of a week already. He hadn't told her how long he'd be away. He never did and she didn't worry, so why was this different? There was nothing else for it, she would have to visit and speak to Mrs Butler. She disliked the thought of being seen with 'that woman', but, after all, that woman had encouraged Willie and, Lizzy believed, entered into a secret plan with him. Well, it was time she was party to their secret. She put on her coat and hat, picked up her handbag, calling to John her eldest to mind the younger children, and set off.

Her neighbour Gertrude Wainright, always on the lookout, popped her head out of her open front door.

"Off somewhere, Mrs Mac?"

Lizzy smiled as graciously as she could manage, pursed her lips, squeezed her handbag and hurried on. Gossiping Gert was bound to find out soon enough. No need to give her a head start. A visit to Mrs Butler would raise eyebrows amongst certain types.

Mrs Butler lived in a different Liverpool to the likes of her and Willie. Lizzy loved her home in Troughten Street, with its two feet of frontage and its own gate separating the door from the street. No sharing, either. The McRoberts family had gone up in the world since they arrived in Liverpool from Scotland with their young son and taken rooms. Willie had been successful, too, since joining the Constabulary, rising from a constable to a detective officer in less than five years and him not even forty years old. Then, the terrible thing happened. Lizzy lived in dread, thinking they would have to leave their neat little house. So she had, naturally, supported Willie's desire to retain his investigative skills, as a private detective. He had been pleased his many friends in the Constabulary, who knew the truth, continued to support him with help and information. At first, the cases were scarce and Lizzy feared he would never be able to earn enough to keep them in the luxury to which she had become accustomed. It was just a little terraced house but it boasted three bedrooms. She had her own kitchen. They didn't have to share the privy out back and there was plenty of room in the kitchen to set up the weekly bath.

But there simply hadn't been enough work for him and he even talked about returning to Scotland, which would have been the lowest admission of failure. Then just when they were on the point of despair, along came Mrs Butler, who made Willie an offer. A wonderfully lucrative offer.

He hadn't told her the details, knowing Lizzy did not approve of Mrs Butler. Lizzy approved of educating women, mind you. Having herself been an illiterate farmer's daughter who had been taught to read and write by her husband, and discovered she too had skill, with numbers. She wanted her daughters to rise above the illiterate class and had insisted they go to school, as well as her boy. Willie agreed. What Mrs Butler did in Liverpool, however, was another matter. As far as Lizzy was concerned, the woman had no shame.

Thinking over the events of the past weeks had taken up the whole of the walk, and she found herself in front of Mrs Butler's house before she had chance to think about what to say. This was the grand, fashionable end of Toxteth. She imagined it would be a good-looking house, but what was now in front of her, viewed through the closed, high, intricate wrought-iron gates, was palatial. Well, she must get in so she would say whatever came to her when she found herself in front of the woman. First dilemma, how to get in? The gates appeared to be locked. Was there a servants' entrance? She'd be more comfortable, but where was it?

As she stood and puzzled a man came out of the front entrance and walked along the drive towards her. He opened one gate with a latch she had not seen and paused.

"Can I help you, my dear woman?"

Lizzy saw a clergyman's collar and was put at ease.

"I wish to speak to Mrs Butler, your... um, Sir." She held her head up, and saw he was frowning. She must have said the wrong thing. "I'm sorry, but..."

"No need to be sorry, my dear." His warm unaccented voice held no contempt for her class. "My wife has gone out in the past hour and I don't believe she will return until late this afternoon. May I be of help?"

His wife! Mrs Butler was married to a clergyman? This was beyond expectation and altogether shocking.

"Mrs Butler has engaged my husband in some work, Sir, and since he went away five days ago I have had no word from him. I was hoping to find out if Mrs Butler has news."

"You must be the detective's wife. Mrs McRoberts?"

"Yes, Sir. That is me."

"I'm sorry to say I cannot help at this moment. If you would allow me to take a note of your address, when my wife returns she can visit you to inform you of any news she has?"

Lizzy shook her head. George Butler hid the smile that came to his lips. He understood perfectly why this woman might not want his wife at her house.

"I can return later, Sir. Perhaps this evening?"

"If you prefer, Mrs McRoberts, we will be pleased to welcome you. Would you, perhaps, dine with us?"

Lizzy's head shook so violently George couldn't hold in the smile.

"No, thank you, Sir," she stammered. "It is kind of you to ask, but I must consider my children. I will visit at six, if that is convenient."

"That would indeed be convenient, Mrs McRoberts. Until later, then." He held out his hand, which she touched lightly with trembling fingers, and walked off in the direction of the city.

Lizzy leaned on the gates to steady her shaking legs. His smile was kind, but the thought of going into that house, through the front door, caused her to clutch her stomach to quell the onset of nausea. But, she had to find out what was happening with Willie. She would come back later and endure.

* * *

The knock on the door came at five, as Lizzy was about to set off to the Butler house. It was a loud, firm knock. She put her bonnet back on the kitchen table and prayed silently Mrs Butler had not decided to pre-empt her visit.

As she walked along the hallway she could see two figures through the glass. The woman must have brought her husband. She took a deep breath and opened the door. Two people stood there, one familiar, George Harbison, Willie's former colleague, now in uniform. The other man was dressed in a good suit and a bowler hat. She stared at them.

"May we come in, Lizzy?" George Harbison said. "We need to speak to you."

"What, why..." Her thoughts were a stampede of confusion. She clung onto the door handle, not moving, not daring to think.

"Inside," the other man said, and pushed past her, followed by Harbison.

They walked towards the kitchen, but she called out, "No, in here," and opened the door to the parlour, which was kept pristine for Sundays and visitors. The children, who had been in the back parlour, came out into the hall, but she frowned and shook her head, directing them back.

"Please sit, Lizzy," George Harbison said, taking her elbow, and gently pushed her into a chair, then he closed the door.

"Who's he?"

"This is Chief Inspector Monaghan, Lizzy."

"You!" She jumped out of the chair. "Get out of my house!" She walked to the door and opened it.

"Sit down, woman," Monaghan barked.

"Lizzy, please," Harbison begged gently.

"I will not sit. You may say what you have to say, then you will leave."

"Very well. Your husband is dead. His body has been found in the river, washed up at the dockside."

"Liar! My husband is away from the city. He has a commission. What are you trying to do now? Is not destroying his career with your lies enough for you?"

As Lizzy and Monaghan stared each other down, the door flew open and a tall youth rushed in. "Ma, what's the matter?"

She took him to stand beside her and put her hand on his shoulder, as much for support as for comfort.

"This man is leaving, John," she said, pointing at Monaghan, "but you may stay, George. You can tell me in truth what has happened."

Without speaking Monaghan nodded to George Harbison and left the room, slamming the front door on his way out, no doubt, Lizzy thought, to ensure the neighbours knew something was amiss.

"Lizzy, why don't we go into the kitchen and make ourselves a cup of tea," George Harbison asked.

She nodded and led the way. Now the hated Monaghan was gone, she could feel the twitching of muscles in her throat. She directed John into the back parlour, ordering him to look after his sisters.

"No tea, George. Tell me what this is about." This time she sat at the table where the family took their meals. He sat to the side of her, scraped his chair forward and took her hand.

"I am so sorry, Lizzy, but it's true. Willie's body was found this morning." He captured both of her shaking hands and squeezed tight.

"I don't believe it. I want to see him." She jerked her hands away.

Harbison shook his head. "Monaghan says no-one can see him. Apparently his body has been in the water for several days and is not fit to be seen by anyone, let alone a woman."

"Monaghan is trying to prevent me, then? I will see this person, who is not my husband." She had been looking into space but turned to rivet her gaze on him. "I must see this person."

Again Harbison shook his head but before he could speak further, there was a loud knock at the front door. Lizzy sighed. "That will be Mrs Wainright, my neighbour. Come to enquire. She cannot bear not to know." But as she approached the door, there were again two figures. She opened the door to the Reverend George Butler and a shortish, emaciated and pale-looking, well-dressed, pretty woman.

George Butler reached out a hand and Lizzy extended hers, as he introduced his wife. She stumbled through a request for them to come in and led the way to the kitchen where George Harbison stood waiting. His eyes widened when he saw who had come to visit. They all stood in silence for a few seconds.

"I have forgotten my manners," Lizzy said. "Reverend and Mrs Butler, this is Constable Harbison who is a friend and former colleague of my husband."

They both extended a hand and George Harbison shook each, never taking his eyes off Mrs Butler.

"My dear Mrs McRoberts," George Butler began. "We received terrible news and have come at once." He looked at Harbison. "I see others are here before us."

"They are telling me my husband is dead, has been found in the river, but they will not let me see the body."

"Who will not allow a woman to see her husband, Mrs McRoberts? Why not?" Mrs Butler asked in a quiet, steady voice.

"Because it is not suitable for a woman, Mrs Butler. According to Chief Inspector Monaghan."

"Him. I see. May I sit, Mrs McRoberts?"

Lizzy shook suddenly. "Of course. We must go into the parlour. Please follow me."

Once they were seated Lizzy spoke first. "It is a nonsense, naturally. He is away from home executing the commission you gave him," she paused and nodded at Mrs Butler, "I was becoming concerned about his long absence and came to your house earlier to ask for news."

"My husband informed me. I am sorry to say I have none, Mrs McRoberts. He sent a telegram on Tuesday to say he had discovered the whereabouts of... something stolen and would be returning as soon as he could reclaim it. There has been no further communication."

"Then he was looking for stolen property?" George Harbison asked.

"In a manner of speaking, yes," Mrs Butler replied.

"What was stolen?" he asked.

"A child," she replied.

Chapter 6

Liverpool 2020

John McRoberts had been more than willing to meet with Nick the following day. Stella had no events at the weekend, January being a quiet month for her, too so Nick booked them a hotel for three nights on the Liverpool waterfront and after travelling on Friday morning they were ready for the meeting with John in the hotel lounge.

"This must be him," Nick said, waving at a short man dressed in a t-shirt, leather jacket and jeans who entered the bar, waved to the barman who waved back, and strolled over to their table. Nick introduced himself and Stella.

"Lovely to meet you at last, after our many chats," John said, looking up at Nick who was half a head taller. "I've brought everything."

"Excellent," Nick replied. He glanced over at the barman. "I'll get you a drink. What will you have?"

"Pint of bitter, please."

"Are you a regular here?" Nick asked.

"Never been here before in me life. Bit posh for me, to be honest. Why do you ask?"

"You and the barman seemed to know each other."

John smiled. "This is Liverpool, Nick. We're friendly people. I'm a friendly bloke."

He had arrived with a large brown envelope under his arm, the contents of which he now deposited on the table they had chosen next to the window overlooking the Mersey River.

"I've had a go at sorting this lot out, Nick," he said. "These are the ones that are going to interest us." He picked three sheets out of the pile and handed them to Nick who opened and scanned the first one, but stopped to check the sender. His eyes widened and he looked back at John.

"Do you know who this is from?"

"Er, yes, a woman. Called Mrs Butler," John replied.

"This isn't just any Mrs Butler," Nick said. "This is Mrs Josephine Butler." He smiled expectantly at John then at Stella. When neither replied he said, " *The* Mrs Josephine Butler?"

"Nope. Sorry, Nick. No idea."

"Me neither, John," Stella added. "But I'm guessing we should know. Was she famous?"

"Not as much as she deserves to be," Nick replied, staring again at the letter. "Josephine Butler was one of the most influential women in the country in terms of the advancement of women's rights in the nineteenth century. She fought on a national level."

"Like the Pankhursts?" Stella asked.

"Not really. She was before their time, although she did support votes for women. The Pankhursts were more interested in the voting rights of middle-class women. Josephine Butler's campaign began here, in Liverpool.

She came from a good middle-class family with high connections. Her parents were principled people and gave her a strong Christian moral base. She moved here with her husband George. He was a clergyman who became principal of a school. Josephine became fixated on the terrible situation of poor destitute women. In particular, women who turned to prostitution to feed themselves and their families." He smiled. "You are sceptical, John."

John McRoberts blushed and scratched his balding head. "Well, working girls, you know. I'm not sure."

"It wasn't the same then," Nick replied. "Poor women generally weren't educated and there were few jobs open to them. When they were widowed, or deserted they had nothing to fall back on. The workhouse or sell themselves were the chief choices. Some got work as servants but that option wasn't available to married women."

"What did this Mrs Butler do?" Stella asked.

"Mainly, at the start, she invited some of the women to come to stay at her own house. Then she opened what she called a 'house of rest' where the women could get respite, learn a trade and go on to a better life. Then she began to campaign for the rights of women and she led the opposition to the Contagious Diseases Act, which was one of the most insidious attacks ever on women's rights." Nick shivered and Stella took his hand.

"I've never heard of it," John said.

"It's a long story and no time to go into it now. There's plenty of material to read. She was also involved in campaigning against the trafficking of young women and girls for use in brothels. People believe this is a modern, imported thing, but it isn't. The Victorians were doing it, but they were exporting, as well as importing.

Victorian trafficking rings took girls as young as twelve, which was the age of consent. They lured them abroad, to Belgium and Paris mainly, with tales of jobs and a good life. Sound familiar?"

"Indeed," Stella said.

"They were sold to brothels and they couldn't get out. The police were in on it, taking their passports and registering them under false names and ages. Josephine Butler was responsible for having the Belgian head of the *Police de Moeurs* removed, prosecuted and imprisoned."

"What's police de... whatsit?" John said.

"Morals police. A special force. They were in on the trade to make sure the girls couldn't get away. Read about it, if you've got a strong stomach. You'll need it."

"And she did this in Victorian times?" Stella asked.

"Exactly," Nick replied. "Victorian women weren't expected to admit sex existed, never mind consider talking about it, in public, too. Apparently Josephine Butler was an electrifying speaker. For such a delicate middle-class woman who was often in poor health, she was a force of nature."

"So, her writing to Lizzy McRoberts was something special," John said.

"We have found ourselves a fascinating mystery," Nick replied and returned to reading the letter.

Stella and John McRoberts sat in silence, on the edge of their seats, until Nick put down the letter.

"OK. John, you've read this?"

"Yeh, but I didn't understand what was going on."

"It seems to me it was written with forethought," Nick replied. "There's as much between the lines as on them."

"Can I see," Stella asked, reaching out for the letter. Nick handed it to her, and she read aloud.

"*My Dear Mrs McRoberts,*

"*I have been to meet with the Chief Inspector. I have also petitioned the Chief Constable. They have agreed to let you see the body and I will accompany you. They are insisting on a verdict of suicide, by reason of shame at his dismissal from the force and the reason for it, no publicity and burial under a pseudonym. In these circumstances they believe an accommodation can be made for a pension for you. I do not believe they can be persuaded away from these terms, despite my encouragement to them to reveal the truth. The Chief Constable informed me there is much at stake, more than he can say. He inquired into the reason for my involvement and I gave him to understand your husband was undertaking a commission on my behalf. At that, he blanched and advised me in the strongest possible terms to leave well alone. I think I must leave the matter in your hands, for only you can decide what is best for yourself and your children. I shall continue to pursue my own discreet enquiries. Please be assured of my willingness to be of any and all assistance to you whenever you might feel the need of it. You have only to ask. May God guide you and be of comfort to you in your difficult hours. Josephine Butler.*"

Nick turned to John McRoberts. "There's your brick wall starting to collapse, John. We couldn't find him because he was buried under a false name."

"But it doesn't give any clue what name, Nick."

"No, but now we accept that's what happened, we can search for clues. We have the approximate date he died. There would have to be an inquest in addition to registration of the death following the inquest. This is all discoverable."

John McRoberts grinned. "So there's an end to it."

"No, John. Think about it. Our information is he was buried on a fallow hillside. Not he drowned in the Mersey."

"Well, that was, you know, a bit dodgy, wasn't it?"

"Maybe not. Here's what I haven't told you, yet." He handed across the table a printout of the newspaper report on the discovery of the skeleton.

John McRoberts read it, his expression at first puzzled, then transforming into amazement. "Fallough Hill. A fallow hillside. So, this could be him?"

Nick nodded. "It's enough of a coincidence for us to check it out."

"This says nothing was found on the skeleton to identify it."

"That's true, but it has a bullet hole through the skull, and William McRoberts was on a commission away from Liverpool. Knowing that, my reading of the letter is something was going on above the level of the Chief Constable. A man of high rank doesn't misidentify and hide a body unless he has a good reason." He paused for a moment. "Look, John, you just asked us to investigate a missing relative. This could go way beyond. If you want to leave it at this, we'll understand."

John McRoberts sat up straight. "No way, mate. I'm in. What do we do next?"

"We make a plan, which I want to mull over. Can we meet again this evening? Would you join us for dinner? And can I have the rest of the papers to read in the meantime?"

"No problem. I've got a few things to do today. I could meet you about seven-ish?"

Nick glanced at Stella who beamed and nodded. "Can't wait," she said.

* * *

Nick and Stella decided on a short stroll before the evening closed in as they were so close to the main attractions of the Liverpool Docks. After walking along the river path to explore the Albert Dock and the Beatles exhibition, the latter having been Stella's long-held ambition, they walked arm in arm along the river to the museums in amiable silence, wrapped in coats, hats and scarves against the biting wind gusting off the Mersey.

Nick stopped for a moment, gazing across the river.

"I do believe you're humming," Stella said. "What's the tune?"

"It's 'Ferry Cross the Mersey'," Nick replied. "I always loved that song. Look, there's the ferry. Let's sit for a moment."

After a few minutes watching the small boat reach the Wirral side of the river Stella asked, "What was in the rest of the papers? Anything useful?"

"There was a letter from someone after William's death, a relative perhaps, because it talks about 'coming back home', which was Scotland. Whoever was writing it advised Lizzy McRoberts to accept the offer, take the pension and get out of Liverpool."

Stella pulled her scarf closer around her neck as a ferocious gust of wind whipped up. "Is that what she did?"

"No, she stayed. She had enough money to open a small corner grocery shop the following year. What we've learned today explains where the money came from. She ended her days living with one of her married daughters, in Walnut Street."

She put her head on his shoulder and slipped her arm through his. "What's the plan, then? You have one, I take it."

"Yes. We should get in touch with the site office at Fallough Hill. I've checked, and there is a number. I'll tell them what we know, or think we do. They'll be pleased to hear that if the skeleton does date to the 1870s there's a chance we can identify it."

"How can it be identified?"

"DNA is the best bet. Let's hope they can extract it, and I'm sure John will give a sample, but I'll check with him tonight."

Stella shivered. The light was fading behind them. "Let's get back to the hotel. I could do with a warm drink and a bath. Ready for more plotting and planning."

He grinned at her as they stood and walked back along the river path.

Chapter 7

Nick's phone call to the site office on Anglesey led to an invite to visit the following day. The site manager told them there was an archaeologist working there who would be grateful to speak to them. John McRoberts was waiting at the hotel the following morning and they set off for the drive under the Mersey and across the River Dee into North Wales.

"Look at the scenery; isn't it beautiful here?" Stella remarked an hour or so later as they crossed the Britannia Bridge onto the island of Anglesey, where there was a clear view of the snow-capped Snowdonia mountains. "And it's so green."

"That's because it rains a lot," Nick replied as he turned the car off the bridge and onto the main road towards Beaumaris. "See there."

Stella sat forward in her seat to see the view between the Britannia and Menai bridges. "How lovely," she said. "We must come back to explore in the summer."

"We used to come here camping every year with the kids," John said from the back seat. "Lovely beaches around the island. We had wonderful times. Now they want warmth and luxury hotels, the great grown-up snowflakes."

Stella looked around and saw he was laughing. "How far now, Nick?"

"About ten minutes. We go through Beaumaris then watch out for a turning on the left. There should be someone at the gate to meet us."

"Isn't there a castle in Beaumaris?" Stella asked.

"Yes, and no we don't have time," Nick replied. "We'll come back in the summer, so don't pout. You'll be able to see it from the car."

After they passed through the town of Beaumaris, slowing so Stella could take in as much as possible of the medieval high street and the fortress castle sitting next to the sea, they reached the turning where, twenty yards along a lane, the site manager was waiting for them. He opened a six-foot-high gate topped with barbed wire and closed and padlocked it once they were through. Then he got into the back of the car with John McRoberts.

"Alexander Fielding, good to meet you all. Sorry about the security. We get a lot of trespassers."

"Why?" Nick asked.

"It's the remains of the house. It's become a popular venue for thrill seekers on the trail of lost houses. You'll see when we get there. Urban Explorers, they call themselves. The idiots have no idea how dangerous it is. Apparently there's an App to find houses like Fallough Hill throughout Wales."

At the top of the drive they reached a small single-storey porta-cabin building. "Here we are," Fielding said and got out, leaving them to follow him inside.

The walls in the small office were covered in plans and drawings. Two computer screens sat on a desk covered with randomly scattered papers.

"Can't invite you to sit, as you can see we don't have enough chairs," Fielding said. "But the boss will be here in a couple of minutes with the archaeologist. They're going to take you to the site of the, err... find."

"Who is the boss?" Stella asked.

"Sir Trystan Wyn Davies. The house and land have been in his family since the seventeenth century. Do you know anything about it?"

"I did a little research," Nick replied. "I thought planning consent was refused?"

"That was a few years ago. We have consent now for a luxury hotel and resort. We'd just started to clear the land when we found your friend. Bit of a shock, as you can imagine. Damn nuisance, actually."

"Mr McRoberts has been searching for his relative for years. Not a nuisance for him," Stella replied.

Fielding had the grace to blush. "Sorry, not thinking."

John McRoberts, who was standing half hidden behind Nick, peered round and smiled apologetically.

Before anyone else could comment, the glass door to the porta-cabin flew open and a man and a woman dashed in. The man was over six feet, taller than Nick and head and shoulders above John. He was dressed in Barbour outdoor gear and wellington boots, and a peaked cap.

The woman was also tall, also in a Barbour but where his was pristine hers was scruffy and covered in mud, as were her boots. Her head wasn't covered but her long grey hair had been pulled back into an untidy bun, emphasising a horsey face, long with a prominent chin.

The man pulled off his cap revealing a head of well-cut black hair and thrust out his hand, which Nick stepped forward to shake.

"Trys Davies. Pleased to meet you." There was a slight inflexion of North Walian accent. The rest was English public school.

Nick made the introductions and turned to the woman, who said, "Felicity Holmes, archaeologist," and nodded at each of them.

Trystan Wyn Davies turned to John. "Our skeleton might be an ancestor of yours, then?"

John bobbed his head and said, "Possibly, um – Sir...
what do I call you? I'm not used to mixing with the
aristocracy."

"Trys is fine. Let's go and observe the scene, shall
we? John, perhaps you can fill me in about your relative
on the way?"

He turned and marched out of the office with John at
his side. Felicity shrugged and fell in behind him. Nick
took Stella's arm, returned her amused smirk, and
followed on.

After they walked through a copse of trees they
crossed what might once have been a lawn, but was now a
muddy, weed-infested, knee-high scrub with the
occasional patch of grass. They were heading towards a
small wood. To their left, at the head of a slight incline,
was a mass of trees, shrubs and bushes. Nick stopped
and called out, "Trys, just a moment, please. Is that the
house?"

Trystan Davies walked back to join him, glancing up
the incline. "Sadly, yes, what's left of it. Nature takes its
revenge seriously. It's been wholly invaded."

"How much can you save?"

"A surprising amount, I'm pleased to say, which
includes the outer façade and most of the main ground
floor rooms. We'll have to replace most of the back, the
kitchens, etcetera, and upwards. The upper interior
floors are gone. Just the main staircase left, but the steps
are rotting. The workforce is clearing around the back
already and shoring it up. That's where we found... it.
Would you like to see the front, when we're done?"

"Love to," Nick replied.

"After we visit the discovery site. Let's go then."

At the far side of the lawn they rounded the edge of
the wood and circled to the left. "I can hear traffic. Are

we close to the road here?" Stella asked. "I've lost my bearings."

"It's another hundred yards or so away. We've come round in an arc from the site office. Here we are."

He stopped in front of a tent, about fifty yards from small digging machinery, at the end a trench leading away from a pile of rubble. "Felicity can take over from here."

"We've put this up to protect the remains from the weather and any damage," Felicity said in a low, gruff voice. "One at a time, please."

"You go first, John," Nick said.

"I'd like you in there with me, Nick."

"Not a problem," Trystan said to the frowning Felicity. "After all, Nick and John have given us a lead on identification." His tone inferred no argument. She scowled, but didn't object, and opened the flap of the tent.

Inside was a tall light shining into a hole in the earth, around four feet deep.

"Must have taken someone a long time to dig by hand," Nick said, peering down.

John edged forward and looked down for a few seconds then straight back up. "I need air," he said and backed away out of the tent. Outside he bent over, hands on his knees, breathing deeply.

Stella ran forward, fearful he was going to collapse. "Are you OK, John? What happened?"

He took a few more breaths and uncurled his body. "Wasn't expecting that," he whispered. "He's a long way down, beaming at me, and a hole in his forehead. His arms are folded on his chest. What does it mean, Stella?"

"I would say it means someone buried him deep in the expectation he wouldn't ever be found, John. Skeletons always look as if they're grinning."

48

Nick emerged from the tent and walked over to them, rubbing dirt from his hands. "I knelt to get a closer look. Do you want to take a look, Stella?"

She paused from a moment, thinking of John's reaction, but curiosity won out. "Just a quick look," she said and entered the tent. Nick and John waited whilst the hum of voices came from inside for a few minutes, before Stella emerged.

"Not much evidence left now, Felicity says. She thinks he would have been shot close by and buried soon after." She turned to John, who was regaining colour. "Whoever did this wanted to be certain he would not be found. There are a few scraps of cloth but they indicate underwear, not outdoor clothing."

"So he was stripped before he was buried," Nick said.

Felicity came out of the tent and joined them. "Yes, he was stripped to his underwear, I suspect. It would have made him harder to identify if he had been found earlier."

"What about the coin?" Nick asked.

"That's an odd thing," Trystan interjected. "It was found underneath his pelvis, as if it was on him when he was buried."

"Unless the person who killed him dropped it," Nick said. "But, we can include it in our investigations. It was a penny, I think Felicity said?"

"Yes. I've looked it up. It's not particularly valuable. It's called a 'young head', dated 1860."

"William died in 1878," Nick said. "Why just the one coin? Did whoever buried him miss it, perhaps?"

"Perhaps. We aren't likely to find out, are we." Felicity Holmes said.

"I wouldn't count on it," Stella replied. "Nick and his colleague Maggie love a conundrum."

Felicity scowled at her but didn't respond.

"What happens next?" John asked.

"We have a forensic anthropologist coming here later today who'll tell us if it's possible to extract DNA from the few strands of hair on the skull still attached, and from the bones and teeth. If you are willing to give a DNA sample, Mr McRoberts, I'm hopeful we can verify the identity," Felicity said.

"Do you have any further information about the victim?" Nick asked.

"I've made a few initial observations, but I would prefer to wait for the expert later," Felicity replied.

"Naturally. You'll let us have any news?"

"Yes, we will," Trystan interjected. "I'll call you myself. Now, if there aren't any more questions, shall we take a closer view of the house?"

Again, he walked off, without checking if they agreed. Felicity Holmes didn't go with them. By the time they crossed the lawn area again Felicity was already back in the tent, oblivious to the outside world, kneeling next to the skeleton, tenderly brushing away more soil.

Trys Davies came to an abrupt halt in front of a twenty-foot-high clump of weed-strangled bushes. "You can't see but the front of the house is just behind this mess here. We can't go inside the structure; too dangerous, but I can show you the frontage."

"Fine with me," Nick said.

"If this is where William died, I'd like to see something of the building," John added.

"OK, follow me."

With the appearance of an explorer entering deepest jungle, Trys began to heave aside overgrown shrubs and step through them. Behind Nick, Stella tripped and stifled a giggle. He looked around at her.

"Dr Livingstone, I presume?" she whispered.

Nick checked a smirk. "Quiet. This is a privilege." Stella adopted a mock serious expression. Nick wagged a finger at her and she poked her tongue out at him, but as they both turned back their expressions changed to awe.

There was enough grey stone showing through the barrage of wild greenery to make out the original size of the mansion. The front portico was half smothered in a tangle of weed, and shrubs had grown in through the windows up to the second floor. The roof was long gone and plants taken root inside, reaching through the floors to the sky. As they stood looking up and down, from side to side, taking in the magnificence of what remained of the structure in its last throes, the atmosphere became abruptly still, no hint of the breeze previously swaying the branches, and a chorus of birds burst into a lament of song. Stella shivered. "Is it haunted?" she asked.

"There are those who say so," Trys answered. "I spend a lot of time here, walking and watching. I've seen many different, odd things. Once for a few seconds someone came rushing down the main stairs behind me without the sound of footsteps. I've thought I'd seen a group of figures staring at me from the first-floor windows. All imagination of course."

"I worked for years as an archivist in Knyghton House, near Newport," Nick said in a low voice. "I know what you mean. Old places can carry an impression of their history."

Trystan Davies gave him an appreciative look. Then he shook himself.

"Well, we can't stand here, so let's get back to the office."

He walked away but Nick noticed John McRoberts was still standing, staring.

51

"John, we're leaving."

"Not yet. Another minute."

"Why?" Nick went back to stand beside him. He looked at John, then called out to the others, "You go on. We'll be there in a few minutes." Then he said, "What are you feeling, John?"

"I'm... not sure, exactly. I don't know how to explain it. Something terrible happened here." He gave Nick a twisted smile. "This is a first for me. You must think I've gone funny."

"Not at all. I've seen something like this before, with my colleague Maggie Gilbert. Is it as if there's an impression of something, that doesn't quite make sense?"

"Sort of, yeh." He shook his head. "I can't explain it."

Nick put a hand on his shoulder. "Let's get back to the office. Once we're on our way back, I can help make some sense of it."

* * *

They agreed Trys would phone them as soon as there was any news from the forensic anthropologist who would organise John's DNA sample. Before they began their journey back to Liverpool, Nick showed Trys the letter from Josephine Butler.

He spent a few minutes reading it through, then he looked at Nick and said, "I was sceptical when you told me about your medium, although I was intrigued. But this..." He shook his head. "This is different. A man came here as a detective and was murdered, by someone at my family's property."

Nick nodded. "Do you want to find the truth, Trys? This has been a game changer for John, too. He had to

52

decide if he wanted to back off. How about you? You understand the implications, I think."

"Of course. It could have been a member of my family. I want to know. Please keep me informed." He nodded at them and left the porta-cabin.

* * *

"So what was it you were going to explain to me, Nick? About what I felt back there?" John asked as soon as they hit the dual carriageway.

"My colleague, Maggie Gilbert, began her work with Maze after an experience bearing similarities to yours. She was working in an unofficial capacity with our founder, Zelah Trevear, at the time. Zelah has a theory about inherited memory. It proved to be the case for Maggie. She had memories inherited from an ancestor of hers who had a child go missing. Because of those memories she was able to discover the fate of the missing child. I'm wondering if you caught glimpse of something which happened at the house."

"It was, like, someone was there trying to tell me something, and there was a shape but I couldn't see any more than an outline. It wasn't an argument, more a discussion. I can't recall what they were saying, like trying to remember a conversation from a dream. It was odd, I can tell you. Never happened to me before."

"Our colleague Zelah says these memories are dormant, until something provokes them into life."

"Hang on a minute, Nick. They can't be related to William, can they? I mean, if that was him back there, and if he never got back home, there wasn't anyone to pass the memory on to, was there."

"No," Nick replied. "I was just thinking about that. It could be someone else went looking for him. His wife, perhaps. Or his son."

"That would be my great great grandad, John McRoberts. A son has always been called John since then. I suppose it's possible. Although he was killed in a tram accident when he was a young man."

"Was he married?" Stella asked.

"Yes, he was, Stella. His son John wasn't born until after his dad died. His wife was pregnant when he died, with my great grandad, who was known as Jake. He was born in 1903. Do you think John could have gone looking for information about William, and something happened?"

Nick turned around in the front passenger seat. "John, is it possible his death wasn't an accident?"

"Oh my God. I don't know. He's supposed to have tripped and fallen in front of a tram. Might he have been pushed? Why?"

"Let's not get too far ahead of ourselves. We'll add it onto the list of things we need to investigate," Nick replied, hearing the tension in John's normally unruffled voice. "I'll keep you informed, of course. We'll have to come back here to visit the central library again but we'll see what we can find online when we get back."

John sat back and closed his eyes. "Thanks. There's something going on here."

"I suspect, John," Nick said, "that we may have something of greater significance on our hands than we expected. Let's go find out what it is."

Chapter 8

Zelah sat at her desk for an hour before she realised she had written less than a hundred words of her latest family history commission. Her weekend away had been enjoyable and fun. She put Maze into the background as she watched her two nephews teach Mischa Quinn how to ski. She went tobogganing with them one afternoon and treated them to expensive meals. Then she left them for another couple of days and returned home, back to her obsession.

These days her mind was almost exclusively on her behind-the-scenes battle with Kennet Quinn. So far she had been successful in having a dozen of his properties condemned as unfit for human habitation. Knowing he would not be interested in the cost of doing them up, she had, through a couple of companies she set up, bought them at rock-bottom prices. In each case he suffered a substantial loss, which pleased her. She would have to invest in them herself and had already begun to do so through a renovation company. Lately, however, her solicitor informed her Kennet Quinn appeared less concerned, shrugging off the losses with apparent unconcern. He must be guessing he was being squeezed out of the market, but had he discovered it was her? She doubted it, she had covered her tracks too well. She enjoyed the stories of his initial annoyance, but wasn't ready yet to reveal she was the cause of his problems. Several his properties would never be subject to being condemned, as he also catered for the higher end of the market to maintain his company's reputation, but Zelah thought she could reduce him to a state of worry, at least, as they fell one by one. Recently, though, the stories being reported back to her were not of anger, but bordering on indifference. That worried her. Had she gone too fast, pushed him down new paths to make up for his losses? She needed to find out what he was up to, but wasn't sure yet how to do it.

When she first told Maggie and Nick about her plan they were enthusiastic, but cautioned great care. The most important thing to be sure of was Kennet Quinn could not find out Maze was in any way connected. Zelah also told Rick Matheson, her close Canadian friend who she met on a visit to Nova Scotia for a Maze case. He, too, cautioned against haste. She knew he was right, of course, but she couldn't help herself. It had been working well, but now, it wasn't. She pondered on whether it might have been because of Rufus' death. It had come as a shock, although Kennet must have realised how ill his father was; but for someone as psychotic as Kennet Quinn, would a death have such a profound effect on him he put a hold on his business? No. Zelah didn't believe he had any more care for his father than for a stranger on the street. Rufus had been out of the business for a couple of years, having handed over the reins to Kennet. Kennet turned it into a nasty but lucrative property letting and management business with the emphasis on tenants at the low end of the market who wouldn't complain, and if they did, found themselves on the business end of a 'discussion' with one of Kennet's so-called property managers, including the also recently deceased Timothy Redland. The discussion began with threats and ended with beatings, sometimes severe and life-threatening, after which they stopped complaining. Perhaps he was planning to diversify. This seemed a more acceptable reason for his behaviour. So, what was he up to? And how was she going to find out? This was the thought obsessing her.

Zelah also knew it was time to give Nick and Maggie an update. The death of Maggie's brother-in-law had distracted them and no-one had asked her about the property plan since then. She wondered if Maggie was now thinking Kennet Quinn might have ordered Graeme's death because he found them out. No-one asked. That might be speaking for itself. Were they still on her side?

She closed her eyes and thought again about how she and Maggie met, in the library at Newport; how Maggie had not then and never since judged her, just accepted her for the person she was. Apart from her husband Martin, no-one had ever treated her so respectfully. She was not generally liked, which never troubled her. She had built a protective wall of indifference around herself, high and impenetrable. Until along came Maggie, then Nick. With them Zelah had discovered the value of trustworthy friendship, but with it came vulnerability.

The opening of the door behind her distracted her train of thought on how she would engineer the conversation.

"You look contemplative," Maggie said, balancing a tray of coffee on one hand as she closed the door with the other.

"What time is Nick getting here?" Zelah asked.

"He said about ten-ish. I guess we're going to have a catch-up."

"He said he's had an interesting weekend. Lots to tell us. I have an update, too."

Maggie paused for a moment, then handed over a mug. Zelah leaned over to fill it with steaming black liquid, stirred in three teaspoons of sugar, as usual causing Maggie to wince, and sat back.

"How's Jack doing?" Zelah asked, putting down the mug.

"Why do I get the feeling you're distracting me?"

"It's a genuine question. He's seemed tense lately."

"He's waiting for his mock exam results. He's got three university offers, but he wants Cardiff, which has the highest requirement. If he can hit it now, he's got his best chance in the summer. He can do it. Worrying, of course." She sat at her desk. "It's tougher on kids now than it used to be. Anyway, I suspect there's a girl involved."

"Usually is," Zelah replied. "He hasn't talked to you?"

"No; it may be something he can talk to Bob about, this time." She took a slow sip of coffee.

"Sex?"

"Likely. He keeps avoiding eye contact."

"He'll be fine. He has a good moral base here, with you and Bob."

"New for Bob, too. First time, in loco parentis, with a man-only conversation. He'll handle it."

"Will he tell you?"

Maggie thought for a moment. "I hope not, for Jack's sake. He needs to know he can trust Bob. If he wants his mother to find out he'll tell me. If not, well, as long as he has confidence in Bob, that's fine with me. How about Mischa?"

"Hell no, she doesn't discuss anything so personal with me. The kid had to make her own way and work it out for herself. Can you imagine her talking to Kennet, or Rufus? But, I thought I saw a closeness between her and Niall, when we were in Austria."

Maggie smiled. "Two souls deeply damaged by their respective parents. Here's Nick. Time to find out about Liverpool."

Once Nick settled himself down, having deposited a stack of papers on the table, they gathered around, ready for him to start.

"You first," Maggie said, nodding at him. "Yours is the most interesting news."

"We have a case here, a big, significant case, one that will bring us a great deal of publicity if we can solve it." He sat back, to Zelah's intense annoyance, but she knew enough about him to know he was mentally preparing his next statement.

"Well, go on, then. What's so special about it?"

"I'll explain, but first, a recap of what we knew before we went to Liverpool. Then what we found out when we got there, and what this might mean, for Maze." He stopped again.

Zelah folded her arms and clamped her lips together. Maggie could see from his tiny darting eye movements Nick was getting the proverbial ducks in a row.

"Right. Recap. We knew John McRoberts' ancestor, the police detective William McRoberts, disappeared without a trace, around 1878. We got the message from Claire Lewis his body was lying on a fallow hillside. Which has most likely turned out to be Fallough Hill, on Anglesey, where a body was found recently with a bullet hole through its forehead, dated to post-1860 by a coin in the grave."

"Was it a deep grave?" Maggie asked.

"Yes, but I'll get to that. At the same time as the Fallough Hill news, John told us a house move by an elderly family member turned up a collection of papers, old papers, from around the time of William's disappearance."

"So the papers can be dated?" Maggie asked.

"No, sorry. That was me getting ahead. Next, Stella and I met with John on Friday in Liverpool. Nice chap. Enthusiastic, or at least, he was on Friday morning."

He paused for a moment. "It's quite different when it's real, in front of you. Once we got to Fallough Hill on Saturday and saw the grave with the skeleton in it, John was in a state of shock. Anyway, I've gone ahead again. When we first arrived there we met the site manager, Alex Fielding. He introduced us to the site owner, Sir Trystan Wyn Davies. Nice man. Plus the archaeologist, Felicity Holmes. Bit dour. Trys and Felicity took us across the estate to where they found the body. The place is an overgrown jungle. Sad. Anyway, Trys let us see the body, or rather the skeleton. Then he took us closer to what's left of the house. Quite a lot, actually, but dangerous. They were expecting a forensic anthropologist later in the day. John has done a DNA sample and they are going to compare it to DNA they hope to extract from the skeleton."

"You were talking about the papers," Zelah said. "Can we go back, please?"

"Sorry, yes. Right. We met with John on Friday afternoon and he brought most of them with him. Some of them weren't connected, but there was one of particular value, and importance. I've made copies for you." He handed them a set of papers from the pile on the table.

"The first, and the important one, is this one." He held up the copy of the handwritten letter, brown with age, that John McRoberts had shown them. "Read it through."

Maggie finished first. "He got a commission from this Mrs Butler, whoever she was. His body was found and I suspect there was something badly wrong with his death. Why a pseudonym and..." She stopped as she caught sight of Zelah's expression of surprise so great Maggie thought her eyes were about to pop out.

"Is this who I think it is?" she said to Nick, ignoring Maggie.

"Yes, it is. We got our hands on one of her never-seen-before letters." He was beaming.

"I seem to be missing out on the inside information here," Maggie said. "Should I recognise this woman?"

"You wouldn't have come across her in mainstream history, although we should know who she is. Josephine Butler was one of the, no, *the* most influential campaigner for the rights of women of her generation." Before Maggie could reply Zelah added, "She cared about poor women, in particular prostitutes. Women whose choice was to sell their body or starve to death. She took them into her home and opened places where they could stay. Houses of rest, they were called. She also campaigned successfully for the repeal of the Contagious Diseases Act."

"Which was?" Maggie asked.

"One of the most disgusting, vile pieces of legislation ever brought into this country against women. It started in towns where there were army and navy barracks, where was an excess of venereal disease. The women the soldiers and sailors used could be taken in at any time and forced to endure an internal examination, or go to prison. The instruments, you can imagine, were... primitive. It was called 'steel rape'."

"But surely they could object?"

"Yes, and be imprisoned until they gave in. There were women who were targeted, called in every week. Apparently, it was agony. They had to be held down. If they didn't put themselves through it, they and the children they supported would starve. The police could take in any woman they thought might be a prostitute." She shook her head. "A lot of young girls were falsely accused and subjected to it."

Maggie was staring open-mouthed at Zelah. "That was happening here, in this country?"

"Yep. Nothing was done against the men who used the prostitutes and were equally guilty of spreading the diseases, of course. Typical Victorian values," Zelah spat. "Josephine Butler fought a long, tough public battle against the act and she won. The Act was repealed. There was so much else she did, exposing the terrible degree of forced child prostitution, the export of British girls as young as ten to brothels in Europe. Horrible."

"She must have been one hell of a woman; scary I imagine," Maggie mused.

"Exactly the opposite," Nick said. "She was fragile and delicate and often ill and she suffered the tragedy of losing a child in a terrible accident."

"What happened?" Maggie asked.

"In the house in which the family lived before they moved to Liverpool, her youngest, a five-year-old, tried to slide down a balcony from the second floor. She fell to the ground floor and died within hours."

Maggie's hand flew to her mouth. "Oh God, how awful."

"Josephine already had a strong sense of social justice," Nick went on, "but when the family moved to Liverpool she needed to do something more, and she found her cause in the plight of helpless poor women."

"That's why you haven't heard of her," Zelah said. "The Pankhursts were for the middle and upper classes. Josephine Butler worked on behalf of all women. The Victorian middle and upper classes thought of her as a bad smell under their nose, although she was one of them and her impulse to help came from deeply held Christian values. She gained a national following of like-minded women."

"And we have a letter from her about a detective who was working on her behalf in Liverpool. That must mean he was doing something for a cause of hers," Maggie said.

"There's a good chance, yes," Nick replied. "It was in the early days of her campaigns, but she had already garnered a following. She held a meeting in a barn once and a group of angry men tried to burn it down with the women still inside. She was involved with setting up the homes for women and she was high profile on child prostitution." He turned to Maggie. "I can loan you a couple of biographies, if you like."

"I'd love to read more, thanks."

"OK, let's get back to the story," Zelah said. "To summarise, Nick, William McRoberts – if this skeleton is him and we aren't a hundred per cent yet – undertook a commission which ended in Fallough Hill on Anglesey, where he was murdered by a shot at close range through the forehead. A body supposed to be his was found in the Mersey. It was registered and buried under a false name, allegedly to protect his family's reputation and his widow was paid off. Is that accurate?"

"Yes, but a lot of questions without answers, yet."

"How did they find the skeleton, Nick?"

"Oh, I forgot to say. It was about a hundred yards or so from the back of the house, in what had been a small copse of trees, which were being cut down to dig a trench for bringing in cables. Lucky they didn't scoop him up. It was deep, about four feet down. Somebody wanted to make sure he wasn't found. They couldn't have considered the need for electricity and gas. It was pure luck, I suppose, the digger took that route for the trench."

Maggie nodded and Nick went on, "As I see it, the main question for Maze is: do we want to take up this case? There's no client. It's just us. Because we can, which is my final point." He turned his head from one to the other. "Thoughts?"

"We must do it," Maggie said without a moment's hesitation. "I don't think we're at the starting point yet, though. We need to know if this is William McRoberts, but, if we assume for now it is, I'll start compiling a list of questions and a timeline and a list of points to investigate..."

"Yes," Zelah said, butting in. "This is all very good but we're not going to get paid, so I want to use this as a marketing exercise and milk it for all it's worth. This could be a bestseller for us."

"And it's in the past, so no present-day repercussions," Maggie said. "We've enough of those to be getting on with."

"And no relation to Kennet Quinn," Nick said.

"Let's hope there's no present-day family in whatever we find," Zelah said. "We might welcome the publicity, but they, if they exist, will most likely not."

Chapter 9

A wave of satisfaction washed over Kennet Quinn as he sat with a glass of the best fine brandy in front of a roaring blaze, in darkness with the curtains closed against blizzarding snow.

He put his head back and sighed with contentment. This was a new, or almost new feeling for him. The first time was eighteen years previously when Gerard was born. Today he was a father again. This time to James Rufus Quinn, seven pounds precisely. His dynasty. Helen had done well. He knew she wasn't maternal. She tried to hide it from him, but it didn't matter. She had played her role perfectly and would soon be surplus to requirements. Women. So pointless except in this one thing. His great great grandfather Adolphus had known what to do with them. Pity intervening generations prevented their meeting.

He would treat Helen well, naturally, in the immediate aftermath of the birth. Unlike the previous one, who turned out to be a woman of immense stupidity, dreaming of love and a happy family. Helen was no fool and could not be treated as one. In a way he admired her, he mused, as he held up the glass to the light and enjoyed the hue and the smell of the rich brown liquid. Not the taste. He never drank alcohol, but this was what a man should do when presented with his heir.

Which brought his thoughts around to Gerard.

The boy was about to turn eighteen and had been brought up with the best Quinn principles. Yet he seemed to have learned nothing. Lately, since Rufus' death, he had caught Gerry looking at him with a hard-to-read expression. Confusion perhaps, anger maybe. The boy was upset by his grandfather's death, but life went on. He screwed up the job he was given, to cause an injury to Maggie Gilbert's brother-in-law, sufficiently to cripple him. But the man died. The idiot boy responsible was now in prison on remand and Kennet knew before long, facing a lengthy period in gaol, the boy would talk, would tell what he knew about Gerry, which would inevitably lead back to himself. This could not be allowed and arrangements were in hand. He expected news any day now.

Gerry had been taken out of the house by Damyan Kostov, one of Kennet's 'property managers' and, in receipt of a false passport, sent to Europe for at least six months. Kennet was sure he would find plenty of amusement. He had been generous. His thoughts turned to his need for a new staff member. He had begun to ask around and had come into possession of information about a young man who might just be suitable. Perfect, in fact. The boy possessed brawn and brain, and a connection which would be strategically and significantly useful. He set a private detective on the case. Again, he was expecting information any day.

His flow of thought was interrupted by a buzzing noise. He put down the glass and fished his mobile phone out of his pocket.

"Quinn."

He listened for a few moments to the voice on the other end.

"I see. Will Mr Kostov recover?"

"That is good news. By whom was he attacked?"

"I am acquainted with no-one of that name. I will send a private ambulance to return Mr Kostov to this country. You said two weeks?"

"Then I will call in one week to ensure your care has been adequate and he will be ready to travel." He took a pen from his pocket and pulled a small table in front of him. "Telephone number and a contact name, please." He wrote them down and ended the call.

The French police wanted to question a Mr Jeremy McCarthy. AKA Gerard Quinn. They were looking for Mr McCarthy to eliminate him from their enquiries. Kennet stood up, picked up the glass and walked towards the fire, where he dripped the contents onto the flames then threw the glass on after it.

He put his hands into his pockets and thought through what to do next. Would the boy attempt to return to the UK? He hadn't checked if Gerry had taken his own passport with him. A mistake. Why might he come back? Something had gone wrong, turning this into another situation to resolve and he was down to just one property manager, but that could be remedied by moving up the investigation into the already identified contender for the role. He would set this in motion in the morning.

In the meantime, he should go to the hospital to visit Helen and James Rufus. He might discuss these events with Helen. She was a clever, devious woman who might even have useful ideas. His latest venture, likely to be most lucrative, had begun when she introduced him to one of her friends.

Rubbing his hands in front of the fire, Kennet gave a few minutes' thought to Maze Investigations and what might be his next move. When they assembled the evidence to prevent his ancestor's statue being put up, the witch, as he now thought of Zelah Trevear, told him Quinn was not his real family name. He had employed his own genealogy investigator to dig out the story. After two months all the man was able to tell him was he had hit a brick wall, that Adolphus Quinn - the real one - died aged seven, tortured and murdered. Kennet knew the most likely suspect was his great great grandfather, the man who stole the boy's identity and become known as Adolphus Quinn. However, the man's attempts to gain information about Adolphus' real identity from living members of the Quinn family had been rebuffed. He suspected the influence of Zelah Trevear, but couldn't yet prove it. He had to admire how Maze put the story together with such rapid efficiency, when his own man was still working on it after two months with little progress. He would find a way to bring down their company and each of them individually. It was just going to take more time than he anticipated.

For now, it could wait. Kostov did not sound to be in danger of his life. Kennet had contacts he could use to find out if Gerry tried to come back into the country. Most importantly, Stephen Dawes, his remaining property manager, could contact the detective and, if all worked out as he anticipated, he would soon be able to greet the boy who would become his latest employee. Maxwell Howell, recently returned to the UK in search of his father, Nick Howell of Maze Investigations.

Chapter 10

By lunchtime on Wednesday Maggie's list of questions filled an A4 sheet of paper. This case was going to be more complex than she thought, but nevertheless she was excited. There hadn't been a suitable opportunity to speak to Zelah and Nick about her idea for taking on the most difficult 'brick wall' cases. It would be a risky venture, financially and in terms of a good success rate. She needed more time to consider how to propose it to them.

Nick had already gone off to meet up with Stella. Zelah was working on one of her story books, although she didn't seem to be attacking it with her usual fierce concentration.

The previous day Bob agreed Maggie could share the news about the boy who had been arrested for the hit-and-run and was now being held on a charge of attempted murder. They were relieved to hear it was a random accident, although no-one said so. He also passed on the news about Kennet's new son.

Following Bob's information Zelah updated Maggie and Nick about the property deals, which gave them pause for thought. They wanted to ultimately take Kennet Quinn down. Knowing it would be a long venture, they hypothesised on the idea he might get sufficiently angry to make a serious mistake, which could potentially bankrupt him and put him behind bars, although this was more hopeful than likely. The man did not act in haste and made few mistakes. They discussed the one weakness they knew about which was his excessive superstition, and were going to give thought to how to exploit it. Nothing was out of bounds where Kennet Quinn was concerned.

Zelah also informed them about being contacted by one of the Irish members of the Quinn family who had helped them to break the case against Rufus and Kennet. She had been offered money to help, but refused it and told the genealogist who contacted her she knew nothing, then phoned Zelah. Was Kennet behind the enquiry? Even if he was, she wasn't too worried. Whatever he found out he could never make public. It would destroy his own family reputation. However, she did suspect he was looking for a way to get to her, a hyena circling prey, trying to find the right moment to pounce and tear flesh.

For her part, Maggie sensed some discomfort about the prospect of doing harm of any kind to another person, but she kept reminding herself this was a man who had so severely beaten his own daughter she lost some sight in one eye, had been responsible also for the death of a tenant when his 'property managers' went too far and worst of all: he was responsible for Bob's near fatal shooting. She worried that, if they did something unethical, they would lower themselves to his level. But then, they were planning to exploit a weakness. They weren't planning to kill anyone.

"Where are you going to start?" Zelah interrupted her train of thought.

"What? Oh, sorry, I was thinking about something else. I'm going to start by assuming this is William McRoberts. Then I'm going to read through these papers Nick got from John. I need a quick break, then I'll get reading."

"I'll join you," Zelah said. "What about the papers? Nick didn't think there was anything helpful."

"Maybe not, but I want to be sure. You know what it's like. You read something, it doesn't seem to mean much, but later it links to something else and you make a leap forward."

"Fair enough."

The slamming of the front door announced an arrival and Maggie held back on her next comment as Bob strode into the kitchen. One look at his thunderous expression told her something bad, terrible even, had occurred. She stood up. "What?"

"The boy is dead."

For a moment she couldn't remember what he was talking about. Then it hit her. "Not...?"

"Yes, him. Hanged himself in his cell, last night. Found this morning." He banged his fist on the table. "They knew he was vulnerable. They should have been keeping a close eye on him."

"Why would he have been left alone long enough; what means did he have...?"

"Exactly." He started to pace around the room and Maggie saw Sherry Martin standing in the kitchen doorway.

"Sherry, I didn't see you there. Come in, please."

The woman smiled and shook her head. "Thanks, but no. We must go. We're due at the gaol. Guv?"

"Yes, yes. Coming." He turned to Maggie. "I wanted to let you know. The family liaison already has the information and will have told your sister. I wanted you to hear it from me."

"What are you thinking," Maggie began, but was interrupted by Zelah.

"Let the man go and do his job, for God's sake, Maggie."

Maggie's head jerked around and she saw, not the anger she'd heard in Zelah's voice but something else. Caution? She turned back to Bob. "Go," she said. "I'll see you later. Any idea what time?"

He shook his head. "I'll give you a call." He kissed her and stomped from the kitchen and out the house.

"I don't like her," Zelah said before Maggie could get a word in. "Don't ask me why. Gut feeling, for whatever it's worth. She wants to know our business. I don't want her to know. That's as much as I can say for now, so don't ask again." She turned to the table and went back to her sandwich and drink.

Maggie sat opposite her. "I can't say I don't like her, but when I see her glance at Bob, I suspect she's calculating something. I think she fancies him."

Zelah grunted. "How much does he know about the property plan?"

Maggie's cheeks reddened. "Very little, actually. I said we have a plan to do with the properties you were leading on, but I haven't elaborated. He told me, as he always does, to keep away from Kennet Quinn. So I told him our plan didn't involve direct confrontation but I didn't go into detail. But I will," she added. "It's time I put him in the picture."

"Not too much detail, please," Zelah said, sandwich in mid-air. "Not that I don't trust him, but he'll worry. If she picks up on his worry she might want to discover more, and if her intentions aren't honourable, she could use it against you; and us."

"A tad melodramatic?"

"Maybe." Zelah shrugged. "I hope so, and if I'm wrong I'll apologise." She put the sandwich back on the plate. "But this isn't good news about the boy's death."

"I agree," Maggie said, sitting back, "but I can't ask Bob to not bring her here. That would sound petty. He trusts her. Let's see how it goes down."

"Good. Let's finish here and get back to work. You've got a lot of questions needing answers."

* * *

After Zelah left for the station to pick up Mischa who was returning from Austria, Maggie resumed her review of her list of questions. She read through the documents Nick brought back from Liverpool and had to agree there wasn't much else to go on. There was a letter from Lizzy McRoberts' sister in Scotland urging her to leave Liverpool and go back to her own family. Maggie knew Lizzy had not done so. If she had to make a guess, it would be the woman hadn't wanted to leave the town where her husband might still be found. The letter made it clear the sister knew nothing about the circumstances in which William was supposed to have died. She referred to the 'tragic accident of your William's death'. If that was the story Lizzy told her family, so be it, Maggie thought.

The remaining correspondence was from later generations. There were references to another 'tragic accident', when William and Lizzy's son John died when he fell under a tram. This was in newspaper clippings from 1903 where it was reported he went out to a meeting and met his unfortunate end, leaving a wife and three children and one more on the way. There was nothing else of interest, apart from a photograph of an old woman with what might have been a couple of grandchildren, dated 1902. Was this Lizzy McRoberts?

She would have been around seventy years old, which looked a possibility for the woman in the photo.

She was about to start on an internet search for the easiest of her questions, when her phone rang. It was Nick, calling to tell her John had been informed the forensic anthropologist reported back that DNA had been successfully extracted from the skeletal remains. The next stage was a comparison to John's DNA, which would be forthcoming in the next couple of days.

"Good news," Maggie said. She told him what she had done already and was about to start, but she had come up against an initial barrier, in that she couldn't discover from the correspondence in what name the supposed body of William McRoberts was buried. "To find out about the inquest, I need the name. I thought it would be in the correspondence, but it doesn't seem to be."

"No, I had the same thought. But, we are aware of approximately when the death took place, down to a couple of days, so I thought, maybe search for deaths and burials within those weeks. It'll be looking for a needle in a haystack but something may jump out at you."

"Well, I can't come up with anything better, so I'll give it a go. I'll call you if anything does jump out, but don't hold your breath. They might have called him John Smith."

Maggie began her search with the 'Free BMD' site, where she put in a time range of the October to December quarter of 1878 and pressed the search button. She stipulated the county Lancashire to start with, and Liverpool, thinking that, as the body was fished out of the Mersey, a Liverpool coroner would have jurisdiction and therefore the man would have been

74

buried within the area. Within seconds the search produced a couple of hundred results in the three-month period, which was as precise as she could narrow it on this site. She looked first for the closest matches to McRoberts: Roberts, Robertson, Robinson. There were a few, but nothing within the right age group, being children and older men. Well, she hadn't expected an instant breakthrough. Next: a William. There were seventeen with that first name, five being within the possible age range. However, none of them had a surname beginning with the letter 'R'. The last thing she could try was the age of the deceased. Knowing William was forty-seven when he died, she looked through all males on the list with an age range between forty and fifty. To be believable, whoever organised and carried out his inquest – if there was one, and unless he too was party to the deception – must have agreed this was a reasonable age for the body, which brought it down to twelve men. All with different names. She wrote them out with their ages and reference numbers.

Still nothing stood out. She sighed. This was going to be impossible. Without some initial point of reference there was likely nothing she could find elsewhere on the internet. She put the list on the table and stood up, about to abandon the search for the night, when something caught her eye. All of the men on the list were aged between forty and fifty. None was called William or Roberts or any variety of the family name, but her eye caught a Robert McWilliams, aged forty-five. Surely not. It couldn't have been so simple. Could it?

She brought up the site for the General Register Office, logged in and cross-checked the reference. It was recorded in the same quarter. This was worth pursuing.

Next she logged on to the Liverpool cemeteries website and put in Robert McWilliams' details. There was just one reference: a Robert McWilliams, buried in the Toxteth cemetery, on the 15th of December 1878 in a communal grave. He was described in the listing as an ex-policeman, with no address listed. Maggie thought of Lizzy McRoberts. If this was the man identified as her husband, such treatment was a shocking abuse of a man's death. It was a strong possibility, though. The date of the burial was just over two weeks after William left home.

Next step, to verify this death against an inquest record, again if there was one. She went onto the Liverpool archives site. She already knew from Nick's previous research police records in Liverpool prior to 1890 no longer existed, according to the police archivist to whom he had spoken. She offered up a plea it wasn't the same for the inquest records. It took a few minutes to find them in the catalogue and she was both delighted and relieved there were some records including 1878, although there weren't any further details confirming which months. Never mind. A quick call the following day might some clarification. A more promising outcome than she could have hoped for at the outset of the search.

* * *

That evening by the time she and Jack had eaten, she had cleared up and Jack begun his tsunami of homework, Maggie was rubbing her eyes to keep herself awake. She still hadn't heard from Bob, but decided to wait for him. She lit a fire in the living room, picked up the new book she was ready to start from her favourite crime author and settled down for what would be a long wait. The news about the boy – she didn't even know his

76

name –disturbed her. She guessed Fiona would have heard by now. Two senseless losses of life. Jack put his head around the door to say goodnight and she carried on reading, fighting the urge to close her eyes, a battle she lost shortly before midnight. Next thing she knew Bob was shaking her arm. She sat up shivering. The fire had long since gone out and the room was bitterly cold. She took hold of his outstretched hand to stand up and yelped.

"Your hands are freezing!"

"It's five degrees below zero out there, and it isn't much better in here. Why are you still up, woman?"

She glanced at her watch and saw it was just after three in the morning. "Why are you so late, man?" She put her arms around him and shivered.

"I'm going to make myself a hot drink then we'll get upstairs. You want one?"

"No thanks. Bring yours along and tell me what's been happening."

In the bedroom she put on warm pyjamas and jumped under the duvet, as Bob came in with a steaming mug of cocoa.

"Look at us; me in winceyette, you with cocoa. More like we're in our eighties than our fifties."

"That can be changed," he said, putting down the cocoa and grinning at her.

"Not at three in the morning when it's freezing." She pulled the duvet up around her neck. "Can you tell me what happened today?"

"It's not clear. He hanged himself with his shirt. The whole thing stinks, and I'm worried."

"Why?"

"He hadn't been recorded at risk of self-harm, for starters. He shouldn't have been alone in a cell and he

77

should have been wearing a prison garment – they can't be torn – not a shirt. The records appear to be OK. He was being regularly checked. What worries me most is earlier in the day he asked to see his solicitor. Didn't say why, just he had something he needed to say."

"What was his name, Bob?"

"Malcolm. Friends called him Malky. He was seventeen." He sat on the side of the bed and Maggie waited. After a couple of minutes he shrugged, got into bed and hugged her. "Hate this part of the job." She smoothed a hand over his stubbly head, and in a few minutes he was asleep.

* * *

Maggie got the call from Nick two days later. The DNA result was back and there was a match. The skeleton was William McRoberts. John McRoberts received the information and phoned the news through.

"Full steam ahead, then," Maggie said. She wanted to punch the air, but kept her hands on the table. After all, this had been murder. She brought Nick up to date on her progress. The Liverpool archives confirmed they held a few inquest reports for December 1878, but these were not digitised and they would have to visit to see the originals.

"Are you up for another trip to Liverpool?" she asked. It was Nick's case, after all.

"I can go next week," he replied. "Tomorrow I have a meeting with someone about Max. They say he's in the country now."

"So we have some time to spend at the weekend refining our questions. We might as well make the most of the trip."

"John wants to be involved. He's told Sir Trystan the news. He wants to find out when he can hold a funeral."

"Do you have a funeral for a skeleton?" Maggie asked. "I've never thought about it."

"We've never had to. Yes, he should be properly buried, under his own name. John is going to contact other family members." He hesitated for a moment, then said, "John wants to inform the local paper the remains have been identified."

"Oh. I don't know what to say about that," Maggie said. "Should we speak to Zelah, see what her take is on it?" Her first thought was if the story got out so soon, some wannabe hotshot reporter could pick it up and take the story away from them. If that was a selfish thought it was too late to ignore it.

"We should," Nick said. "It may be a selfish thought, but..."

"No, I was thinking the same," Maggie replied. "And I suspect Zelah will agree. Let me speak to her and I'll call you back."

She got Zelah on the phone five minutes later, told her the news and waited for the resultant blast of expletives to die down, before she ended the call and rang Nick back.

"She agrees with us. You'll have to convince John to wait. Can you do that?"

"I'm sure I can. He trusts us. I'm going to be honest with him, though."

"I would not expect anything less of you," Maggie replied. "Tell me what he says."

Twenty minutes later he called her again. "He's in. He doesn't want some reporter, especially some tabloid journo who will sensationalise it, to have anything to do with it. As far as he's concerned it's his ancestor and our case. He wants it done properly, with respect. He called at once and told Sir Trystan the same, and he agreed, too. No fuss, no news, but Trys wants to be kept informed."

"He can help us, too," Maggie replied. "This is going to focus, initially, on him as much as it is on us. After all, we don't know yet whether it was his ancestor who fired the gun."

"Yes, I explained to John he might remind Trys of the possibility. He's offered to do whatever he can to help."

"Good. I've done a timeline. It's flexible for now, but once we've been to Liverpool I can tighten it up."

"Then let's get going. I want to solve this one," Nick said. "Anything else?"

Maggie told him what she thought might be a possibility for the name under which William's death was registered.

"Definite possibility, as Bob would say. Shall we order it on priority?"

"How about you call John and ask him to go into the registrar's office on Monday and wait for a copy? It'll be more expensive, but if we can verify it's the same man, it'll be a significant leap forward."

"Good idea, I'll call him now."

Maggie ended the call with, "It's going to be an interesting case, Nick."

She sat back smiling. To prepare Nick and Zelah for her proposed new venture, solving this case would be perfect. All she had to do now, was solve it.

Chapter 11

Liverpool 1878

Lizzy McRoberts sat in her kitchen. She hadn't taken her hat off, or even her coat. Josephine Butler made a pot of tea and poured a cup for each of them. She now sat in silence next to Lizzy, instinctively knowing she should wait until Lizzy could lift her head to speak.

It took a further ten minutes, before she whispered, "You met him, Mrs Butler."

"Yes, Mrs McRoberts, I did meet him."

"Was the corpse my husband, in your opinion?"

"I believe we both have already the answer to that question, Mrs McRoberts."

"Is there anything we can do?"

Josephine Butler shook her head.

"Did I do the right thing, Mrs Butler?"

"My inclination, although outraged at these events, is to say you did, Mrs McRoberts. You are a young woman. You have a family to care for, to bring up. I have told you of my suspicion, what I think happened." She paused, paling. "I sent him away."

Lizzy McRoberts looked up. "You did nothing wrong, Mrs Butler. What you have told me is beyond shocking. It is... outrageous, horrifying, frightening. I admit it, I am frightened. I cannot challenge them, as you do."

"In this case, Mrs McRoberts, I, too, would not challenge further. There would be no chance of success. It goes too high." She stood. "I must go. My family will be wanting me." She took Lizzy's hand. "You can rely on me for support, at any time. Just send a note."

Lizzy saw Josephine Butler to the door, then returned to the kitchen. She would not ask for the woman's help again, although she knew she could.

Josephine Butler was a special person, a true Christian dedicated to helping poor women and fighting terrible injustice which Lizzy now understood as she previously had not. Willie had played a part in fighting injustice, and paid for it with his life. How did she feel about that? Proud of him. Proud he stood up to the forces of evil. She could see now he had no chance, right from the start. As soon as the first woman had spoken to him of the events happening in the city to young girls and children, and he had taken it seriously enough to speak to his superiors, he lost his job. He been sacked in disgrace and named as the perpetrator. Shamed in front of his colleagues; not that many of them believed it, although many were frightened enough to shun him, forcing him to take on the role of a private investigator. Josephine Butler knew, too, something bad was happening, heard about Willie and asked him to investigate further, which he did. Willie was dead, Lizzy had no doubt now. Where, and why and how? And who.

She sighed. She would take their pension; she could not refuse. She would buy a small corner shop and start a business. She was good with numbers. Her children would not suffer. Would she leave it there? Could she? No, of course not. Mrs Butler told her the name of the woman who first approached Willie. She would speak to the woman, find out everything she could. Discreetly, of course. She feared *they* might watch her. She would leave it some time. Six months, perhaps. That should satisfy *them* she had moved on. A voice interrupted her musings.

"Ma, is father truly gone?" whispered the boy, standing in the doorway gripping the doorpost with white knuckles.

"Yes, John. You are the man of the family now. Come here and sit with me." The boy sat at the table. She took his shaking hand and kissed it.

"What happened to him, Ma? Do you know what happened to him?"

He was a sharp boy and she couldn't lie to him. "No, my son. Not yet, but I will. When it's time I will tell you the whole story. When you are grown up. Perhaps you will be the one who finds justice for him. I fear it cannot be me. Now, will you help me with the chores?"

"Of course," the boy replied. "May I ask....?"

"No," she replied, then put an arm around his shoulders and squeezed gently, fearing she had been too harsh. "Not yet. One day you will know. I must go out now. I have some arrangements to make. Look after your sisters. I will not be above an hour."

John McRoberts nodded and stood at the door, watching her walk along the street. He took deep breaths, each one not calming, but increasing his rage until he thought his head would boil. Someone had deliberately disgraced and killed his father. At thirteen there was nothing he could do, but his time would come. He would have his vengeance on *them*, whoever *they* were and if he couldn't manage it, he would ensure somehow William McRoberts would be given justice and vengeance.

Chapter 12

The weekend had been quiet. Maggie had worked on her ever-growing list of questions in between enjoying time out with Alice. Zelah was nowhere to be seen. Nor was Nick until Sunday evening, after Maggie drove Alice back to school in Cheltenham, when he appeared unannounced and more pensive than usual.

"Just a quick visit. I want to print out some papers. I'll be out of your hair in no time."

"Help yourself," Maggie replied. "Anything you want to talk about?"

"No. Well, actually, I've been thinking about Max."

She sat up and turned off the sound on the TV. "What about him?"

"He's disappeared again. He's in the country. I thought he might try to contact me and I have some anxiety about why he hasn't."

"Is there some way you can reach out to him? Social media?"

"I'm not comfortable. If he wants to keep to himself for now I must respect his wish. I just wish I understood why." He shook his head and stood in the doorway for a few moments, staring at the fire. "I'll get my printing done."

Maggie left him to it. Listening to the rhythmic churning out of pages on the printer, she felt for him. A son he barely knew, who might harbour as much resentment as love.

At least he was talking about his feelings. In the few years she had been acquainted with him, Nick had become more communicative but still there were many silences and periods of staring into space. She knew this was his way; he weighed everything before he spoke, so he never intentionally gave offence. Although the silences were sometimes long she had learned not to feel obliged to fill them. Now she always knew whether he had finished speaking or if there was more to come. It was worth waiting for. Nick rarely spoke frivolously.

The printer stopped. He appeared back in the room. "I'll leave you now." He went to turn away but Maggie stopped him.

"Nick, if there's anything I can do to help..."

"I have only to ask. Yes, and I will, but for now, there isn't anything. I must go now. We still OK to go to Liverpool on Tuesday?"

"Can't wait," she replied.

After he left Maggie put more logs on the fire, watched them catch and throw up crackling flames and decided not to return to the TV but to take another look at her list. Now they knew the skeleton was William McRoberts, she could steam ahead like a racing ship, but with luck not the *Titanic*.

The first items on her list were about the inquest, starting with: did one take place and, if so, what date was it carried out in relation to the discovery of the body? At what point was the identification of 'Robert McWilliams' made? Who made the identification?

Some of this information would come from the death certificate, which John McRoberts was going to order and collect in Liverpool as soon as the office opened in the morning and phone Nick when he had it. Earlier she completed some background reading about inquests and discovered, if there were no suspicious circumstances, the coroner could decide not to hold an inquest, instead granting permission for the burial to go ahead. She would also search for such a report in any coroner's inquest reports, but it was the outcome she needed.

She also wanted to discover what she could about the death of William and Lizzy's son John. John told them his family believed it was a 'tragic accident', which meant there would have been at least an inquiry to establish the circumstances.

Going back to William, how she could find out more about his journey to Anglesey, primarily why he went there? She had spent time over the weekend with biographies of Josephine Butler, but found no mention of the engaging of a detective. She noted at the time the Butlers hadn't been long in Liverpool and Josephine Butler was mainly involved in setting up her 'house of rest' to help women get off the streets and attain work skills. But another campaign in which she was involved, one Zelah mentioned, was the highlighting of the extent of under-age prostitution throughout the country and the fact girls as young as ten or twelve were being exported abroad, sometimes enticed by inaccurate advertisements, sometimes kidnapped, sometimes sold by unscrupulous parents to groups of men who ran the 'business'. This latter she found astonishing: some were working-class street gangs, but others were not working-class street men, but middle and upper class so-called 'gentlemen'. She had read about gangs bringing unsuspecting young women into Britain these days, but had no idea this was an old practice. An idea was beginning to form about the 'commission' William McRoberts had undertaken.

That they would have to go back to Fallough Hill was a given. She now divided her list into three parts, the first around William, the second around Fallough Hill, the third around the accidental death of the first John McRoberts. It would be interesting to meet Sir Trystan

Wyn Davies and to find out the history of the estate from someone close to it, not from the pages of Wikipedia and other online sources. Might he have some estate papers and historical documents from the late 1870s? It was a question she was itching to answer and would check with Nick tomorrow.

In addition to understanding why William went to Fallough Hill, she wanted to learn his history, as much as Nick had been able to find out. Where he came from, what took him to Liverpool, when he had joined the force and when he had become a detective. Nick said there was little information about him apart from a record of his attendance at the funeral of a senior colleague and a report of him arresting a man who stabbed another outside a Liverpool pub.

She needed background information, about the police in Liverpool at the time and about the role of a private detective. This was something she could get on with whilst she waited for Bob to come home. Retrieving her laptop from the office, Maggie soon found a wealth of information on the Liverpool police in the nineteenth century and on the role of the Victorian private investigator.

An informative blog provided her with information about the role of the PI. The main work seemed to be in assisting defence solicitors to find witness evidence for a trial. They welcomed the services of an ex-detective who would have possessed such skills. There was also the 'bread-and-butter' work of finding evidence of unfaithful spouses, bigamy and divorce. Would William have been the sort of man to relish such work, after the cut and thrust of the life of a detective who regularly engaged in head-on clashes with the criminal fraternity in Liverpool?

The blog suggested the role of a PI was a thriving profession with many men taking it on, some former professionals, some amateurs who had time and interest. Many were employed by solicitors, but, she mused, if they weren't, how did they find employment or commissions? A story told of one man who learned about crimes through his former police colleagues and visited the victims to see if they needed help in bringing the perpetrators to justice, with the proviso when he met the victims they had the wherewithal to pay for his services. This might have been what William was relying on, but given he had been dismissed, would his former colleagues have been willing to pass on such information, for their own safety?

What else could he have done? Advertise, perhaps? She opened the British Newspaper Archive site and brought up the Liverpool newspapers in the relevant decade. Entering key words 'Private Detective' and 'Private Investigator' in the advertisements section, she hit the return button.

This produced over a hundred hits, but they were all in London in the *Evening Standard* and nothing before 1880. Was it because it wasn't respectable to advertise in the previous decade, outside of London, or because the newspapers weren't available for 1878? This was something else to add to the search list in the Liverpool central library and archives. Reading through some of the advertisements for 1880, it was clear the line of work was thriving in the capital city. The various agencies and individuals expressed their credentials as ex-policemen and advertised such services as 'suspected persons watched', 'missing friends found' and 'divorce and confidential cases secretly conducted'. It was a fascinating insight into Victorian life and she couldn't help reading on, although there was nothing to connect to William McRoberts or Liverpool directly. But this was the life he was entering and he must have known this was what he would be doing as a profession. In the private sphere he would not have the power of arrest nor would he be able to act in serious criminal cases. It must have been something of a comedown.

She yawned, closed the laptop and went to check on Jack, to find he was already asleep. It was now close to eleven and no sign of nor word from Bob.

As she undressed and got into bed she thought again about her sister and wondered if she should make another attempt to contact her. Maggie understood she should be the one to reach out. Perhaps now Fiona knew it was a hit-and-run and the boy responsible was dead, she would stop blaming Maggie and Maze. Was this another selfish thought? Yes, but at the same time she genuinely wanted to help her sister in any way she could.

She would call her in the morning.

Chapter 13

Monday mornings in the Gilbert household were rarely an enjoyable experience, but this one was a particular nightmare and Maggie was relieved when everyone was gone.

Jack, expecting the results of his mock exams, was tight-lipped and when he dropped a tea mug he swore and pushed Maggie out of the way as he tried to pick up the broken pieces. She sent him on his way early with a lecture about rudeness ringing in his ears, together with Bob, who had had less than four hours sleep and was also tense and grumpy. She felt for both, but wanted some peace and space.

Jack was going to text when he received his results and Maggie was anxious, too, as she had been during their trip to Cornwall when he was awaiting his GCSE results. To fill in the time she went back to her lists and sub-divided them yet again, constantly watching the time, noting when Jack would have arrived at his sixth-form college in Cardiff.

Finding she couldn't concentrate on work yet, she decided to grasp the nettle and picked up the house phone to call her sister's number. It rang out and continued to ring until the answerphone kicked in. Maggie wasn't sure if she was disappointed or relieved. She left a brief message saying it was her and the time of the call and she would call back later.

A few minutes later her mobile pinged. Thinking it was Jack she ran to the kitchen and grabbed it. It wasn't Jack. It was Fiona and the message read: '*Don't bother*'. She flung the phone onto the table as tears smarted her eyes.

There was nothing for it now but to wait and five minutes later the phone pinged again. This time it was Jack and the message read: '*Call me. Now*'. With some trepidation she dialled his number. When he answered his voice was quiet and detached. Fearing the worst, she asked, "Well, tell me. It can't be that bad."

There was a pause, long enough for Maggie to want to reach down the phone, grab his shoulders and shake. He needed one Grade A*, two Grade As and one Grade B. What had gone wrong?

Then he spoke. "Three A*s. One A."

She breathed and yelled. "What the... Jack, brilliant. Aren't you pleased? It's fantastic!"

Another pause, then, "Yeh. I can't believe it. Talk to you later." And he ended the call.

For a few seconds she was disconcerted. Then she decided he was shocked, too, and he would call back later when he had taken it in. She'd have to be patient.

In the following half hour Nick and Zelah arrived and she told them Jack's news, welcoming their delight.

"Does he want to go to university?" Nick asked when she told them Jack didn't sound as pleased as she thought he might have been. "He still enjoys researching with us, and he's good. He has an eye for detail unusual for his age, and he can think through a scenario with maturity. Again, unusual."

"He's changed in the past couple of years," Maggie said. "I have to see him as an adult now, Bob says, but for me he'll always be my little boy."

During the day Maggie and Nick focussed on their trip to Liverpool and Anglesey. They would be leaving the following morning. Hotels were booked, meetings arranged. Now they were waiting for John McRoberts to call with details of the death certificate for 'Robert McWilliams'. The call came just after lunch.

"I've come home and scanned the certificate, Nick. I've emailed it to you."

"OK, hold on a moment." Nick opened his emails and saw it was waiting. "Great, thanks, John. Give me five minutes and I'll call you back."

"Right, here goes," he said to Maggie. He opened the attachment, scanned it, and then put it up on the white board for her and Zelah to read.

"Wow," Maggie said a few seconds later, staring at the enlarged picture as Nick was getting John back on the phone.

When he connected Nick said, "We should go through this box by box; is everyone in agreement? Good, let's start. John, you have the original copy in front of you?"

"Sure have, Nick."

"First box: Date of death and place. They were already recording actual address as well as date, fortunately. He died on 15th of December 1878 in Liverpool. Not especially informative. Name and surname: Robert McWilliams. Sex: Male. Age: 45 years. Rank or Profession: former police officer. Cause of death: suicide by drowning whilst intoxicated. Signature, description and residence of informant: Joseph Monaghan, Coroner. When registered: 18th of December 1878. Signature of Registrar: can't decipher."

He sat back. "Thoughts, anyone?"

"It fits," Maggie said. "It's the story in the letter to Lizzy McRoberts."

John's voice came from the squawk box in the centre of the table. "I agree, Maggie. Can I call you Maggie?"

"Of course," she replied.

"They kept the profession, so it could appear to be William. The age was about right. What about this coroner, though? Why was he the informant?"

"Because there was some level of inquiry," Maggie said. "We don't know if there was an autopsy. I think not, if you look at the dates between the death and the burial. Sorry, John, I haven't passed on this information yet. He was buried a couple of days after his body was found."

"That's quick, which suggests no autopsy," Nick said.

"From what I read, if the coroner decided there were no suspicious circumstances, he could proceed to instruct the registrar without forcing an autopsy," Maggie said.

"Do we suspect the coroner was involved?" Zelah asked.

"We don't know, yet," Maggie replied. "We should look when we get to Liverpool. Is there anything else we can get from this, today?"

Nobody spoke.

"Then I suggest we wrap it up, for now," Nick said. "John, Maggie and I will be travelling tomorrow morning, which will give us time to get started at the central library archives for a couple of hours tomorrow afternoon. We can stay until Friday afternoon. Shall I call you later?"

"Yes, please. I'm going to take a couple of days off work. Many hands, etcetera."

"We're going to need them, especially if we're going to get over to Anglesey as well. See you tomorrow, then."

* * *

Maggie and Nick were underway the following morning as soon as Bob saw Jack off to school. Jack hadn't talked much about his exam success and Maggie picked up the vibe not to ask too many questions. Bob said he would talk to him whilst she was away. Between Bob and Zelah, who was also going to stop over at Maggie's for a couple of days, Jack would have sufficient sympathetic, non-judgemental listeners if he chose to open up. It was strange for her, but he was officially an adult now and his choices deserved her respect.

The journey to Liverpool was uneventful. En route Nick told Maggie there was some evidence Max had reached Newport in the past couple of weeks, but then had been lost sight of.

"He must be trying to get close to you, Nick," Maggie said. "He hasn't seen you since he was a little boy, so perhaps he's trying to get some information about you."

"I hope so."

They found John McRoberts in the snack bar on the ground floor of the Liverpool central library, a file tucked under his arm.

"I've been here since they opened," he said. "I've found a couple of things. It's good, this researchin', isn't it?" He glanced over at Maggie, whose head was tipped back, staring up at the five-floor open rotunda. "Amazing, isn't it," he said with pride. "Best in the country."

"It's a great space," Nick said, grinning at Maggie's open mouth.

Maggie shook her head. "Amazing. Which is the researching floor?"

"Up on the third. I've booked tables together for us."

"What have you found so far, John?" Nick asked as they made their way up on the central staircase.

"There's not much in the papers. Perhaps they worked to keep it out. There's just a mention in the *Echo* about a body being found in the Mersey. Could have been the right one. I've got it printed out. What are we going to do for the rest of the day?"

"Coroners' inquests and reports to start with," Maggie replied. "For William and for John, your great great grandfather."

"Oh yeh, which reminds me. My dad wants to meet you, if you've got time. He's fired up about this. His grandad Jake passed down some stories of his own father's accident and death."

"Is he mobile?" Maggie asked.

John nodded. "He doesn't get out much, he's nearly eighty, but this is the most excitement he's had in years."

"Could you bring him to dinner at the hotel tonight?" Nick asked.

"He'd love to. Right, here we are. Let's get going." He bounced off the elevator, Nick and Maggie following.

A couple of hours later they took a short break to compare notes. Maggie had found out about both coroners' inquests. Nick decided to go out to the register office, which was just a few minutes' walk away, to get the death certificate for John McRoberts in 1903. John was going through the digitised copies of the *Liverpool Echo* and other papers to see if he could find any news or other information on and around both deaths.

Back on the third floor Nick gestured to them to join him at a seated area close to the lift, where they could talk without being overheard or annoying any of the other researchers. He waved the certificate and they gathered around.

"This is interesting. Accidental death. There was a coroner's inquest this time, following a post-mortem. He suffered fatal crush injuries. The death certificate was reported and signed by the coroner. No family member involved or mentioned. But the address, if I'm not mistaken, is the same family home your uncle recently moved out of, John."

"Yes, it is, in Troughten Street. Family's been there for ages. Not my dad, mind. He's a younger brother. He lives in the next street but one."

"What will happen to the house, now your uncle's gone?" Maggie asked.

"Not sure yet, Maggie. Family conference coming up. We thought one of his kids might want to move in, but they aren't keen. Me uncle couldn't manage the upkeep. I did me best, a few odd repairs here and there, but it needs a big refurb. I'll be sorry to see it go, but I'm not sure any of us can afford the cost."

"Does it belong to your uncle?" Nick asked.

"Shared between him and my dad."

"Big decisions ahead, then." Nick yawned. "What have you found out, Maggie?"

"Good news and bad," she replied. "The bad news, there's nothing here about an inquest for 'Robert McWilliams'. I suspect the coroner went along with the police story and didn't convene a jury. The good news, there was a post-mortem examination and an inquest for John McRoberts, after the tram incident. I've printed out a copy for each of us of the official report."

"Anything from your newspaper search, John?"

"I've found a few mentions of the accident. There's something interesting," he said, raising his eyebrows.

"Might you be going to tell us the same as I found in the coroner's report," Maggie said. "About the person they couldn't trace?"

"Exactly," John said in a conspiratorial whisper.

"Someone care to fill me in?"

96

"Sorry, Nick. Yes. Maggie, you go first. The newspaper reports are not going to be as accurate as the coroner's report."

"They'll give a different angle, which may be important," she said. "Anyway, according to the coroner it was an accident. The post-mortem revealed serious crush injuries. Plus one of his legs was practically severed. Massive blood loss."

"Poor sod," John whispered.

"Hopefully, the shock stopped him feeling too much pain before he died, which was mercifully quick. An ambulance was sent for, but he was dead by the time it arrived. A crowd gathered around and there was a nurse in the crowd who tried to help him, but his injuries were too great. There was another man, who rushed forward to drag him away from the tramlines. A witness said – and this is the interesting thing –the man appeared to go through John McRoberts' pockets. Policemen were on site within minutes and held back people who witnessed what had happened. They got names and addresses, but it turned out none of them was the man who went through John McRoberts' coat pockets. He disappeared in the melee. No-one was able to give a good description of him, but—"

"There's a description in the newspapers. There was a reward offered," John interrupted. "Sorry, Maggie, carry on."

"There's not much more," she said. "The jury, directed by the coroner, agreed on a verdict of accidental death. The pocket search was written off as the work of an opportunistic thief. That was it."

"But someone didn't think so," Nick said. "Tell us about the newspapers and the reward, John."

"Well, the accident was reported in the papers at the time. Mentions his name, his wife and his children, and his profession. He was a worker at the Albert Dock. A cotton porter."

"Interesting," Nick said.

"Why interesting? In what context?" Maggie asked.

"It was one of the hardest jobs on the dock. They humped great bales of cotton arriving on ships, mainly from America. They had to be strong so I'm guessing he was a big, strong man."

"And?"

"He would have been sure-footed on the edge of a kerb and it would have to have been a big push to tip him headlong in front of tram he would have seen coming. How did they justify an accidental push? Is there no mention of his height and weight in the report?"

Maggie went back through the paperwork. "Yes, there is. The autopsy report says he was six feet two inches tall, of a strong build and in a healthy condition. I didn't consider when I read it."

"Context," Nick said, sitting back and rubbing his hands together.

"Why didn't it get picked up?" John asked.

"Because we have a different context for asking the question. They wouldn't have known his back-story. The coroner asked questions about the witness who went missing, but if it happened a lot – let's assume it wasn't a rarity people didn't want to get involved, or there were such opportunistic thieves – he wouldn't have any reason to question the accidental aspect of the fall."

"But we do," John said. He was sitting on the edge of his chair, tapping his fingers on the arms. "There's more to this, isn't there?"

"I think so," Nick said. "However, we've done as much as we can here. Everyone agree?" They both nodded. "I want to spend some time reflecting. We can meet again this evening, talk over where we've reached, and what we do next."

They stood, packed up their papers, each deep in thought, and left the library, agreeing to meet in the hotel at seven.

Maggie and Nick decided to walk back to the hotel along the riverfront, both agreeing they needed some fresh air and exercise after sitting for several hours.

Nick walked in silence with a fierce frown of concentration and Maggie grabbed his arm as he stepped forward to cross a road, to stop him walking into the path of an oncoming bicycle. He stopped abruptly, shook his head and looked around as if surprised by his surroundings.

"Where was your head?" Maggie demanded.

"There's something," he said. "Actually more than one something. Some facts I must get hold of and put together. You did say you'd written a full family tree and timeline?"

"Yes, I have, but I'm hoping to get more information from John's dad tonight. Are two and two about to make five?" she replied, smiling.

"I believe they are."

* * *

On the dot of seven o'clock Maggie and Nick stood to welcome the two men heading towards them. John stood a little behind the man who couldn't be anyone but his father; older, slightly bent, shorter than his son and with silver hair but with an identical shining ruddy face. He marched up to Nick and Maggie and shook their hands with such a firm grip Maggie winced.

"This is Jacka, my dad," John said, raising his eyebrows with a smirk at Maggie who was trying to surreptitiously massage her aching palm. "He's excited about this meeting."

"As are we," Nick replied. "Let's go through to the restaurant. Our table is ready."

Once they got past the initial small talk, ordered meals and received drinks, Nick was itching to start the substantive conversation.

"I'm guessing, Jacka, John has filled you in about our research and what we've discovered about your great great grandfather, William?"

"Oh aye. Pretty shocking, isn't it," the old man replied with a gleeful grin. "Villainy at work, I think."

"Indeed a possibility," Nick replied, unable to prevent himself from grinning back. "We're going to attempt to find out what happened to him. You know," he hesitated for a moment, "how we received the initial information about William's body being at a place we identified as Fallough Hill?"

Jacka frowned, then remembered. "Right, the medium. OK with me, fella. I've seen and heard a few things in my time." He sat back and folded his arms. "I suppose I am a bit sceptical. Once had a neighbour who used to hold séances and claim she spoke to the dead. But it was her husband behind a curtain, with a lot of smoke and a mirror and recorded noises." He winked at Maggie. "But, we none of us have the inside track, do we?"

"Quite right," she replied. "Always good to keep an open mind."

Nick gave a short cough. "There's something particular I'd like to ask you about," he said, taking back control of the discussion. "I've looked at the family tree – by the way, after dinner Maggie's going to ask you to help her fill in more names and dates – and I saw your great grandfather John died just a month after his own mother Lizzy died. This struck me as being, what shall I say, something to explore? I was wondering if your grandfather – I believe he was known as Jake - ever told you any stories about those two deaths being so close together."

The old man loosened his tie and rubbed his chin. "As a matter of fact, Nick, he did, or rather my own dad Jonno did, passed on from Jake. Jake died young, just thirty-five when he died. I never knew him."

John McRoberts' head whipped around to stare at his father. "You've never told me anything about that! I've been on this research for over a year and now you mention this?"

Jacka shrugged. "You never asked. Honestly, son, I didn't remember until now."

Maggie, fearing a row was about to break out, intervened with, "It happens sometimes. Our memory gets a sharp nudge which pushes up something from the depths to the surface. What did Jonno tell you, Jacka?"

"He told me about the will, and the letter. The one that went missing."

John sat back, arms folded, scowling, then he suddenly leaned forward and was about to say something Maggie thought he might later regret, when two waiters arrived with their starters.

"Can you tell us about it, Jacka?" Maggie said.

"I'll give it me best shot, love. It's not a long story." He unfolded a napkin onto his lap, gave a platter of tempura prawns an interested examination and put a few onto his plate.

"When John's mother Lizzy died she left a will. Not a lot of money, just a bit of savings. Some for each of her kids and grandkids. With the will was a letter. Apparently she always promised to tell my great grandad John what she knew about what happened and what she found out when his dad died. He was thirteen when it happened and she wouldn't tell him at the time. When he got older she kept refusing and in the end he gave up ever expecting to find the truth. When the will was read he found she'd written it down."

"Did he tell anyone what was in it?" Maggie asked.

"No, he didn't but he was supposed to have been moody for days. They put it down to grief, like. John got on fine with his old mum, my dad said; he was distraught when she died. Me dad thought there might have been more to it. Then John went away for a couple of days and when he got back he was miserable. That was until someone got in touch and asked to meet him. A couple of days later he went off to the meeting."

"Why did he go to the meeting?" Nick asked.

"Apparently grandad never said. But grandad's mum Evelyn, John's wife, told him someone had been in touch when John got back from wherever he'd gone. Wanted to meet him. The family thought he'd taken the letter with him. That's the end of it." He leaned forward, picked up a hot battered prawn and began to crunch on it. "These are good, aren't they?"

There was silence for the next ten minutes as they digested the information with the food. Nick was the first to restart the conversation.

"I'm just throwing out an idea here, but Jacka, was there anything else after his death, and after his funeral?

Anything strange happen? Did anyone come to the house?"

"No; no strangers. An insurance bloke did come around. Story is that grandad was just a small kid, but he remembered my Great Grandma Evelyn saw the bloke off. He thought it was a funny story. Some bloke in a suit saying he needed to check through great grandad's papers to find his insurance document." He laughed. "Grandad's dad didn't have insurance. He was a docker. He didn't read much. Insurance be damned." He made a snorting noise.

"Then who was it?" Nick asked.

"No idea. But whoever it was never came back. Great Grandma Evelyn made sure, with the business end of her broom. Dad said you didn't get on the wrong side of Great Grandma Evelyn. God help anyone who tried."

"That's interesting, Jacka. Do you have access to your brother's house?"

"You mean do I have a key? Yes. I do."

"We have to go to Anglesey tomorrow, but when we get back, could we take a look?"

"Sure. What do you want to see?"

"Anywhere your great grandad might have hidden the letter, Jacka. There's a chance it's still there."

Chapter 14

Liverpool 1879

Lizzy McRoberts sat in her kitchen, elbows on the table, hands wrapping her head. In the year since the body which wasn't William had been buried she had been going about asking discreet questions, talking to women on the streets. Josephine Butler gave her some names and had offered to help, but Lizzy had refused. She wanted her enquiries to be inconspicuous and, as much as she had come to admire, appreciate and on a personal level like Mrs Butler, her presence would give the matter unwanted attention. Mrs Butler understood and accepted further intervention on her part was neither required nor necessary and Lizzy had not heard from her since.

It was dark outside, and cold. Almost a year since the last day, when Willie kissed her and walked out of the front door, saying he would be back in a few days. She walked to the window and jerked the curtains closed, put on a few more coals, then sat again, pulling her shawl around her shoulders.

The children were asleep. Her John, against her wishes, had left school at fourteen and found work at the Docks. On the one hand she was proud he wanted to be her support; on the other, he could read and write just enough but she wanted more for him.

It wasn't all bad. She had her little grocery and tobacco shop. There were good, reliable, constant customers. She worked hard to make it the success it had become and there was the start of some decent profit, enough for Lizzy to put aside some savings. There were many years of work ahead, at least another twenty or twenty-five. It took enough of her time and energy to stop too many painful thoughts, but the price she paid sometimes felt too high. When she was least expecting it, her heart would suddenly ache, bile rising into her throat and she fought to suppress the overpowering anger that rushed in like a roaring flame and blotted out her sanity. Willie should have been with her. A working man, looking after his family. It was all he ever wanted. Now she knew what had happened, there were moments when she wanted to buy a gun and shoot the people whose names she had accumulated over the past twelve months. But what good would such actions do? Leave a fourteen-year-old boy to look after three sisters? The truth would never be made public anyway, could not be. The more Lizzy learned the more she understood what she was up against. It was monstrous, but too big for her to fight, for any one individual to take on. Silence was the price she would have to pay for her comfort and security for the rest of her life. They bought her off, she thought again, always with anguish. Perhaps, one day, someone could, and would, get justice for Willie. One day she would tell John the truth. She promised him. But how? And when would it be safe?

She stood and put the kettle on the hob. An idea started to come to her, but her thoughts were interrupted by a knock at the back door. Gossiping Gert. Her neighbour had been helpful, she couldn't complain, but Gert didn't read signals, subtle or not, such as when Lizzy was bone-weary and wanted peace and silence.

Sure enough, Gertrude Wainright was on the back doorstep, nose pressed against the glass. With a sigh, Lizzy let her in.

"Nice and warm in here, Lizzy," Gertrude began as she swept past into the kitchen. "Not like the Alpersons. Shivering in there, I was." She eyed the kettle which was just starting to hiss.

"Cup of tea, Gert?"

"Love one, my sweet. Haven't seen you around for a few days. Just wanted to check you're alright, like."

"Why wouldn't I be, Gert?" she replied with her back to the woman, who was settling herself in a chair and heaving her expansive forearms onto the table.

"Well, that man who was asking about you. Who was he, then?"

Lizzy froze, kettle in mid-air. The heat reached her palm and she dropped it back on the hob with a clatter which made Gert sit up and spin around.

"You alright there, Lizzy?"

Lizzy took a few seconds to collect herself. "Fine. Handle was a bit too hot. I'll use the cloth."

She didn't speak whilst she put the tea into the pot and poured on the water, nor when she brought the cups from the dresser, giving herself vital minutes to inhale calmness before she turned around, making an effort to appear relaxed.

"What man was that, Gert? What was he asking?"

Gert's instant wide smile and the flickering eyes told Lizzy this was the best piece of gossip the woman had heard in a while. Gert reached out for her teacup, took a long gulp as Lizzy returned to the table and banged the cup down, too engrossed in how to convey her news to her own best advantage to notice Lizzy's shaking hands.

"Tallish, heavy overcoat and a bowler. Wearing gloves, too. I thought perhaps he was one of those lawyers, come with good news." She smiled expectantly.

"He was asking for our address?"

"Yes, and your shop, Lizzy. Is it good news, then?"

"He hasn't found me yet. I expect it will be about the insurance." She spoke in the most disinterested voice she could muster. A small tremor on the surface of her tea betrayed her turmoil, but Gert didn't notice.

"Oh. That all? Explains why he was asking about your children." She picked up her cup again and put it to her lips.

Lizzy jumped up. "Sorry, Gert," she snatched the cup out of Gert's grasp, "I've things to do. You know what it's like. Busy, busy. Come back tomorrow."

Gert found herself propelled by a firm hand on her elbow out of the back door. Lizzy could guess at the amount of self-righteous indignation to be relieved by a visit to houses along the street to report back on Lizzy McRoberts' unpleasant behaviour. She did have things, or rather, one thing to do. It was time. They were checking on her. Something of her visits and talks must have reached them. She would have to stop, but she had gained enough information now. She would pass on what she could to Mrs Butler. Her last remaining opportunity was to write down everything she knew, for John. This was a daunting task for a woman who hadn't learned how to read and write until after her marriage, but there was time. She went into the parlour to collect Willie's writing box. Sitting back at the kitchen table, pen in hand she began.

'*My Darling John, you will see this when I am gone. This is for your safety, and your sisters. As I write we are being watched. It is a year since your beloved father died. I want to tell you what I have learned in this year about the circumstances around your father's death. I know what he was doing, why he was killed, who did it. You may have guessed already that the body we buried was not your father. I am sorry I have not spoken about it. I have promised myself I will never speak about it. I will now tell you everything...'*

Chapter 15

"Are you saying you knew who my father was when you offered me this job?"

Kennet Quinn smiled at the boy sitting in front of him. He crossed one elegantly shod leg over the other and picked up his glass of water from the table to his side, not breaking eye contact. The boy was trying to appear calm, but Kennet saw the twitching of the eyelids, the dilated pupils, the unconscious tap of the heel on the floor.

"Why? Does it matter?"

The boy hesitated for a moment, biting his lips. "I just want to hear it from you, that's all."

"But that is not all, nor is it enough. Words are important. When you work for me you must always choose your words with care. You never know who is listening."

Max Howell shrugged. "OK, I want to find out everything I can about him."

"Then why don't you tell me what you have already, and I will fill in some gaps in your information, if I can. Or if I want to." Kennet sat back, his hands on the arms of his chair, and waited.

Max stared at him for a few moments, but soon blinked. In his youth Kennet perfected the art of staring without blinking, drilling into the gaze of whoever was opposite him, black pupils unmoving. It unnerved people and Max succumbed.

"He killed my mother." Max's turn to sit back.

"I see. How did he do that? I understood your mother died from an excess of drink and drugs. She was an unreconstructed old hippie who thought LSD would let her live forever and that was before she got onto cocaine. Didn't she die in India? At a retreat run by a bunch of do-gooders who told her fasting and prayer would cure her addiction?"

His lips betrayed the slimmest of smiles as Max trembled with each sentence.

"He abandoned us. He said he would get help. He told us to wait. He never came back."

"How old were you then?"

"Ten."

"Did she wait?"

Max put his head down, speaking into his chest, fists gripping the sides of the chairs. "For a while. Until she couldn't."

"Why couldn't she wait?"

"Because she needed help." Max put his hands up to his head, rubbing the sides of his eyes. "She was in a bad way. Someone else came along. He took us to the ashram."

"And they took care of you both."

"You're joking! We had to work. She couldn't get her drugs. She got crazy. They were trying to make her go cold turkey. She couldn't do it."

"And what happened then?"

The boy turned his brown eyes to the ceiling, reliving the memory. "The ashram was on a hill above a river, a fast flowing, narrow river, led into a gulley. One day she got up early, went to the river and threw herself in."

"And you?"

"She left me a note. Said it was his fault. He should have come back and got us out."

"You stayed there?"

110

"I was ten. I didn't have choices then. I had to work if I wanted to eat and live. But only until I didn't need them any more."

"How did you get away?"

"I killed one of them when I was fifteen. Then I ran."

"Why did you kill? Was it a man or a woman?" Kennet asked in a tone of polite disinterest, as if the matter was purely academic.

Max's hands trembled and he pulled them into his lap, tight together. "One of them tried it on with me when I was eleven. I don't... I can't...". His head was twitching and shaking.

"I understand. It went on for four years before you killed him."

Max nodded.

"How did you kill him?"

"He took me to the river, as usual. I struggled, I pushed out at him and he fell in. Like my mother."

"And you have been looking for your father since then. Do you want to kill him, too?"

The boy looked at Kennet, nodded, eyes blazing. "Why do you want me to work for you?"

"Simple," Kennet replied. "He was responsible for my father's death. Him and his colleagues. I want justice in the same way you do. I want to bring their business down; I want to ruin their reputation as they are trying to ruin mine. I have two questions for you. I need answers. If you cannot answer them, or cannot accept the premise of my questions, then I cannot help you."

"Then ask me."

"Are you prepared to do whatever I ask without question? You may not appreciate some aspects of my business. I have to be tough."

"If it gets me closer to finishing off my father, yes."

"Good. Can you remain at a distance from your father, until I tell you otherwise?"

The boy hesitated, then said with a snarl, "If you can guarantee I can be there at the end. I can be the one to do it."

"I make no promises. But you can be sure he will realise you were the one who brought about his downfall, and that of his friends and colleagues."

"OK."

"Good. You can go now. You are satisfied with your accommodation?"

"It's great, thanks," Max replied, standing and starting to make for the door.

"I am placing trust in you, Maxwell. If you let me down, I do not forget. Wait for my call."

Max nodded without turning around. As he left the room Helen passed him in the hall, carrying the baby. She nodded briefly to him and joined Kennet.

"Who was he?"

"A new recruit. A valuable one, until I need to remove him. We can discuss it when the boy here is fed. Give him to me. Have you brought the bottle?"

"It's just cooling. I'll get it now."

Kennet took James Rufus in his arms. "You are going to be the new king of the castle, my boy," he cooed to the baby, stroking the sleeping head, waking him up. "There, there. Pa's going to feed you now."

Helen paused at the door, smiled to herself and went downstairs to the kitchen. If Kennet were entertaining any idea of removing her from the scene, he would soon be disabused of the idea.

Chapter 16

Maggie's first view of Fallough Hill was through a hailstorm.

Travelling to North Wales from Liverpool, the weather became progressively worse. She and Nick had travelled by train and hired a car in Liverpool. The amount of snow on the ground had decreased the further north they progressed. By the time they reached Liverpool there was no snow, but it had been replaced by a wind so bitter Maggie wrapped herself up like a Siberian hunter when the time came to leave the hotel.

She had heard about the stark beauty of the Snowdonia Mountains but there was nothing to see as they crossed the Britannia Bridge onto Anglesey, thanks to a low cloud base. The wind blew with sudden gusts so strong Nick had to fight with the steering wheel to keep the car on the road. His vision was impeded by rain that kept turning to hail, and hailstones that felt as if they were being fired from a cannon directly at the windscreen.

The gate was open for them and as they pulled up to the porta-cabin Trys Wyn Davies was there waiting to hold the door open to let them in.

Introductions were made as they dripped over the floor. Maggie shuddered and said, "This is terrible, isn't it?"

"This is average. You should see it when it's really bad," Trystan said with a blank expression, leaving Maggie nonplussed. Then he guffawed. "Sorry. Yes, it's grim. The weather can take its spite out on us here on the island. But we forgive it in the summer, when it behaves itself beautifully."

"It sounds lovely."

"Don't take your coat off. This isn't going to get any better, so let's get outside again. Nick and John, do you want to come with me?"

"I'll give it a miss, thanks," John replied. Nick nodded agreement with John. "Take Maggie. Show her the grave site and the house. Both skeletons," he said.

Maggie glanced over at the glass door of the porta-cabin which was now shaking on its hinges. But, she hadn't come all this way to chicken out because of the weather. "OK, Sir Trystan. Let's go."

"It's Trys." He walked over to the door, then turned back to Nick and John. "Make yourselves comfortable. It's just us today. I'm glad you've come. When we're done here we're going back to my house for lunch. My mother wants to meet you, and I've found something interesting for you to see."

He pulled up his hood and Maggie did the same, pulling her gloves back on and covering her mouth with her scarf. As they both stepped outside the door crashed shut behind them.

She could just see ahead as Trys led the way across the path through the weed-infested tangle of the former lawn and around to the back of the house. Although the tent over the skeleton had been given extra stability with thick ropes held on iron pegs, it still flapped and cracked with each blast of wind. They made their way inside. The rain had not penetrated the tent and the skeleton was lying peacefully unaware of what was raging above him.

"When will you get him out of here?"

"We were hoping today, but it's been put off until tomorrow," Trys replied. "We don't want to risk damaging him."

Maggie nodded, then dropped to kneel beside the grave. "Poor man. He came here thinking he'd picked up a good commission. What were his last thoughts, facing the gun, do you think?"

Trys rubbed water off his cheeks with both hands. "I hadn't thought about it. Family, I would guess. People he loved, as all of us would. I hope it was quick."

Maggie stood up. "Did he have nothing on him to identify him?"

"No. There were just a few scraps of material, that our anthropologist said was underwear, typical Victorian long-johns. Cheap variety, likely mass-produced. His other clothes were removed before he was buried. There was the coin underneath him. Well, sort of underneath him."

Maggie had been staring into the grave, fixated on the grinning man with the hole in his head. She turned to Trys. "What does that mean?"

"It was lying directly beneath his pelvis, as if it were part of him. Strange, now I think more about it, given he was dressed just in underwear."

"Were there buttons, from the underwear?"

"Yes, a couple. They hadn't been disturbed either. Is this significant, do you think?"

"As yet, I have no idea." The wind whipped the tent flap open. "We're being urged to go," Maggie said. "Can I see a little of the house?"

He led the way back around and through the jungle of bushes and trees to the front façade. Maggie paused, staring up as the hail hit her exposed skin.

"It's beautiful, Trys. I'm so pleased you can save some of it."

"It's been in my family for four hundred years. I'm pleased, too. It's taken some time to get the plans agreed, and the funding. My dream is to return the lawn back to a good enough state for guests to be able to play croquet."

115

Maggie laughed. "Good luck with that. It'll take a couple of seasons, but I'd love to come back when you open it. Will you tell guests about the skeleton?"

"I hadn't thought about it. It would be excellent publicity, but can you finish the story, solve the mystery?"

"It's what we do," she replied. "We'll do our best. We should go now. I can't feel my hands."

* * *

They made their way back across the Britannia Bridge, following Trys' Land Rover along the A5 road, noting the signs in Welsh and English relating its place in history.

In response to John's question Nick replied, "It was the first national road since Roman times and it follows the route of the Roman Watling Street. Laid out by Thomas Telford. He built the original bridge, the Menai. Quite a feat of engineering in its time."

"How long would it have taken by coach from London to Holyhead?" Maggie asked.

"By stagecoach, about three or four days, I expect. Oh, here we go."

Ahead of them, after they passed a sharp bend in the road over a busy river and driven uphill for about half a mile, Trys turned left and they followed a track, at first steep then on a lesser incline through an avenue of tree-lined fields, where sheep huddled against the wind. After a few minutes they reached more cultivated tall shrubs, where the track opened out in front of a house. Trys jumped out and shouted, "Park anywhere."

It was a traditional Snowdonia stone, double mansard house; dark, solid and imposing. Trys led the way through the main front door to a porch where they

116

disposed of coats and boots. Once through a half-glass door, they entered a hallway with a double width staircase at the end, doors leading off on both sides, and a corridor on the right.

"This hall's the size of my living room," John whispered to Maggie.

"Impressive." She nodded, glancing around at the portraits hanging on the walls.

A door to their left opened and a woman walked out. She was tiny, both in height and figure, slightly bent, white-haired and bright-eyed, dressed in beige slacks and a light beige sweater. She held out a hand to each of them and said in a reedy voice trembling with age, "Helen Wyn Davies. Trystan is keeping me up to date on developments. It's fascinating. Follow me."

Maggie raised an eyebrow at Nick and John and they followed the old lady to the door next to the one from which she entered the hall. Hand on the handle, she said, "This is our library."

Their gasps of surprise and "wow" from John as the door opened caused Maggie to bump into Nick, who stopped dead as he entered the room.

It was around thirty feet square, with a ceiling height Maggie guessed as being at least twenty feet with an imposing three-tiered glass chandelier at its centre. Opposite them was a set of three long sash windows looking out onto the garden at the side of the house. Every inch of the remaining walls was filled with bookshelves from floor to ceiling. Two old desks sat back-to-back in the middle of the room, a laptop open on one of them.

There were some novels, but also biographies, books of maps ancient and modern, medical texts, travel books. Books on philosophy, history and geography.

"May I," John asked, standing in front of a shelf of king-size, tall books.

"Of course," the old lady said. "They were meant to be read and studied."

"I love maps," John said, taking down one of the largest books and laying it on a nearby desk. "This is old. It's the lands of the Bible, isn't it?"

"My father was a traveller in the Middle East," Helen Wyn Davies said. "A diplomat. He spent time in the Arab countries, including Palestine in the 1930s. He began the collection. My late husband carried it on. I've told Trystan, who also loves books, to stop now. We have enough." She walked over to stand next to John. "That one dates from the nineteenth century. Fascinating, isn't it?"

Maggie was staring around but noticed something on one of the desks caught Nick's attention. "What's that, Nick?"

"Estate papers, I think. Lady Wyn Davies?"

Helen joined him. "That's what I wanted you to come here to see. Trystan told me about the death of the poor man and I understand you have been able to date it. These should help you. You may borrow them. When you have finished I want them back, mind."

"Do they relate to something relevant?" Maggie asked, craning her neck to see what Nick was doing as he flipped through the pages.

Trystan, who disappeared when they entered the house, now joined them, kissed his mother on the head and said, "I see she's got there before me. Has mother explained?"

"I was just doing so, my dear. On the weekend the man died, there was a Christmas celebration at Fallough Hill. An annual event, for the family and special guests, old friends. Plus some business guests. Sir Richard always had an eye to an investor." She winked at Maggie.

"This is an inventory of the costs of the food and drink," Nick said, still flipping pages.

"And this," Helen said, picking up an A4-sized book with a monogrammed cover and a clasp holding it shut, "is the daily journal kept by Sir Richard's wife. It was fashionable then to keep such a thing. I could never do it. Too boring for me, recording the minutiae of your everyday life, but Victorian and Edwardian women did it. You'll find her opinion on their festivities and..." She paused, a theatrical pause, gaining her audience's attention. "The names of every guest who was at the house over the weekend. Together with her opinion on the actions and character of each of them."

"Does this mean we have the name of the person who shot William McRoberts, right here?" Maggie picked up the journal and stared hard at it as if her intensity would force it to reveal its secret.

"Quite possibly," Helen said, nodding emphatically.

"Sorry to break this up, but lunch is ready," Trys said. "Let's eat and we can discuss what you're going to do next. John, are you coming? Can you tear yourself away?"

"Hardly," John replied, reluctantly closing the huge book of ancient Middle East maps. "But I am starving. Let's go. Let's plan."

* * *

On the way back to Liverpool they decided to do nothing else together for the rest of the day. The main plan was to read what was in the diary – Maggie – and the household accounts – Nick – during the evening, then

119

meet the following morning with John and Jacka at the family house to begin the search for the letter.

"You OK, John?" Nick asked, turning his head, smiling.

John was hugging a large package close to his chest. At the end of their lunch, when they were saying goodbye to Trys and Helen, John asked if he could take another, final look at the book of Middle Eastern maps.

"No, you can't," Helen replied and was met with an expression of surprised hurt and disappointment, which turned to excitement when she went on. "You can take it with you. Just a loan, mind you. Show it to your father. And bring him with you when you come back. It will be good to talk to someone who has memories, even if they are second hand."

John explained over lunch his grandfather Jonno, Jacka's father, had been in the RAF during World War Two, and spent most of his time as a mechanic in North Africa, servicing aircraft. Following the War, he had been posted to Palestine.

"What did he think about it?" Helen asked.

"Jacka says his dad didn't say much, told him some stories, but no detail."

"Interesting," Helen replied. "Did your grandfather like the countries?"

"Loved all of them, Helen. He took photos, small black-and-white snaps, of the sphinx and the pyramids. He liked the people too. And the mosque with the golden roof and the wall. In Jerusalem he felt like he was walking in the steps of the Bible, which was special for him, because he was Catholic."

"Did he ever go back?"

"No, never did. He was content with his memories and he loved maps. He's dead a few years now and he didn't enjoy travelling much. He didn't leave the country after he got back in 1948. He liked Blackpool. Although he did go to Devon once. Me dad's the same."

She laughed and took his hands in hers. "Bring your father here sometime. He sounds an interesting character and I'd love to hear about his father's memories and see the photographs."

"I will do. He'd like you too. Just don't talk politics, Helen. He's a dyed-in-the-wool Scouse lefty socialist. I don't think you'll have that in common, will you?"

She glanced around to make sure her son couldn't hear, and leaned in towards him. "You'd be surprised, dear boy," she replied with a wink.

* * *

After dropping off John and his prize, Nick and Maggie went back to the hotel to read their documents before meeting for dinner.

They decided to eat in the bar at one of the low tables by the window, so they could spread out their documents and make notes as each told the other what they found. Nick went first.

"If this was a small informal gathering, as Helen said, I can't imagine what a big one was like. The preparation was immense. They hired extra staff for the three days, maids, kitchen support staff, general servants, plus planning for the staff who travelled with the guests. The butler and the housekeeper were in charge. These accounts could be a script from *Downton Abbey*."

"Does it help us?" Maggie asked.

"Not sure. There are some names here, allocation of bedrooms for accompanying staff, some are named, which might be useful."

"How would they know the names of the accompanying staff in advance?" Maggie asked.

"Good question. Perhaps they were regulars at these events. Maybe they had their own rooms and requirements already known to the family, and each time they visited it was the same."

"Can we assemble a complete list, do you think, of everyone who was there over the weekend?"

He turned over a few more pages on the table. "No, not from this. We do have a list of staff wages here, which is helpful. I'm just not sure if we can pinpoint this weekend, but we can give it a go, if we need to. How about you?"

Maggie picked up the diary and her notes. "This is illuminating. The practice of the hostess was to comment on everyone who attended. Some she liked, some she didn't. She doesn't hold back."

"Useful insights?" Nick asked.

"Yes, but tempered by some prejudice and high-handed opinions. I've made some notes. These are the highlights and I thought perhaps we can swap documents tonight. I'll read the inventories, you read the diary."

"Good idea."

"OK," she took up her notes, "here goes. There were thirty-five in all. Now for quantifying and naming the people who were there. The family, obviously. I did a quick check on the census and the Wyn Davies' had five children. In 1878 they would have ranged in age between ten and seventeen. I got their names from the census. According to the diary they were at home. In addition, the paternal matriarch was there, plus Lady Wyn Davies' parents and her sister, sister's husband and their two children. That makes fourteen. There were also two younger Wyn Davies daughters, Sir Richard's sisters, and their husbands and children. Three children between them. Twenty-one. One impoverished elderly cousin on the wife's side. Twenty-two. Two local landowners plus wives. Twenty-six. And..." She paused and looked up. "What I think may be the significant one: three business guests of Sir Richard Wyn Davies. Each with a wife and three children between them."

"Why are those more significant than the rest?"

"Because of what she says about them. Although, I agree we can't discount all the others, but we can discount some of the children, and some others."

"Go on," he replied.

"Let's discount the children first. Would you agree we can ignore those who were under eighteen?"

He nodded.

"That takes out thirteen. We're down to twenty-two. I would say we can take out the elderly impoverished female cousin, the sisters and the local wives and the elderly relatives. I mean, I don't believe the matriarch would have been involved. She was in her seventies. And Lady Wyn Davies' parents. Agreed?" Nick thought for a few seconds then nodded again. "Good, another nine gone, which gets us to thirteen."

"Who were?"

"Sir Richard Wyn Davies, Lady Virginia, the three brothers-in-law. The two local landowners. And six of the special guests."

"Nine men and four women. Is there anything in the diary to let us discount any more of them?" Nick asked. "It's still a lot of potential suspects."

"Well, according to Lady Virginia Wyn Davies, the brothers-in-law barely owned a brain cell to share between them. Nick, why don't we leave it there for tonight? Let's read each other's papers and info and regroup in the morning, before we head off to John's house. Here comes the food. Let's eat, then I need to sleep. It's been a long day."

Chapter 17

Maggie was halfway through a full English breakfast when Nick arrived with a bowl of fruit and a mug of coffee.

"Don't give me the look," she said, waving a piece of sausage on a fork.

"I wasn't going to. Shall we add 'don't tell Bob you ate that' to the list of things to do when we get back?"

She put the food in her mouth.

"I will take your lack of protest as a yes. I read the diary last night. There's a few more people we can rule out." He dug into his bowl of fruit.

Maggie swallowed the sausage, paused, scowled at the plate, pushed it away, and picked up her cup of tea. "Who and why?"

"I agree we can rule out the children. They were all under eighteen. I can't see how teenagers, even a couple of them working together, could have shot a man and buried him so deeply without anyone noticing. It would have taken a lot of effort and time."

"OK, agreed, unless later we find out something about any of them. Who else?"

"The two local landowners. One was blind and the other had been wounded, temporarily incapacitated with a broken arm. And I agree about the brothers-in-law. I wouldn't rule them out totally at this point, but there are better possibilities. Oh, yes and Lady Wyn Davies."

"Why her?"

"She was writing about all of them. Something about the tone, I suppose. Part amused, part catty. But her worst comments were kept for the extra guests. So, I have two lists: an A list and a B list. On the A list is Sir Richard, the three special guests and one of their wives.

On the B list: the brothers-in-law, so five on list A and three on list B."

"Why is one of the wives still in?" Maggie asked.

"Because Lady Wyn Davies was particularly rude about her. She knew the other two and thought them boring and stuffy." He glanced at his watch. "We should get going. John and Jacka will be waiting for us."

It took twenty minutes to check out of the hotel and ten minutes later they reached the McRoberts family home, north-west of the city centre but close enough to walk to it. As expected, John and Jacka were already there. It was a terraced house in a long road and must once have been an aspiring, up-and-coming street. This was the area to which William McRoberts chose to bring his family. It turned out to be their last move, around 1877 and over a hundred and forty years later the family was still there.

Maggie knew some of the back-story of when the McRoberts family first came to Liverpool from Scotland. They moved through digs and rooms, into bigger rooms, then into their first small house which was a walk-in from the street and, following William's promotion, to this more spacious three-bedroom house with its own little garden. Originally the toilet, the 'privy', would have been outdoors in the backyard. As they walked through, Maggie could see an extension had been added, allowing for a bigger kitchen and an upstairs bathroom. The paintwork was scuffed and the wallpaper dark and loose in places. The front door was original, but wooden double-glazed windows had been put in. The décor was 1960s. It was what an estate agent would call a house 'with potential', what Maggie thought of as a good 'doer-upper'.

Jacka was waiting at the living room door at the front of the house. "Me and him started a bit of a search, like." He beamed. "We've been checking the walls, seeing if there's any hollow bits. Nothing yet."

"Let's go through to the kitchen," John said. He led them past the staircase on their left and through a small dining room where a wall was knocked through at the back to become part of the new kitchen/diner extension.

At the end of the building was a set of old wooden French doors through which she glimpsed a small patioed garden.

"It's a nice house, John," Maggie said, standing at the exit to the garden. "It needs some doing up, but it could be lovely. Mine was the same when I moved in."

"I know, Maggie, but the roof leaks," John replied, "the guttering's full of leaks, too, and there's a lot of damp. It was built in 1877. It needs replastering and it hasn't been rewired since 1950. Check out the Bakelite switches. They're antiques. William was the first tenant and Lizzy became the owner in the 1880s. She passed it onto her son John. We have the original documents."

"Let's consider what we're going to do here, and organise a search," Nick said. "Would it be possible for you to show us around the house, John, and point out the original parts and what's changed since Lizzy and John died?"

John led them back out of the kitchen to the stairs. "It's an odd shape," John said as they reached the top of the first flight of stairs before the staircase turned a hundred and eighty degrees. There was a small square landing with a door leading off. John threw it open, to reveal a bedroom.

"This is like a mezzanine," Maggie said. "I've seen something similar before. My grandmother's house in

Newport was similar. This is an original part of the house."

At the top of the second set of stairs was a bathroom to the left and facing them another door. When opened, this revealed a large bedroom stretching across the frontage of the house. The stairs then turned again and went up another floor, ending at a door which in turn led into another bedroom, built into the roof space.

"When was this added?" Nick asked.

"Nineteen sixties," John replied. "It was the attic, at the beginning. Mind the light switches. They wobble. The screws holding them in have gone."

Although the room had the same 1960s décor as the rest of the house, there was no sign of the original attic space. It smelled of damp and there were two buckets strategically placed to collect dripping rainwater, both of which needed emptying.

"This would have been cleared out in the sixties. So if Lizzy put the document anywhere here, is there any chance whatever it was contained in would still be around?"

Jacka shook his head. "I helped clear it. We chucked most of it."

"Can you pinpoint the time, Jacka?" Maggie asked.

"Um, let me think." He gazed at the roof, rubbing his stubbly chin. "It would have been about 1968. Me and Julie had been married for a year. We got our own place in sixty-seven, after living here with mam and dad for the first year. Grandma Mary was still there, then. She was ancient, or so I thought at the time, although younger then than I am now. Me mam and dad wanted the extra room for me sister and her husband. They'd just got married and had a kid on the way."

"It was a busy household." Maggie smiled.

"Yeh," Jacka replied. "Let me think... when we were here there was mam and dad, Grandma Mary. She was dad's mum. Me and Julie, and little brother Norman. He shared with Grandma Mary until she died. No more crowded than most around here. Our Norman never left. He's just moved out in the past couple of weeks. He's in a home now. Dementia. He's three years younger than me."

Nick glanced around again. "There's not much point in searching here. Shall we go back to the kitchen and draw up a plan?"

* * *

Over coffee and biscuits Nick sketched out a quick plan of the house, marking which rooms were original and which were new and updated.

"There's no point searching the updated part," he said. "We should concentrate on the original rooms."

"What are you thinking, Nick, and be careful," John said, flicking his head at his father. "I don't want him attacking walls with a hammer or a screwdriver."

"We're looking for just a few pieces of paper. They will be old and delicate. If we're right and John McRoberts left them in the house before setting off to his meeting, he must have had some suspicion and would have taken care to ensure they couldn't be easily found or couldn't be damaged. It would have been somewhere he could get at when he got back, which he expected to do. Thoughts, anyone?"

"In that case, behind a wall isn't an option," Maggie said, eliciting a sigh of relief from John. "But maybe a floorboard, or a skirting board?"

"The front hall has tiles, but the skirting boards are original. In the parlour the floor and the boards are original, and the fireplace."

"Upstairs, the front bedroom is the same," Jacka added, "and the halfway room. The bathroom was converted from a bedroom when the loft extension was done."

"What about this room?" Maggie asked.

"This was the old kitchen," John replied. "The door used to lead out straight onto the yard. It hasn't been used for years."

"Shall we start at the top, then, and work our way down?" Nick asked.

* * *

After two hours of tapping, prodding and taking up some floorboards, nothing had been found apart from a few old coins, some sweet wrappers and a few desiccated mice.

"Let's take a quick lunch break, then try the ground floor," Maggie said. She sent Jacka out to buy sandwiches from the small take-away shop at the end of the road.

"This isn't looking good," she said to John, over cheese and pickle and ham sandwiches.

"Well, trying to find something hidden for almost a hundred and twenty years wasn't going to be easy. Dad'll be disappointed if we don't come up with anything, but we can only do our best."

They cleared up and started again from the back of the house, moving forward. The last room was the parlour. After half an hour of going over the entire space twice and Jacka getting as far as he could up the chimney, they found nothing.

Maggie sat back in one of the fifties armchairs, her eyes closed, as Nick and John decided there was no point carrying on and they should lock up and leave.

"We'll have to go over the evidence we have, John," Nick said. "Sorry this turned out to be a wild goose chase." He turned to Maggie. "You ready to go." She didn't reply. "Maggie?"

"I'm thinking. Wait a minute. There's something. Keep quiet, all of you."

The three men stood in the doorway, giving each other puzzled looks, but not speaking. Jacka opened his mouth after a couple of minutes, but was forestalled when Maggie jumped out of the chair.

"Jacka, you said when you emptied the loft back in the sixties, you chucked 'most of it' out. Do you mean you kept some things?"

"Just a couple of old bits. Nothing special."

"What did you keep?"

"I can't say about the others, but I've got a few bits."

"Like that tacky old suitcase, the miniature one, and the old box thing?" John asked.

"Yeh. I keep them on the shelf in me front room, in mam's old cupboard, with some of her china."

"Can we come to your house to see them?" Maggie asked.

"Certainly, love. Let's go."

* * *

Jacka's mother's 'old cupboard' turned out to be a stylish 1930s art deco cabinet. It contained a top shelf of pieces of china, including what Maggie recognised as Clarice Cliff.

"These are lovely, Jacka," she said, bending down to examine them close up.

"Bit gaudy for me, but me mam loved them. Got them from her mother. I expect my kids will chuck them out when I'm gone."

"Not if they've got any sense," she replied. "There's over a grand's worth of china here, maybe more."

She bent down to the bottom shelf, to the old case, the box and a lady's dressing table set of mirror, brush and glass powder jar.

"Let's take these out." She removed the case and the box and set them gently on the coffee table. The lid slipped from the wooden box and Nick caught it in time to stop it crashing to the floor. He grimaced, put it down and opened the small suitcase. It was old leather, no more than a foot wide, eight or nine inches across and about six inches deep, with two clasps and a handle at the front.

"This is a document case," he said, opening the clasps. "It's empty, but it's lined. Can we see if there's anything hidden in the lining?"

John nodded. Jacka was still staring open-mouthed at his mother's 'gaudy' china.

The lining was loose in a few places, just enough for Nick to slip a finger underneath to separate it. After a few goes he shook his head. "Nothing doing. It's stuck fast. If there was anything hidden under here it would have disintegrated years ago."

He moved it aside and placed the wooden box in front of him, opened the wobbly lid and propped it with a cushion. "This looks handmade. See how the lid is cut on a slope. When it was opened it would have sat square on the table. It's a writing box."

Nick removed the cushion and laid the box flat open. The wood on the bottom was flimsier than the top and it had split almost in half. The top half was empty and unlined. The bottom half, however, was built in sections. Closest to him was a section across the width of the box, about four inches wide and itself divided into three sections. In the first compartment on the left was the ink well, with an old bottle of ink still sitting jammed in it, unmovably stuck. Next to it was another small square section, of the same size, with a piece of wood blocking it. Nick prized out the wood. There was nothing underneath. The final section was longer. "This was where the pens were kept," he said. The remainder of the box was covered by a frame lined with a flimsy piece of red felt. "They would have written on this and, if I'm not mistaken..." He lifted the frame to reveal a space, again empty. "This is where any documents would have been kept. So, nothing here I'm afraid. What a shame." He went to put the lid back on, but Maggie's touch on his arm stopped him.

"Just a minute. Can I take a look?" He moved out of the way and she took his place in front of the box. She took the inner frame out again and ran her fingers around the edges of the bottom of the box, peered in, then looked up. "This pen holder section isn't the same depth as the document holder."

Three heads simultaneously moved forward.

"You're right," Nick said. He nudged his finger at the piece of wood separating the pen holder from the rest of the box. It gave a fraction of an inch, but wouldn't move further. He looked at John and Jacka. "What do you think? I'll have to give it a good pull to get it out. It may destroy the box."

John looked at Jacka, who nodded. "Do it, Nick."

133

"Right. Let's see." He took the thin sliver of wood between his thumb and forefinger and tweaked it back and forth until there was a small crack of the glue giving up. Nick breathed out a sigh of relief as he gently eased it out of the box. It hadn't broken. So far so good. He put it on the table and peered into the space. Now for the base section. This time he pushed on one end and again there was a crack, sharper this time. His fingers shot back out of the space.

"It needs smaller fingers. Maggie, your turn."

Maggie flexed and curled her fingers and put a forefinger down to press on one side. It moved down, enough to get the nail on her other forefinger under the opposite edge and ease it up, then out. As the wood came out she peered down. "There is something here. It could be paper."

Again she tried with her fingers to tease it up, but to no avail. "It's stuck to the bottom and if I pull too hard I'll tear it." She paused for a moment, then turned to Jacka. "Tweezers?"

He ran out of the room. They listened in silence to the thundering steps up the stairs, a pause accompanied by the banging of a door opening and closing, and the feet thundered again. Jacka appeared with a smile of triumph, panting and hoisting a set of rusty tweezers.

Maggie took them from him and turned her attention back to the box. For what seemed an hour but was no more than a couple of minutes, her fingers beginning to tense and tingle, she teased looser edges of paper away from their confinement, until she was able to slip a finger underneath. "It's paper. Let me just... here! Got it."

Her fingers emerged from the space, between her thumb and forefinger a parchment hanging, yellow with age, folded several times.

"Open it up, then," Jacka said, but Nick wagged a finger at him. "We have to be careful and take our time, Jacka. Maggie, one fold at a time."

She flicked her head once, then peeled back the first fold with the tips of her fingers. "It's still in one piece, I think." Then the next one, and the next. Then the final fold. With the lightest possible touch, she took out a tissue and smoothed it over the paper. It was covered in tiny handwriting, the ink brown and light in places, but still legible.

"How many pages?" Nick asked.

"Two," she replied. "I have some acid-free pockets back at the hotel. We'll need to get them in as soon as possible. It's to make sure the moisture from our hands doesn't do any damage," she explained to a puzzled John and Jacka. She peered down. "I can make out some words, but it's not easy. Jacka, how about a magnifying glass?"

He ran out of the room again, this time just next door where the sound of a drawer opening and the clunks and bangs of objects being flung out caused Nick to chortle, before Jacka reappeared.

"Good enough for Sherlock Holmes," Maggie said, taking the oversized round-handled glass from the old man. "Let's see what we've got." She paused. "John, would you read it first? If this is Lizzy's letter, it's yours by right."

"No, you do it, Maggie. My hands are shaking."

"OK, here goes."

She leaned in with the magnifying glass and began to read in a voice loud enough for all to hear clearly:

"My Darling John, you will see this when I am gone. This is for your safety, and your sisters'. As I write we are being watched. It is a year since your dear father died. I want to tell you what I have learned in this year about the circumstances around your father's death. I know now what he was doing, why he was killed, who did it. You may have guessed already that the body we buried was not your father. I am sorry I have not spoken about it. I have promised myself I will never speak about it. I will now tell you everything..."

Chapter 18

"Hey, glumface, what the fuck is up with you?"

On Friday morning, Zelah stood in the kitchen watching Jack trudge around looking for something to eat for breakfast. She wasn't even sure he wanted to find anything, as he opened and closed cupboards so randomly he couldn't have looked properly. Eventually he pulled a bottle of chocolate milk out of the fridge and turned to leave the kitchen without acknowledging her.

"Not so fast," she said, scuttling over to block the doorway.

"Let me out, Zelah," he replied, swigging the drink from the bottle and not looking at her.

"No, I don't think I will. Unless you plan to push me out of the way."

He looked at her. "I could, you know."

"But you won't. You're not that kind of boy. Which is why you've been such a pain the arse lately. Isn't it about time you got it out? Whatever 'it' is."

"You wouldn't understand."

She threw up her hands in mock horror. "Indeed. I am an old woman who never had any teenage experiences. Apart from running away when I was sixteen, living on the streets, getting in trouble with the police, and so on. Now, sit down. We are going to talk. Now!"

She saw tears start to glisten. Taking him by the elbow she pushed him towards the chair, where he plonked himself down. His hands grasped the plastic bottle so hard it dented and made an ominous cracking sound.

"You're cleaning up if it breaks," she said. "Jack, just tell me what's wrong. Please."

He put the bottle down. "It's my girlfriend. Or at least, I thought she was."

"You've been dumped?"

"No."

"Oh my God, she's not pregnant?"

"No! I'm not so stupid."

"Well, you are some kind of stupid. What about your girlfriend. What's her name?"

"Sophie. Sophie Britton." His voice softened and a dreamy look appeared.

"Judging by the soppy look, she's still your girlfriend. What has she done?"

"Her exam results were terrible but she doesn't care about university. She wants us to get engaged, get jobs and find somewhere to live together."

"You mean, she doesn't want you to go to university?"

"Yeh. But I want to, Zelah. It's my ambition now, but she says I have to choose."

Zelah nodded slowly. Then she stood up. "What time do you finish today?"

"Lunchtime. Why?"

"Because I am going to pick you up and we are going back to my flat. I need to check it's OK and you are going to talk to Mischa, because you need an alternative point of view. No point me saying what I think. You wouldn't like it."

"Bob thinks I should dump her."

Zelah agreed, but thought this wasn't the right moment to say so. And such an action needed to be the boy's decision.

"Right. Off, you. I'll see you later. Be ready." She shooed him out of the kitchen.

"The little bitch," she muttered. She needed to talk to Mischa, to fill her in and get her input on how to help

138

Jack. It was seven in the morning. Too early to call Mischa. She began to put last night's dishes into the dishwasher. Maggie and Nick were due back later, having spent a final evening in Liverpool with John and Jacka to discuss their discoveries. Alice was going to a friend overnight then back for Saturday and Sunday.

Zelah needed the peace of her own space. Mischa was going back to Ireland this evening. She could take her and Jack out for an early dinner, drop Mischa at the airport, Jack at home, then retire to her own place. She breathed a sigh of relief at the thought, as Bob raced in and out of the kitchen and he and Jack left the house.

A peaceful weekend coming up.

* * *

Zelah and Jack got back to the flat near Caerleon at two o'clock where Mischa was waiting for them. She decided to leave her car on the road instead of in the secure underground garage. At five she emerged again, with Jack and Mischa, and drove off.

They were laughing over a joke Mischa made and Zelah was pleased Jack listened to what the girl had to say, so much so she didn't notice the small black car parked further along the road, with a head and shoulders hunkered in the driver's seat. The driver watched with envy and anger at the laughing group but made no attempt to follow them. Patience had become a necessary virtue. It would have to wait until Zelah Trevear was alone.

* * *

Zelah left a message for Maggie to say she, Jack and Mischa were having dinner out and would be back around seven-ish. Bob also messaged to say he was working late, not back before midnight. So, when Maggie deposited Nick with Stella and let herself into an empty house late-afternoon she was relieved to have a couple of hours alone.

Leaving her bags in the hall, she went into the kitchen to put the kettle on and with a supply of tea in the biggest mug she could find, she put her coat back on and let herself out into the garden to wander around and process what she and Nick had learned in Liverpool and North Wales. There had been no more snow since she went away and what was lying on the ground was starting to melt so it no longer formed a blanket, but a series of small islands. Dodging through them, Maggie went straight to the end of the garden and gazed over into the canal.

"I wish I could have some time to move at your speed," she muttered to the motionless black water, her hands curled around the cup to keep her fingers warm. "Then again, no-one knows what's going on beneath your surface in your stillness."

During the five-hour journey home she and Nick discussed a tentative plan of what to do with the information they had discovered in the letter from Lizzy McRoberts to her son. They agreed Maggie should give Zelah the details as soon as possible and begin their research. She was now more certain than ever this was going to be a major case for Maze to solve and as soon as they could reveal the details, the better. The publicity would be fantastic. Maggie could begin her venture into 'brick wall' cases openly and in earnest. Most importantly, this case was based entirely in the past, with no possible repercussions in the present day. Or so they hoped. There was a possibility there could be embarrassment for a present-day family, but they would do their best to be sensitive, should it turn out to be the case. Hopefully, the distance of time wouldn't make whatever they found seem too bad to a modern-day descendant.

She had begun a list of tasks in her head and she went through them again now, before turning to go back into the house when a voice startled her.

"Talking to the canal water? That's an odd one, even for you."

She spun around to find Bob standing behind her, wearing the bobble hat with strings he had worn when she first met him. He hugged his arms around himself.

"I thought you were going to be late." She shivered. "This teacup is not doing its job. Come on, let's go in. It's getting dark already."

"Sure. Nice to see you, too. And you can tell me why you were talking to the water."

"I'd stick my tongue out at you if I didn't think it might freeze in mid-air."

In response he gathered a handful of snow, fashioned it into a snowball and they laughed as he chased her back up the garden, catching her at the door and attempting to stuff the snowball down the back of her neck. She screamed and laughed, fighting him off, then put her arms around his neck. "We've got a few hours," she whispered, but her smile died as she saw Sherry Martin standing in the hall doorway.

"Oh, hello, Sherry. I didn't realise you were here." She poked Bob in the ribs and he stifled a smirk.

If there was a joke, or anything vaguely amusing, Sherry Martin didn't see it. For a moment she looked as if she was sneering at them, but the expression turned into a smile, although it didn't rise beyond her mouth.

"We just called by so Bob could see if you were home and give you an update on the investigation into Malcolm Thomas' death," she said.

Maggie had to think for a second. "Oh, the boy, Malky." She turned to Bob. "Could it wait until later, Bob? I've been back literally ten minutes. Zelah should be on her way over with Jack before long and I want to update her on the outcome of the Liverpool trip. I'll wait for you," she added.

"Up to you. I might be late, though."

"I'll wait," she said, smiling. Sherry Martin shuffled in the doorway.

"See you later," Bob whispered with a grin and a wink.

* * *

After she closed the door on them, Maggie warmed up her tea and took it into the office. She had kept up to date with emails and messages during the trip, so there was nothing requiring her attention. She decided to begin her 'to-do' list but after writing two items, she found her intent to be diligent knocked off course by consideration of Sherry Martin.

There was something perplexing about Sherry. Not unlike the canal water, calm enough on top but the suspicion of something else going on beneath the surface, something murky. Maggie had no wish to get to know Sherry better, but perhaps getting to understand her could help allay the feeling of disquiet she felt whenever she and Sherry were in the same room. She knew Zelah sensed it, too. How to bring it about in a natural way?

She thought for a few minutes, then picked up the phone.

"Bob, are you and Sherry still on the move?"

"Yes, why?"

"I was wondering if she would join us for dinner tomorrow night. Alice will be home, Zelah can come over, and Nick and Stella. You and she are likely to be working together for some time, so it's a chance for her to get to know us better. Is she there? What does she say?"

Maggie was hoping that asking the question without giving Sherry too much time to think of an excuse would force her to accept. She was right.

"Excellent. I'll get it set up. It'll be informal. No need for her to bring anything. See you later."

She ended the call with a smile. She would make sure the others didn't suspect her ulterior motive. *Let's examine you in more detail on my territory, Sherry Martin*, she thought. She went back to her list making.

* * *

Zelah and Jack made a noisy entrance just after seven. After hugging his mother Jack went to his bedroom. Zelah stayed in the hallway, without taking off her coat. "I'm going straight home," she said. "It's been fine here, before you ask, and now I need my own space."

"OK," Maggie replied. "I was going to ask you to stay for half an hour so I can bring you up to speed on the Liverpool trip. Up to you. Actually," she paused, "how about you come back tomorrow after lunch? I'm collecting Alice in the morning from Abergavenny. There's something I need your help with, later tomorrow."

"Go on," Zelah said, head to one side.

"I've, err, I've invited Sherry Martin to dinner tomorrow night. Nick and Stella are coming, too."

"You don't like her, nor do I. Why is she coming to dinner?"

"Because I want to find out why I don't like her," Maggie explained. "If it's just about Bob, or if there's something else. I've got a... you know, a feeling. I can't explain better, not yet."

She expected Zelah to jibe or to challenge. Zelah did neither. "Yes, I agree. There's something off. On one condition, though."

"Which is?"

"We agree in advance what we give away, about the cases we're working on, and nothing about the Quinns. Agreed?"

Maggie returned an emphatic nod.

"OK. Should be interesting. Give me a precis on Liverpool. Good trip?"

"Very. Amazing, in fact."

Zelah paused. "Great. Now I'm torn. I want to go home and I want to hear what happened."

"How about I read you the letter we found? Then tomorrow we can give you the full story."

"Let's go." Zelah turned and walked into the office. Maggie followed her. She had been examining the letter again and making yet another list and had left the paperwork on the table. Zelah sat, arms folded and Maggie began.

"I'll go into detail tomorrow about how we found it, but the content is a gobsmacker. Here goes:

"*My Darling John, you will see this when I am gone. This is for your safety, and your sisters'. As I write we are*

144

being watched. It is a year since your dear father died. I want to tell you what I have learned in this year about the circumstances around your father's death. I know now what he was doing, why he was killed, who did it. You may have guessed already the body we buried was not your father. I am sorry I have not spoken about it. I have promised myself I will never speak about it. I will now tell you everything.

" Your father was an excellent policeman with a good record. He was popular with his colleagues and was approved of by his superiors. He never put a foot wrong in the seven years he was a uniformed man, nor when he became a detective. I was so proud of him.

"One day he was called to an incident at a house in the Ropeworks. A woman there, a woman known as an inebriate, was claiming a man had abducted her child, a girl of twelve years. Your father asked some questions and spoke to the neighbours. It turned out the woman had sold the child, when in a state of drunkenness. When she became sober she wanted the child back. She asked around and was given the name of the man but she said he would not give the child back and later left the city. Willie made some enquiries. The information he gained was other girls had been kidnapped or sold and had not been found. One had previously been reported to the police but they had done little to find her. That girl was ten years old. Willie found out the name of the man and it was the same man. He reported his findings to his superiors. Five days later he was dismissed, for "associating with prostitutes". They said more than one made a complaint about him. The officer who dismissed him was Chief Inspector Charles Monaghan. Your father of course protested his innocence and asked to see the evidence of the complaints. Statements were shown to *him, but they were written by Monaghan with the names of the women who signed with their mark. I have since spoken to these women. They told me they either made no complaint, or were forced to make their mark. They did not have relations of any kind with your father. A few of his friends stood by him. Dear George Harbison was one. He tried to get more information, but was warned off.*

" Your dear father worried about how he would support us. We had not long moved into this house. How could he afford the rent? He decided to try his luck at the work of a private detective investigator. At first he had little luck, then a few cases came along. But he despised what he was forced to do. Following men suspected of adultery, discovering evidence of minor discretions on behalf of merchants and the like against their workers. Some of his former colleagues tipped him off about criminals and he was able to gain some work helping the police, until Monaghan found out.

" Then, one day, Mrs Josephine Butler came to ask him to help her. You will no doubt know Mrs Butler's name. She has become famous now. Back then, she had just moved to Liverpool and was working on behalf of the street women. She was not popular. She asked your father to undertake a commission to find a child who was missing. This was the child of a common woman but Mrs Butler was not affected by her lowly class. The child, whose name was Elsie, was twelve years old and was supposedly beautiful. The man promised Elsie would be trained as a Ladies' Maid in London. The mother admitted to taking money from the man who bought her, but when the effect of the drink was gone, regretted her action and wanted her child back.

"She gave Mrs Butler a description of the man who bought Elsie. Mrs Butler engaged your father and offered him a good payment for the commission of finding out who the man was and bringing the child back to her mother, generous indeed. Your father discovered the man had left the city and gone to a house on the island of Anglesey in Wales, called Fallough Hill. He told Mrs Butler he was going to follow on, but did not give her his suspect's name. He set off on that fateful day in December. I never saw him again.

"When George Harbison came to see me, with that man Monaghan, to tell me a body had been found in the river, I knew it could not be your father. Monaghan tried to stop me from seeing the body, but Mrs Butler prevailed. I do not know how. She accompanied me. Whoever the poor man was, he was not your father. How do I know this? Easily! They told me the body was dressed in underclothes, which I asked to be returned to me. It was not his. Do you remember how your sister gave your father a lucky penny? He promised he would always keep it on him. I sewed it into a pocket in his underclothes. I sewed firmly. Your sister watched me, with great fun. He promised he would never lose it. There was no pocket in what was returned to me. Yet I know he set off with the penny sewn into his garments.

"What could I do? Little, I am so sorry to say. I allowed them to silence me with a promise of your father's pension. I allowed a poor unknown man to be buried in your father's place. There have been many times I have regretted this. I have cried long into many nights. But I accepted the bribe. I had you and your sisters to look after. Had I not accepted we would have been destitute. Monaghan also hinted he would make sure your father's reputation was publicly ruined if I did not. So I took their money.

"But I could not rest. After some time I went again to see Mrs Butler. She gave me the name of the woman whose child disappeared and a description of the man who Willie was searching for, an Englishman, wealthy and respectable. I do not know if your father ever reached the house in Wales, or if he was killed before he even left our city. I must accept that he is dead. I went to speak to the child's mother. Her name was Margaret Doherty. She has never seen or heard from her daughter again. She was not helpful. I believe she was frightened. She went to ask for help from the police but was taken in front of Monaghan, called a liar and a drunk. He threatened to arrest her and remove her to an asylum and her remaining children to the workhouse. In the past months I have been asking around and about, regarding missing children. There is something terrible happening in this wonderful city of ours. It is done by rich men. They are close by.

"It is now almost a year since your father left us. Today I have been told a man has been around asking about us. I believe they have found out I have been asking questions. This means I must stop my search. I do not know what they could do to us, but I believe in my heart and in the depth of my soul they murdered your father to not have their wickedness revealed.

"I am writing this letter to you in the knowledge you will not read it until I am gone. I hope you will understand why I have held back this information for so long.

"If you decide to discover more about what happened to your father you have my blessing, but beg you to be *very, very careful. These men are still depraved and dangerous.*

"*May God bless you and keep you safe, my darling son.*"

For a few moments Zelah sat silently, she and Maggie staring at each other.

"Are you thinking what I'm thinking?" Maggie asked. "And what Nick is thinking?"

Zelah nodded slowly. "Organised child prostitution. Not much shocks me, but hearing that was shocking." She stood up. "I presume you're already drawing up a list of actions?"

Maggie nodded.

"Good. Tomorrow we'll go through the whole story again. Do you have any idea who the buyer might have been?" She wrinkled her nose.

"Yes, we do. Or at least we have a list of potential suspects. That's part of the story."

"Then I'll look forward to tomorrow. Now, I'm off. For a quiet evening and lot of thinking. Well done."

* * *

Zelah took a copy of the letter to review at length and when she let herself into her own flat, feeling an immediate rush of relaxation, she threw her bag and coat on the closest armchair, followed by the letter. She went to her drinks cabinet to pour herself a gin and tonic. In the kitchen, loading the glass with ice, her concentration on the contents of the letter. As she picked up the glass and turned back towards the sitting room, her doorbell rang. Not expecting anyone she went to the door with some caution, peeped through the spyhole and saw a delivery courier holding a package.

"Delivery for Miss Quinn?"

She cursed. Mischa hadn't told Zelah she was expecting anything. Drat the girl. She took off the security chain and opened the door.

Before she knew what was happening the courier rushed at her, punched her in the head and grabbed her by her hair. Before she could stop him he pulled her hands behind her and grabbed them with his other hand.

He knocked her onto her knees and stood behind her, pulling her hair backwards. The glass dropped onto the carpet and she was momentarily distracted by trying to focus on it. Then her brain kicked in. *Get a grip, Zelah.* She took a deep breath. *Focus and think.* She could fight this once she could master the pain from the blow and from whoever this was, trying to pull her hair out.

"What do you want?"

"Information, witch bitch."

Then she knew. She blew out another long breath.

"Then let go of my head and we can talk about it."

"No chance." He was trying to mutter through a pulled-up scarf which was slipping from his mouth. He attempted to take one hand away from Zelah's head to grab hold of the scarf and slide it back up. This was her chance. She was too quick for him. Focussing on the glass, she 'saw' it jump, which it did, straight at him.

With a cry he let go of her hands, as the glass hit him on the side of his head. Zelah whipped around. His face was now covered by the scarf, but it was too late.

His eyes widened with horror, expecting her to do something terrible to him. Instead, his head whipped back as Zelah laughed.

"Oh, for God's sake, you idiotic stupid boy. If you wanted information about your mother you should have just knocked on the door." She gestured to an armchair next to him. "Sit there. I'm going to clean up this mess and get us both a drink. Beer?"

Gerry Quinn fell into the chair. Unable to take his eyes off her, he nodded. He sat still. He couldn't have moved if he tried. But he didn't want to move. Too many thoughts bouncing around in his head, none of which he could fully pin down. He'd got it all wrong. What was she going to do next? He had planned to extract the information he wanted and make a fast get-away. Why did his plans never work out? Maybe she would be willing to tell him what he wanted to hear about without the involvement of threat and violence. This was a new concept. He continued to stare at her. There was so much she might be able to tell him, but so much he couldn't tell her, things she mustn't find out. He would have to be vigilant, think about what he was about to say. Not easy for him. If he said the wrong thing, he was quite sure Armageddon would be dumped on his head. Time to find out.

Chapter 19

Zelah returned with an opened beer bottle which she put on a small glass table next to his chair, then sat on the matching armchair, another gin and tonic in hand, this time heavier on the gin.

Gerry stared at her, waiting for Zelah to make the first move, open the game. Grandad had taught him how to play chess. He had never quite got the hang of it, but he knew enough to think more than one move ahead.

"Go on, then, ask me a question," Zelah began. She held back a smirk at his frown of concentration.

"How much will you tell me?"

"I don't know until you start asking me questions, Gerry. Depends on the subject, doesn't it?"

He sat halfway up. "Where's my mother?"

"Australia. Next question?"

"It's a big country."

"Well spotted. She's in Melbourne, which is a big city. Next?"

There was a long pause during which neither of them moved, but Gerry's expression formed itself into a grimace, then turned red.

"Did he do what you said he did?"

"Yes."

"Why?" he shouted, eyes blazing. "Why?"

"Because she was no longer useful; he was bored with her; she served her purpose. Take your pick. You know him better than I. If she hadn't got away he would have had her committed to a private mental facility, or if he didn't want the cost, he would have had her killed. That's what he does to people who are no longer useful. What he had in mind for your sister, wasn't it?" It was her turn to sit up. "Why did you laugh when he beat her more than half to death?"

"I want to talk about my mother."

"Oh, didn't I explain? Perhaps not clearly enough. This is going to be an exchange of information. Quid pro quo." She started to explain but he got in first.

"I know what it means."

"Good."

She went to stand but he jumped out of his chair and stood in front of her. "We aren't done."

"Not nearly. I'm going to close the curtains. This is going to be a long night." She dodged around him and shut off the floor-length picture window with sets of heavy white curtains, before returning to her seat and picking up her drink. "Next question?"

Gerry stuck out his bottom lip. "I want to speak to my sister."

"That's not a question, and it would be up to her, not you. Are you going to apologise to her?"

"I want to ask her about our mother."

Zelah took a long slug of her drink, the ice rattling in the glass as she gulped it down. "I said quid pro quo. I'm willing to tell her you've been in contact with me. That's as much as you're going to get for now. Next?"

He started to wander around the room and stopped in front of the group of three of Martin's landscapes on the far wall. Zelah realised she hadn't checked if he was carrying a weapon. Would he threaten to slash the pictures to force more information out of her?

His head moved from side to side, contemplating. "This is nice."

Not what she was expecting. She stood and joined him. "My husband was an artist. An exceptionally good one, as you can see."

The next sentence was totally unexpected. "I miss my grandad." She glanced fleetingly at him and for the briefest moment she experienced a feeling of compassion, but killed it before it could take hold.

"But not your father?"

He didn't reply, and went to sit again. Zelah heard a low grumbling sound, which at first she thought was coming from his mouth, then realised it was his stomach.

"When did you last eat?"

He shrugged. "Can't remember." His stomach rumbled again, loudly. He rubbed it and winced.

She knew what she was about to do was wrong in so many ways, but said, "Wait there." She went into the kitchen and returned with two bags of crisps and an out-of-date bacon, lettuce and tomato sandwich. "Best I can do."

He ate voraciously for a couple of minutes, making sure he got every crumb in each of the crisp packets.

"Where have you been sleeping? You stink and I'm guessing by your scruffy appearance you've been sleeping rough."

Again, he shrugged.

"Does your father have any idea you're here? What has happened to you, Gerry?"

"He sent me away." He paused and wiped a crumb from his mouth. "He gave me a job to do, but I screwed up. He sent me to France with the moron Kostov." He put the beer bottle to his lips, taking just a small mouthful, never looking at her.

"What were you supposed to do? It must have been a serious screw-up for him to send you out of the country?"

Instantly she regretted asking the question. Never ask a question if you might not want to hear the answer. He might be able to tell her something about his father's business on one hand, but on the other... she felt a flutter of fear.

Gerry shook his head. "I can't talk about it."

"OK, then don't. Let's move on." He looked at her now, surprise and interrogation replacing the cocky look.

She needed to rethink where to go next. "I've noticed lately your father seems to be up to something, a new business venture, maybe. What do you know about it?"

"Not much. He didn't involve me. He's got a new boy on the team. Kid called Max something. He's on the new stuff."

For a second Zelah froze. A coincidence? She didn't believe in them. "Max what?"

The boy shrugged again, letting his arms fall over the sides of the chair. She batted down an urge to jump up and grab hold of his shoulders.

"Don't know. Never heard his other name."

Zelah put her elbow on the arm of the chair and rested her closed fist on her forehead. She was about to try another tack when Gerry yawned, loudly enough to distract her. She needed more time.

"Where are you staying? At home?"

"Fuck, no. Pa thinks I'm in France. I had to get away from Kostov. He kept calling me a stupid loser and saying he wanted to come back, but had to stay to babysit me."

"How did you get away?"

"I hit him over the head, took my bag and scarpered."

Zelah's eyes widened. "Is he OK?"

"Dunno. I called an ambulance."

"So... you might have killed him."

Again, the irritating shrug. "Maybe. Don't think so, though. He was groaning when I left."

155

She raised her eyes to the ceiling. "You could be on the run from the French police, if he's seriously injured."

"Yeh, could be." She wasn't sure if he was unconcerned, or unaware of the depth of the trouble he might be in. He yawned again. She made another decision.

"OK. Just for tonight, you can stay here. You can have a shower. I don't want the smell on my settee. I'll give you an old dressing gown of my husband's. You give me your clothes to put through the wash. Tomorrow morning, we'll pick up again. I may – I say *may* – speak to your sister and your mother this evening. OK?"

He nodded, went to stand up, staggered slightly, and said, "Why are you doing this for me? You should be hating me."

"Easy. Quid pro quo."

He trudged off to the bathroom, took a shower and reappeared in the old pyjama bottoms and dressing gown of Martin's that Zelah retrieved the back of a cupboard. She put blankets and pillows on the settee. Within five minutes he was asleep.

Zelah watched him for a few moments, before locking the front door to make sure he couldn't get out, then locking herself in her bedroom. She knew she wouldn't sleep yet. What he said hinted at trouble. She needed to talk to him again about what he had already told her about the night of Bob Pugh's shooting. She would also call Michelle in Canberra – she lied about the city – and work out what to say to Mischa. That might have to wait.

She had to admit he was going to be useful to her, with what she needed to know. But at the same time, she was becoming more fearful about finding out things she didn't want to know, that could compromise her with both Maggie and Nick.

It was going to be a long night.

* * *

Five miles away Kennet Quinn put down the phone, asked Helen to leave the room and sat with James Rufus in his arms. He stroked the baby's nose, which wrinkled and gave out a sneeze that sounded more a kitten than a human. Kennet smiled.

The boy must have re-entered the country with a passport he, Kennet, had not provided. Gerard was proving himself to be capable and in one way Kennet was impressed.

In another way, he had to control himself to not crush the baby in his spasming hands. His body shuddered. The boy had defied him. His contact couldn't tell him the precise date, but guessed Gerard had come straight back to Wales from France after disabling Kostov, which meant he had been back for at least two days. So where was he? Gerard didn't have many friends and he was sure if he tried to hide with any of them, none would be so stupid as to keep such information from Kennet. They knew where their interests lay, best friend or no best friend.

There was another niggle in the back of his mind. Since Rufus died Gerard had become more distant. He even asked Kennet once about Michelle. Of course, Kennet slammed shut the subject, told him his mother was a drug-addled slut who he had thought was dead; imagine his surprise to find out she was alive. He thought he had convinced the boy. Now, he wasn't so sure. It occurred to him the few people from whom Gerry could find out more information was the witch and her colleagues, and the girl, as he now thought of his daughter.

He picked up the phone again, dialled back the person to whom he had just spoken, issued his instructions and returned to the baby.

He smiled as the tiny nose snuffled again.

Chapter 20

The next morning Maggie set off for Abergavenny to meet Alice and bring her home for an overnight stay. At the same time Zelah was sitting with Gerry in the living room of her flat, silently drinking hot chocolate and eating croissants, each engrossed in thought.

Neither had slept well.

As soon as Zelah had called Michelle in Australia and explained Gerry was in her flat, Michelle demanded to speak to her son. Zelah gave him the phone and left them to it. No point in her trying to referee or intervene. Either it would work out, or it wouldn't. She expected the latter, but couldn't have been more wrong. They spent two hours talking to each other. By the end of the call, they had decided Gerry should get to Australia as soon as possible, preferably within days.

The call with Mischa hadn't gone so well. Zelah expected the girl to be upset, which was nowhere close to her reaction as soon as Zelah told her Gerry had turned up. It went downhill from there. Mischa refused to speak to him, shouted at Zelah and put the phone down. Zelah wouldn't have been surprised if, at the end of the call, Mischa threw the phone across the room. She tried to call back, but each attempt went straight to voicemail. Gerry seemed philosophical about his sister's refusal to speak to him.

"She hates me. Suppose I can't blame her. Doesn't trust me at all."

"I'm not sure I do," Zelah replied. "I don't believe in conversions on the road to Damascus."

"I want a new life," he said. "I don't like this one any more."

159

Apart from thinking about how to get Gerry out of the country and how to get back in touch with Mischa, Zelah was reeling from the information the boy had given her. There were two significant pieces of information.

In exchange for her agreeing to fund his airline fare he told her about his father's new business venture, of which he knew practically nothing. But he was aware Kennet thought the venture would be far more profitable than the property business, especially as he was having trouble and had had to sell several of the properties at a loss. She asked him who he sold them to, but Gerry didn't know. *Just as well*, she thought. She asked if Kennet knew, but Gerry was quite sure he didn't. Kennet tried to find out but had come up against a wall of offshore banking bureaucracy. Zelah kept her expression uninterested, she hoped.

The information worrying her the most was her growing certainty the new property manager, Max, was Max Howell. But she could not work out how Kennet could have known about him at all, never mind find him. Was it just chance? She didn't believe in coincidence and not in a coincidence of this magnitude.

The most horrifying information was that Malky Thomas' death was down to Kennet and led her to suspect Gerry was involved in the so-called accident. It was like trying to get blood out of a stone and in the end she stopped pushing him. His anxiety on the subject caused him to have a panic attack and it had taken some time to get him to calm himself and take slow breaths. She did it in the end by telling him if he didn't she'd have to take him to hospital, which would alert Kennet to his being back in town. That got through.

Still there was a nagging doubt this was an elaborate trick by Kennet to find out about the property plan and get something on her. She was racking her brains over how to find out. Just after ten in the morning she got the answer.

Gerry was looking decidedly sleepy and having finished his breakfast was heading over to the settee to sleep.

When she opened the curtains earlier, Zelah saw something to increase the doubt. Time to find out. She walked over to the window and began to close the curtains.

"I have to go out," she said over her shoulder. "I'll come back again around teatime, with some food for you. Then I have to go out again. Don't go near the window."

He nodded and gave out a yawn that reverberated around the room.

"Because one of your father's men, Stephen Dawes, has been sitting outside in a car for a couple of hours."

His reaction told her everything. He leapt off the settee and ran to stand next to the door into the hallway, his back rigid, arms by his sides, eyes wide, his lips clamped together. Zelah knew Gerry was not a good actor. This was real fear.

"He can't see you," she said. Even if you stood right in front of the window he couldn't see you, not through these windows."

"Can he get in?" His voice shook.

"No, not unless someone carelessly opens the door, as I did last night. He might get into the building, but he can't get past my security. When I go out I'll lock you in. The door is steel re-enforced. I'm not expecting anyone, so if anyone does ring the bell, just ignore it. Here." She handed him a mobile phone. "It's for emergencies. Just my number in it." It was the phone she had first given to Mischa. "If anyone does come to the door, call me. And don't even think about trying to ring any of your friends. I've it set to alert me." She hadn't, but guessed he wasn't tech savvy enough to know.

Gerry peeled himself off the wall and lumbered back to the settee.

"Get some sleep. You're exhausted. Text me when you wake up. I'm expecting Dawes to follow me. If he does, it means he's interested in me, not you. I will text if it happens. Now, sleep. Oh, yes. Don't be tempted to check, in case he's still there. He might see the curtains twitch and if I'm not there it will tell him someone else is."

He nodded rapidly and closed his eyes.

For the next hour, as the boy slept, Zelah made three decisions.

First, she would have to tell Nick his son was working for Kennet Quinn. It would horrify him and she couldn't second-guess what he would do. But this was not a problem for her to solve right now. It could wait a little while longer.

Second, she was going to have to live with the knowledge Kennet organised the accident that had killed Maggie's brother-in-law, and could never tell any of her friends and colleagues she knew. It would be a heavy burden but just another one to add to the load she already carried. Gerry hadn't told her in so many words. He was traumatised about the entire affair and it was clear this was what decided Kennet on sending him to France. She knew, too, she was perverting the course of justice by keeping the information about Malky Thomas' death from Bob.

Third, there was something she would have to tell Bob. Gerry managed to recall the 'import' business in which Kennet was becoming involved was to do with bringing merchandise into the country. The business partner was called Mr Wall, or something similar. He had overheard a conversation about moving the goods. He also knew Rufus hadn't liked it, and told Gerry to keep away from it. Zelah suspected drugs. She wouldn't put it past Kennet.

What she didn't want to tell Bob yet was Gerry's confirmation he didn't shoot Bob. There was someone else there that night. The person ran past Gerry as Bob fell to the ground. The person was a woman. Gerry had no idea who she was, but Zelah knew. Her crazy niece, Emer McCarthy Miller. Her failed attempt to kill Bob had probably kept her away for the past six months but Zelah knew enough about her to believe she would try again, with another family member, somewhere, sometime.

With a heavy heart and a conscience firing rocks at the inside of her brain, she set off for Maggie's house for the lunchtime meeting about the McRoberts case. Stephen Dawes followed her. At least that was one less worry. She paused briefly to text Gerry Dawes was no longer in front of the flat. There was no reply. Guessing he would sleep into the evening she pushed on, but decided to return home between the meeting and the family dinner. Just in case he tried to abscond. She still didn't trust him, despite everything he had told her.

Chapter 21

"Zelah! Could you please bring yourself back to earth?" Zelah jumped at Maggie's sharp tone and realised she had zoned out.

"Things on my mind. What were you saying?"

Maggie sighed. "I said there are three main suspects in the murder of William McRoberts. Four if you count the houseowner, but we can keep him on hold for now, until we learn more about the three more likely contenders." She paused. "I am getting a strong impression you aren't invested in this case."

"I'm interested on an academic level. In the end my input doesn't matter, does it? You've got this."

Nick shuffled in his seat and gave Maggie a questioning glance. Maggie, about to reply, stopped as Jack rushed through the door, followed by Alice.

"Can we listen in? I wouldn't mind helping out on the research with this one."

"We're going to need the help," she replied, not wanting to have a go at Zelah in front of Jack and Alice. "Sit yourselves down."

"As I was saying, there are three suspects. They were staying at Fallough Hill on the weekend of the Christmas party. Lady Wyn Davies didn't write nicely about any of them. They were business associates of her husband, although there's little information about the nature of their business. I've put together what I have on each of them. It's just rough notes so far, but we can work on fleshing it out next week. What we do know, or believe, from the information in Lizzy McRoberts' letter, is that the man who took Elsie was an Englishman, not a Welsh man."

She pulled up a sheet of handwritten paper onto the display board.

"They are firstly, Mr Nathan Rosen, a factory owner from Manchester. He was accompanied by his wife and teenage daughter plus the daughter's friend. Second, Sir George Wakelin, plus his wife. Sir George was a London merchant. And third, the Honourable Christopher Camberwell, fourth son of a Lord, Baron something, a politician. I can't remember the actual title and name. He was accompanied by his fiancée and his niece. He seems to be the Victorian equivalent of a brainless playboy. His entry in *Burke's Peerage* is minimal."

"Her Ladyship's comments were pretty scathing about each of them," Nick added. "She was a snob, looked down on anyone who came from 'trade' and hated the fact they were successful and her husband needed money."

"Camberwell wasn't from 'trade', was he? Why didn't she like him?" Alice asked.

"Envy, I think," Nick replied. "She was jealous of his being higher on the peerage scale which got him respect and invitations, but in her opinion he was as close to a happy idiot as one might find."

"Like that chap on *Blackadder*, what was his name?" Jack asked.

"You mean the Lieutenant George St Barleigh," Nick replied, grinning. "The Bertie Wooster character?"

"Not sure who Bertie thingy is, but yes, George, that's the one, in the trenches."

"Which is how she portrays Camberwell. I'm not sure she got it right, though."

"Why not, Nick?" Jack asked.

165

"Because of what she says about the fiancée and the niece. The three didn't seem to gel. I can't get any closer to it."

"Can I research him?" Jack asked. "He sounds fun."

"OK with me," Maggie said. She looked around the room. Nick nodded. Zelah was looking out of the window. "What about the other two?"

"I'll take Rosen," Nick said. "Might be interesting about the history of industrial development in Manchester."

"Which leaves me with Wakelin. I am assuming, Zelah, you do not wish to be involved in this research? Zelah? Zelah!"

"I was listening. Why would any of them shoot a police detective? Main issue for me is: they didn't know he was coming to the house, so whoever did it, must have panicked when he turned up. Therefore, I suspect he asked for them by name. That's my main concern with the letter from Lizzy McRoberts to her son. She didn't give him a name to go on, but the evidence we have suggests she must have known. Why didn't she write it down?"

"Maybe, maybe not. I'm not convinced she knew. Lizzy might have found out from the women she spoke to in the year after William's death, that's a possibility, but perhaps she didn't have strong enough proof or was frightened of putting it in writing," Nick replied. "Thoughts, anyone?"

"She was protecting him," Jack suggested. "She thought if she said who it was he could get into big trouble if he went after the person."

"Yes, good thought," Maggie replied. "But she also said she thought he might be the person to get justice for his father. By not giving him the name, if she had it, she was tying at least one arm behind his back."

"How about, she wanted to make him think about it," Alice put in. "She gave him clues. She wrote this letter in two parts."

"Why do you say that?" Zelah asked.

"She starts off saying it's a year since he died. The last bit sounds different, though, as if she's added it just before she died. She's telling him to investigate and warning him again about dangerous men. She says they have always been dangerous and depraved. I don't know, it just sounds like it was written later." She shrugged.

Nick scanned it again. "You could be right, Alice. She says, '*these men are still depraved and dangerous*'. I didn't spot it at first. But it doesn't explain why she didn't tell him who they are."

"Let's break it down, from the historical point of view, not William's death," Maggie said. "She says there is something going on in Liverpool. It's at a high level. She was bought off. It also appears Chief Inspector Monaghan was involved, somehow. It involved the buying and kidnapping of young girls. This could have been a paedophile ring, or a slavery ring, or both. She says they are rich and powerful men."

"But Lizzy doesn't give the name," Nick interjected. "Why not?"

"For protection," Zelah said. "When William never came back, what proof was there? A disgraced police detective who turned up dead in the river and a story based on the rantings of a drunken street woman. No chance. There's nothing written about this case anywhere else, is there?"

"Not that I've been able to find," Nick replied.

"But it does move the investigation further forward, doesn't it?" Maggie said. "The perpetrator was an Englishman, wealthy and respectable. Which means, in terms of the guests at the Christmas party, not the host nor his local guests, nor any of the women."

"Which just leaves the brothers-in-law and the business guests. And if we can discount the brothers-in-law for the brainless idiots her ladyship believed them to be, we're left with the invited guests. Rosen, Wakelin and Camberwell. All wealthy, respectable Englishmen."

"Let battle commence," Zelah said. "I'm going to go home for an hour or so. Personal stuff. I'll be back in time for dinner."

"She wasn't like this yesterday. What's up with her?" Jack asked after Zelah had gone.

"Who knows?" Maggie replied. "Whatever it is, she'll tell us when she's ready, if it concerns us. Or not at all if it doesn't. Now, I must get on with dinner. Anyone coming to help?"

The speed their heads went down and their excuses came up gave her the answer. She sighed.

"I'll be in the kitchen, if anyone needs me."

* * *

Zelah arrived back at the house just before seven. Nick and Stella were already there and both Jack and Alice had dressed more formally than usual. Bob arrived home in a hurry at six thirty and presented himself downstairs shortly after seven, just as the doorbell rang.

"Let another battle commence," Zelah muttered under her breath, at which Alice grinned and Jack told her to shush.

Maggie answered, showed Sherry into the living room and Bob got her a drink, scowling at Zelah when she smirked at Sherry's request for sparkling water, then went back to the kitchen.

After some polite but stilted conversation, Maggie appeared again to invite them through to the dining area. She had made a special effort with the table, using her mother's inherited 'best' china and silver cutlery.

"Wow, just like Christmas," Jack remarked as he sat down.

Maggie told everyone to sit wherever they chose, but it became tribal. The table easily sat eight. Bob took one seat at the head with three at each side. On his immediate right and left were Maggie and Sherry. Next to Sherry, Stella then Nick. Next to Maggie, Alice and Jack. Zelah sat at the opposite end facing Bob.

Maggie had cooked both a vegetarian option, for Alice who was experimenting, and a non-vegetarian option for everyone else. They all complimented Maggie on the cooking – a novel experience for her – but she noticed Sherry, whilst making the right noises, picked around bits of food and put most of them back on the plate. It was the same for the final course. She'd made Eton Mess, Jack and Bob's favourite, and a home-made crème caramel, which to her surprise and relief had turned out well. Sherry asked for fruit.

During dinner they discussed the pre-agreed 'safe' topics, but Maggie wanted to find a way to get Sherry to let down her guard. Apart from a few nods and smiles she contributed nothing more than the odd word. What happened next came as a surprise to all.

Sherry had been looking around the table, surreptitiously, Maggie thought, weighing up everyone, including Jack and Alice.

Jack was talking about his A level exams in the coming May and June and his hopes for university. Maggie asked Sherry if she had been to university.

"No."

"Did you join the police straight from school?"

"No."

"What made it the right career choice for you, Sherry?"

"I can't remember."

"But you enjoy the work?"

"Oh, yes."

Stella had a similar experience of being rebuffed, following which no-one else tried. Maggie was on the point of giving up when Alice said, "You may not get to do the final exams, bro." Everyone looked at her and she added, "It's about what's coming, isn't it? The virus. Like in China."

"What do you mean, Alice?" Nick asked. "I've seen some reports there's another virus, like SARS, in one part of China. Isn't this the same thing?"

"No. That's the problem. This is a novel virus. It's killing hundreds and hundreds of people. They've locked the city of Wuhan down. No-one's allowed to go outside."

"But we've contained viruses before," Stella said. "What's different about this?"

"It's not just novel. It means there's no treatment or anything. It's... how did it get described? Yes, the most highly transmissible virus anyone has ever seen. The World Health Organisation is warning people. They're advising it will spread everywhere fast."

They were distracted by a shout of laughter, which came from Sherry. "That's the stupidest thing I've ever heard. As if this country couldn't deal with some piddly flu virus." Her expression of contempt as she looked at Alice shocked Maggie. Alice didn't seem phased.

"It's not flu," she replied. "There's no treatment and it spreads like wildfire. Look it up. People in China are dying. It's horrible."

"And how do you think it's going to get here, young lady?"

Bob scowled at Sherry, but she didn't notice.

"It will already be here," Alice replied. "You know, aeroplanes." Now she was mocking.

"What's the transmission rate, do they think, Alice? The 'R nought' number." This was Zelah, who caught on that Alice had some worthwhile knowledge and needed a chance to show it.

"It's at least three, maybe four," Alice replied, smirking at the obvious lack of understanding around the table, but letting her glance rest a moment longer on Sherry, who clearly resented being caught out.

"Shit," Zelah said. "And no treatment. She's right. This could be big trouble."

"There's a film," Alice said. "Called *Contagion*. Worth a watch."

"Right, so you're getting this from Hollywood," Sherry said. "Not fact."

"The film is based on a well-known prediction at some point there will be another novel virus, like Spanish flu, except that wasn't flu and not Spanish. But that's not the point. Anyway, it's based on science. The WHO says so. They're worried."

"Well, I'm not," Sherry replied. "Bob, it's time for me to go. We have an early start tomorrow." She stood and pushed back her chair. "Nice to meet you all. Thank you for the dinner," with a nod to Maggie, "and the interesting education," with a mock bow at Alice. Bob saw her to the door.

As soon as he returned the conversation began again. None of it was complimentary.

"What did we do wrong?" Jack asked. "Why was she so rude to Alice?"

"She's not used to intelligent kids," Bob replied. "The sort she deals with are more likely to hurl abuse than scientific information."

"You deal with the same kids," Nick replied, in what was for him a sharp tone. "You don't assume they're all the same until they prove themselves to be OK."

Bob went to speak, then sat. "Sorry," he said. "I'll speak to her tomorrow. Sorry, Maggie. You were just trying to make her welcome."

Maggie glanced at Zelah who looked away, knowing Maggie's intention was nothing of the sort.

They didn't let Sherry's behaviour spoil the evening. They ended the evening playing board games and having fun, no-one putting it into words, but relieved she was gone. 'Articulate' would not have been Sherry's cup of tea, no more than 'Boggle' and 'Cluedo'.

When Alice and Jack went off to play computer games, Maggie and Zelah cleared up in the kitchen. Maggie could see Bob was upset but trying to chat to Nick and Stella. Stella would be able to steer the conversation in a more pleasant direction.

"She did it with a purpose," Zelah said, handing plates to Maggie to put into the dishwasher. "She wanted to ensure she wouldn't be invited again."

"Well, she's upset Bob, so any hopes she had in his direction are well and truly destroyed."

Zelah stood for a moment, an empty casserole dish in hand. "I don't believe she had any, Maggie. She wants to avoid us. I wonder why?"

"I don't care," Maggie said, slamming the door shut.

"I do," Zelah replied. "She did it for a reason. If she thought it would make us disinterested in her, she's wrong. Makes me more curious, not less. I'll do some snooping."

"She certainly wasn't keen to talk about her past."

"I noticed. Silly way to behave in front of a group of genealogists." She put the dish in the sink. "I have to go. I'm going to London tomorrow then over to Ireland. Personal stuff."

"Anything we need to know?" She expected Zelah to say no.

"Maybe. I'll talk to you when I get back in a few days. I'm not needed at the moment. You can spare me. Say goodnight to the others for me."

Later, after Nick and Stella left and Maggie and Bob were alone, she approached him with a glass of his favourite whisky. "Strange evening. What was that about, do you think?"

He said nothing for a few minutes and she allowed him the time, watching as he took sips of the amber liquid.

"She wasn't enthusiastic about being here, but you ambushed her and she had no choice."

Maggie went to protest, but stopped, knowing it was true. Best to admit it. "OK, yes I did. But she had a choice. Don't say she didn't. She's intelligent enough to have thought up an on-the-spot excuse. Can I tell you why I did it the way I did?"

"I was hoping you would."

"I've been puzzled about her since she partnered with you. I've seen the way she looks at you sometimes. I thought she fancied you."

He had been staring into the glass but now looked at her, questioning. "Why didn't you tell me? We could have discussed it without having to go through this evening."

"I'm not sure. Maybe I was a bit jealous. She spends more time with you than I do, these days."

"I thought we were solid."

"Me, too," she replied. After a short pause she went on. "I'm sorry. I wanted to find out more about her. I'm a bit ashamed of myself now."

"And what is your conclusion?"

"Apart from knowing myself to be a jealous woman, which is a humiliating discovery? I still don't like her."

He laughed, put down the glass and took her hands in his. "I love you. I don't mind about the jealousy. Flattering, actually. Maggie, she's no threat to you. Now I'm going to tell you something you can never repeat or I'll have to kill you."

She nodded, not sure what to expect.

"I don't like her, either."

A burst of laughter broke the ice that was already thawing. It came with a wave of relief.

"Good. She's odd, you know. Zelah thought she behaved the way she did to put us off. Well, that worked. But you know Zelah. It's made her curious to find out why."

Bob rolled his eyes. "Typical of you lot. What would put other people right off attracts you closer to them. You're moths to a flame." He stood up, stretched his shoulders back and gave out a yawn lasting several seconds, then held out his hand. She took it and he pulled her out of her seat. "Come on, let's go up. One thing Sherry was right about – I've got an early start. I'm on at six."

They walked out of the room and as they reached the stairs he stopped. "Maggie, should Zelah's snooping find something, I want to know, right?"

Chapter 22

Anglesey 1903

It took John McRoberts the best part of a day to reach Fallough Hill. He couldn't get home before nightfall and would have to find a room, but it didn't matter. He knew his mother's letter off by heart. Spurred on by anger and righteous indignation, he was confident and prepared for whatever would be the outcome of this visit. Or, he thought so, until he found himself at the top of the drive standing at the edge of the lawn, looking up at the house.

For a moment he swayed on his feet as his breathing quickened in time to his hands clenching and unclenching. He had never been close to such a place before, let alone think of speaking to its occupants. Yet he sensed an awareness of having been here before, having already looked at this imposing view. He shook his head and began to move again, following the path around the edge of the lawn to the front door, picking up his pace as he went, in time with the thump of blood beating in his ears.

There was a large black knocker on the double front door. He hammered three times and stood waiting, mouth dry but adopting a smile to give an appearance of confidence. No-one came. After a few minutes of hovering and wondering if he should knock again he heard approaching footsteps from the other side of the door. As the door opened his immediate view was of an outer porch with an inner glass door through which he could see an imposing hallway. There were many doors leading off, and a double width staircase to the immediate left of the entrance, leading to a galleried first-floor landing. All this John took in as the stony-faced servant, who opened the door, stood waiting.

"How may I help you, Sir?"

John removed his hat and held it in both hands at his chest. "I wish to see Sir Richard Wyn Davies. Please."

"Sir Richard is not at home," said the imperturbable face. "Shall I take a message, Sir?"

John froze, uncertain how to proceed. As he agitated over his response, a door in the background opened and a voice said, "Who is there, Ashley?"

"A person to see Sir Richard," the servant replied. "I have informed the person Sir Richard is not at home."

John heard the contempt as the voice pronounced *the person* and blushed, but stood his ground, despite the rain, which had been threatening as he reached the estate, now fell heavily on him.

An old woman, dressed in purple and black and leaning heavily on a stick, advanced towards the door. She looked him up and down, gave him a superior smile and said, "What do you want with my husband?"

"I want to ask him about my father's visit here, Milady. It was many years ago. My father never came home. I am trying to find what happened to him. I am John McRoberts. My father was police detective William McRoberts."

"How intriguing. Do come into the hall before you become thoroughly soaked. Now, tell me what this is about."

Conscious of his inability to stop dripping on her ladyship's hall floor, John gave his story as succinctly as he could, ending with, "My mother's letter gave this as the address to which my father came in search of the child."

177

"And what do you think we might know? I can assure you no street child ever came to this house from Liverpool. I would remember." She paused. "Just a moment. The date, the 16th of December 1878 you say. About two weeks before Christmas?"

"Yes, Milady."

"In those days we held a house party on the weekend two weeks before Christmas." She turned to the servant. "Ashley, ask Evans to come here. I believe he is somewhere upstairs." The servant acknowledged with the slightest of nods and departed.

"Now, Mr McRoberts. We'll ask Evans, our butler, when he arrives. He was a young man back then. He might recall. In the meantime, I shall find my old diaries. There may be something in them."

"This is kind of you, Milady."

"Not at all. It will be interesting. So little is, these days."

So she was going to help him more out of alleviation of her own boredom than his need, but whatever the case, any help was appreciated. He went to thank her, but stopped mid-thought, as a wave of darkness overcame him. He swayed on his feet, began to sweat and realised the darkness was a pulsating orb of fear, filling his lungs. He wiped his sweating palms on the sides of his raincoat. As his heartbeat increased he looked up at the staircase. A man was walking down, tall and thin, shoulders appearing to be pinned back, arms at his sides. By the time he reached them John was shaking.

Lady Virginia Wyn Davies appeared perfectly at ease. "Ah, Evans. Mr McRoberts, this is our butler Mr Ebenezer Evans. He was a young footman at the time you are describing." She turned to the man who stood impassively at her side. "Evans, this is Mr John

McRoberts from Liverpool. He says his father came here in seventy-eight on a detective mission, to bring home a young street girl who went missing and was believed to be here. Can you recall anything?"

The man Evans allowed the sides of his mouth to curl up. "I cannot recall such an event, Milady. It was a long time ago, but I would remember such an unusual event. When in seventy-eight?" he said to John.

"The 16th of December," Lady Wyn Davies interrupted. "The weekend we would have held one of our Christmas parties." She peered at John. "You are pale, Mr McRoberts. Can we fetch a glass of water?"

John shook his head and managed to say, "No, thank you. I am tired after a long walk." He couldn't bring himself to look at the butler.

"Good. Well, I have an idea." She beamed. "I will review my diary for that weekend. If anything out of the ordinary occurred, I shall see if I wrote about it. I suggest you return this time next week, Mr McRoberts. I will inform you of my discoveries."

"Thank you, Milady."

"Yes. Well, it has been interesting to meet you, Mr McRoberts. Evans will see you out." She went back to the door from which she first appeared, stood for a few seconds with her hand on the handle and a puzzled look. She shook her head then turned back and went to another door.

The butler raised his hand in the direction of the entrance. "This way, Sir." John walked ahead of him. At the door he paused, still unable to even glance up. He desperately wanted to look the butler in the eye, but fear kept him back.

"We shall see you again next week, Sir." The door closed behind him.

Taking deep breaths to calm himself, John walked to the end of the drive as fast as he could, trying not to run, in case anyone should be watching him. He didn't understand what had just happened, but he had the coming night and a long journey home to think it over.

Inside the house from behind a curtain, Ebenezer Evans watched the figure stride down the drive and out of sight. He went to check on Lady Wyn Davies, who was now snoozing in front of a fire in the parlour. No need to worry about her. When she woke she would have forgotten the man had been here. When he was certain the other servants were occupied elsewhere he went to the telephone cabinet in the servant's corridor and put through a call.

"What do *you* want?" the voice at the other end murmured as the operator connected them.

"The possibility we discussed? It has occurred. The old woman has talked about a diary she kept. She invited him to return next week."

"A diary? This is inconvenient. Find it and make it disappear. Now, give me every detail you have about the man, and I shall take it from here."

Chapter 23

Making her way back to her flat after dinner, Zelah was troubled.

At home in between the afternoon meeting and the dinner she booked a flight to Sydney for Gerry, leaving the following evening at eight. She hadn't told him yet, as he slept through her visit. Her plan was to stay at home Sunday morning, then leave around three, to get him to the airport on time and to allow her time to catch a flight to Dublin. She still hadn't been able to speak to Mischa and this was the significant part of her worry.

Another growing concern was Sherry Martin. Something was wrong there. She couldn't put her finger on it, but Zelah's nose was twitching with an unpleasant peppery sensation. This was way more than a case of sex and, or, jealousy. Having watched her throughout the dinner Zelah could sense an agenda. It was true some of the looks Sherry gave Maggie did suggest resentment but Zelah sensed more to it than that. The fact she singled Alice out to ensure her determination to not be invited again told her Maggie was the target, not Alice. Alice had been the device. Zelah noticed, in the two hours they had been together, Sherry hadn't looked at Bob with any kind of interest. The woman also, when she thought no-one was looking, couldn't hold back her anger towards Nick. Just one small comment, that Zelah hoped no-one else noticed. She wondered if Nick had noticed. She'd ask him, when she got back from Ireland.

Stephen Dawes was still following her as she turned the car into the secure underground garage at her apartment block. She would have to work out how to get rid of him before she and Gerry took off for the airport tomorrow. This wouldn't be too difficult, Dawes not likely to have been gifted with much intelligence in her opinion.

Gerry was shocked to learn he was flying to Australia in less than twenty-four hours, but relieved. The fact she booked business class was sufficient to give him something to look forward to. Zelah had to take him through the plan several times on how to get him out of the country without his father noticing. One of her concerns was he could not enter the country on a false passport. He would have to use his own, which he kept with him. The false one she would retain and destroy. His initial entry would be for three months on a standard visitor's visa. Michelle had done the same and already extended her stay to twelve months. This should give them breathing space to decide if they could get on. Then they could plan.

But there was a price. Zelah's price was Gerry's record of everything he knew about his father's business, his contacts and his finances. She would ask the questions and record his answers. He agreed, after some consideration and with reluctance. He was eventually swayed by the idea of being half a world away and learning how to surf, which was sufficiently enticing to overcome his fear of his father finding out he had co-operated with Zelah Trevear.

* * *

The next morning they were ready from midday, bags packed and ready to run out of the door to the garage. Gerry couldn't sit still. Zelah told him her plan to ensure Stephen Dawes could not follow them, but they had to wait on the timing and hope it was before three o'clock –

the latest she determined they could leave and still make their flights.

It happened at one thirty. A police car drove up to Stephen Dawes' car and the officers began to question him. At the same time, an elderly man joined them, gesticulating and shouting. This was it.

As Zelah drove out of the garage, with Gerry hiding in the footwell of the back seat until they reached the end of the road, through the open car window she could hear Stephen Dawes trying to defend himself to the two police officers against the angry blustering of the chairman of the local Neighbourhood Watch, who had received anonymous reports of a man, a non-resident, sitting in a car and watching the apartment block for two days. Dawes saw her and scowled, but there was nothing he could do.

Zelah had arranged flights where they both departed from the same terminal at Heathrow so were able to enter the terminal building together before they split up. Gerry was leaving first, Zelah had an additional hour to wait for her flight, and she was able to accompany him to his gate.

"Good luck with your mother," she said. "Let me know how it goes. And tell me you've arrived safely. I'll be expecting a text."

He nodded and stepped forward. For a moment she thought he was going to hug her, but the moment ended with Gerry turning his back and walking through the departure gate and out of sight.

"Ungrateful little bastard," she muttered, knowing he wasn't, really. Now for the other sibling. This was going to be much harder. She headed for the first-class lounge and spent the waiting time drinking champagne and starting her check on the life and times of Sherry Martin.

Chapter 24

Zelah texted Maggie and Nick on Sunday before her flight to say she wouldn't be back until Wednesday at least, and they should hold the fort without her.

"What else does she think we'd do?" Maggie muttered as they got to work on Monday morning.

Nick smiled but didn't reply. "What about what Alice was saying on Saturday?" he asked her.

"You mean this virus thing?"

"Yes. I did some research. She's right, it could become quite serious."

"What do you mean by serious?" She stopped and turned around to face him.

"The last time anything comparable happened was the Spanish flu in 1918, which as Alice said wasn't flu and wasn't Spanish. It killed up to fifty million people worldwide. Many of them young. Of course, it's now thought to have been an H1N1 virus, not like this Coronavirus."

"What does that even mean?" Maggie asked.

"I don't know enough about it. But, if it's anything like the speed at which that one transmitted, a terrible thing is coming."

Maggie shivered. "Let's hope we can get hold of it soon, then. I mean, we've managed to contain H1N1 and SARS and Ebola, haven't we?"

"Yes, but this seems different. If it is a novel virus, there's neither treatment nor cure. The Chinese and the WHO are worried."

Maggie shrugged. "Well, perhaps it's just a storm in a teacup." She stopped. "What if it isn't, Nick? What would happen?"

"Well, in China they've locked down a whole city. No-one allowed out of their home, but it's already spread to nearby countries."

"I can't imagine it happening here."

"I can. We should think about it."

"Well, all we can do for now is carry on, see what happens, how it progresses. What do you say?"

"Yes. If it's easily transmitted, then planes will likely carry it around the world, to start with." He saw she was agitated. "We won't worry for now, OK?"

"We'd better get on with this case, then." She turned back to her laptop and recommenced the search into Sir George Wakelin.

Thus far she had established that when Sir George and Lady Maud Wakelin attended the Christmas party at Fallough Hill, he was fifty-five years old and Maud forty-seven. He was knighted three years previously in 1875, having been the owner of a string of a new type of shop popping up across the north of England, the forerunner of the Department Store. He had been born in 1823 to a Draper called Joseph Wakelin, on the outskirts of Manchester. Joseph's profession, as each of his children was baptised, was recorded as a both a Hawker and a Draper, which meant at some point he sold cloth from a barrow. He must have moved on to a small single shop, as on the 1841 census Joseph was recorded as a 'Storekeeper' aged fifty and eighteen-year-old George, the youngest of the five Wakelin children, as a 'Shopkeeper's Assistant'.

By 1851 Joseph was gone; Maggie found his death the previous year. George, now twenty-eight, married Maud

Sikes and was a Store Proprietor. They had two children aged two and one month. George's fortunes grew over the next ten years, as he opened more drapery stores and began to sell additional items. Sadly, tragedy struck somewhere during the decade. Both children died and by 1861 there was no further mention of any more being born.

By the time of the 1871 census, George and Maud lived in an imposing house in Chester, with a total of ten drapery stores in Liverpool and Manchester and the Mancunian suburb towns. His name was well known and he was a 'respected citizen', according to newspaper accounts of his activities. By the time he received his knighthood George Wakelin had retired, sold off his stores, bought the mansion in Chester on the banks of the River Dee and was trying his utmost to forge his path into higher society. According to Lady Virginia Wyn Davies' diary in 1878, he was not making any headway. Successful as his business ventures were, according to Lady Virginia he remained '*an unpleasant little parvenu with a fondness for his own voice and opinions which he gives at every opportunity on every subject. He neither respects the opinions of others, nor receives them with good grace*'.

Maggie also discovered Sir George loved a good fight, through the legal system. He issued many injunctions suing for slander, the most interesting of which was against Michael Camberwell, the eldest of the four Camberwell brothers. Claiming the Honourable Michael Camberwell had damaged his reputation by calling him an imposter and a 'wolf in sheep's clothing', they settled the case out of court in 1880, which Sir George was also fond of doing. As far as Maggie could discover, none of

186

his claims for defamation ever made it to the courtroom floor.

By the end of the day, when Jack arrived home from school, she had a good, rounded picture of Sir George Wakelin to discuss together when Zelah got back from Ireland.

Nick had begun to research Nathan Rosen and Jack joined them to put in an hour before dinner on Christopher Camberwell.

"Nathan Rosen is something of an enigma," Nick said as Maggie got up and was about to leave the room.

"I'm just going to forage for dinner, but how so?"

"He had a finger in many pies, some of which might have been shady business enterprises."

"Do you need to discuss this now?" she asked.

"No, it can wait." He closed his computer. "How about in the morning? I've updated my notes."

"I'll do the same," Jack said. "Carry on foraging, mum. I'm starving."

Nick chuckled. "Keep the workforce happy. I'll see you tomorrow."

Bob hadn't returned all day and hadn't messaged Maggie about when he might be back, so she and Jack went ahead and ate together.

"What have you found about young Camberwell?"

"I'm doing it how you said, mum, getting as much background as I can from the census returns and other records. He was twenty-six when he went to the party, so he was born in 1852. He was one of seven children, he had three older brothers and one older sister and two younger sisters. I've got census returns for 1861 and 1871 but they don't tell you much."

"Why not?" Maggie asked, although she could guess the answer.

"Well, he was just nine at the time of the 1861 census. He was at boarding school."

"The upper classes liked to get rid of their children as soon as possible," Maggie said. "And 1871?"

"He was at a college in Oxford. Studying law."

"Naturally. I expect he went to Eton or Harrow in between."

"Actually no, he's not listed at either of them," Jack replied.

"Well, another public school, then," Maggie said. "Keep checking; it will be recorded, somewhere."

"Does it matter, mum?"

"Everything matters," she replied. "It might turn out to be irrelevant, but we gather it up anyway. You never know where a story might go."

"OK. I'm done for tonight. I've got an essay to finish."

"Off you go, then," Maggie said. "I'll clear up."

Before going to bed she tried to switch her brain off by watching one of her favourite foreign language police dramas, but gave in after half an hour. Choices were either go to bed, or take another run through the research. Research got the vote. She didn't believe she'd be able to sleep, anyway. On and off through the day, Maggie found herself thinking about Zelah and her withdrawal, not just from the case but from Maze in general. She was sure it was nothing to do with the case itself, but as Zelah gave nothing away about any concerns she might have, it was impossible to guess what was absorbing her. It must be something to do with Mischa Quinn, as she had announced her decision to go to Ireland in an abrupt way. And Maggie thought Zelah looked tired and tense, which was also unusual.

She had just started her laptop onto the Ancestry site to find out more information about George Wakelin, when the quiet opening and closing of the front door announced Bob's return.

"Burning the midnight oil?" he said as he slumped onto the settee next to her desk. Maggie thought he looked tired and tense, too.

"You look as if you could do with a drink."

She stood up to go to the kitchen, but he stopped her with a touch on her arm. "Where's Zelah?"

"Gone to Ireland for a couple of days. Why? Is there a problem?"

"When you ask, you know there is one."

She sat on the settee next to him. "Can you tell me? Is it something official?"

"Yes and no." He yawned and sank deeper into the seat, his head leaning so far back he was looking at the ceiling. "I shouldn't, but I need you to tell me if you hear anything."

"You've got me worried, Bob."

Without looking at her he said, "We've been looking for Gerard Quinn recently. I can't tell you why. We haven't been able to find him for a week or so. Gone off the radar. Yesterday, he suddenly reappeared and flew to Australia."

"What's that got to do with Zelah?"

"She paid for his ticket. She has questions to answer."

Chapter 25

"That's impossible," Maggie said. "Just... impossible. He hates her and she's been winding him up. This must be a trick."

"Where did she fly from?" Bob asked.

"Heathrow." Maggie opened her mouth to say something else, then stopped. "Oh."

"If she went with British Airways it would have been from Terminal Five. The same terminal for flights to Australia."

Maggie stood and paced around the room. "She's been distracted lately, not with us on this research into Fallough Hill. I knew there was something on her mind." She went back to the settee and flopped down next to him, turning her head towards him. "What the hell has she been up to? What has she done?"

"This could be connected to Kennet Quinn," Bob replied. "I wouldn't put it past her to get his son on board then send him far away."

"Can't you tell me anything about why you were watching him?" Maggie asked.

He gave her back a long stare. "No."

Knowing when she was beaten Maggie said, "I haven't told you much about what she's been doing about Kennet Quinn. It's time I give you the full story."

He raised an eyebrow. "Don't leave anything out."

* * *

Bob listened to everything Maggie told him without asking questions, then gone to get them both a drink. When he got back he handed her the glass.

"The most interesting thing for me in what you've said is he doesn't seem too bothered, which tells me he has other plans on the go."

"Do you know what they are?"

"No not yet, but there's been some suspicious activity. Can't say any more. Right, I'm going to bed. I'm knackered. You coming up?"

"In a minute," she replied. "I just want to think this through."

After a few minutes of numbness, Maggie began to consider what Bob had just told her. What was Zelah playing at? Gerard Quinn was a nasty, vicious boy who hated Zelah. There were more questions, too. She knew Kennet's estranged wife, Michelle Morgan Quinn, had gone to Australia. Zelah had let it slip. Had Gerard gone to join her? If so, why would Zelah have organised the flight? If her intention were to get him away from his father, this would lead to trouble for her and Nick as soon as Kennet found out. And he would find out, Maggie was sure about that. There was one answer she needed. She left her glass on the table and headed upstairs.

"Who else knows Zelah paid for the ticket?"

Bob gave her a fixed stare, understanding what she was asking. "No-one. I'm keeping it quiet, for now. But I can't keep it back for long."

Maggie nodded. Zelah certainly did have questions to answer and she suspected they weren't going to like the answers.

* * *

In the meantime, there was work to do. She discussed it with Bob and he agreed she could tell Nick about

Zelah's largesse, which she did the following morning. She wasn't going to tell Jack or Alice, who would be home again at the weekend.

Nick teased his fingers through his hair. "I can't believe she would approach Gerard Quinn," he said.

"Maybe he approached her."

"Um... possible. When she first told him his mother wasn't dead he didn't believe her, but he must have been puzzled."

Maggie nodded. "And when he heard the story about how Kennet deliberately burned Michelle's hands it must have set him thinking. But if he approached her after that, why didn't she tell us?"

"Typical Zelah," Nick muttered. "How many times have we said so?"

"Too many," Maggie replied. "This time, though, she may be in more trouble than even she can handle."

"Not the first time we've thought it, either. Anyway, let's get on. This is becoming interesting. I have some questions for us to consider."

"Fire away."

Nick folded his arms and stretched his legs out under the desk.

"OK. First, what prompted Sir Richard Wyn Davies to invite these particular three? When did he invite them? Was it at the same time or separately? Were they in Liverpool at the time? When was the child 'bought' in relation to the date of the house party? Why did the person who took the child need to take her with him or her? William went in search of the purchaser and the child and his lead took him to Fallough Hill. His plan was to bring the child back. How could the child have remained at Fallough Hill and not be noticed over the course of a weekend?"

"That's a lot of questions. Why don't we focus on the child, see what we can find about her as the centre of the issue? We've been thinking about William and the Christmas party, but what about the child?"

"Reasonable idea. What do we know about her already?"

Maggie shuffled through the papers on the table and picked up a copy of Lizzy McRoberts' letter to her son John. She scanned it and said, "She was called Elsie and she was twelve years old. Ah, yes, her mother was Mrs Margaret Doherty, so she was Elsie Doherty. The policeman Monaghan was involved, again."

"I'll look her up on the 1871 census," Nick said. "She'd have been about six." After a few minutes' searching he said, "I can't find any mention of them. Let's try another site."

"They might not have been in Liverpool at the time," Maggie said. "Or you could search for another spelling of Doherty. I had one of those once. I found it under 'Dorty' after months of searching. Must have been how they pronounced it and the enumerator just spelled what he heard. Enter a variation of the spelling."

"OK. Yes, got them. They were in Lydia Street, which was a tenement." He switched his computer view onto the white board. "Seven family members. Mr Patrick Doughty – another change of spelling – was a docks worker, Mrs Margaret Doughty, no profession. Then there was David, aged eight, Elsie aged six, so born around 1865/6, Mary Anne aged five, Patrick aged three and a ten-month-old baby called Michael."

"And in 1881 and 1891?" Maggie asked.

Nick checked each one. "No Mr Doughty in 1881 or 1891. But there are another three children born between 1871 and 1876. I'm going to check if he died." After a few minutes he said, "Yes, here's a Patrick Doughty, died in 1877. So, Mrs Doughty was left a widow with eight children. The eldest boy David would have been old enough to work, and Elsie, too, but even so..."

"No other means of support," Maggie interjected. "Six young children to feed and the potential income from one boy and one girl. You know, they used to sometimes put the little ones on the street to see what scraps they could find to sell to passers-by. God knows how they survived."

"Well, it would appear Mrs Doughty took to drink, because the letter says she sold Elsie when she was drunk."

"Don't judge her," Maggie said sharply. "She did make an effort to get the girl back when she sobered up. She must have been desperate."

"I'll give her the benefit of the doubt," Nick replied. "But not too much. Right, I'm going to see what else I can find about the Doughty family descendants. If we can find a living one, there might be an old family story, you never know."

"I'll take a look for any mention of Elsie Doughty under any spelling, in the census reports, and anywhere else I can think to look."

It didn't take long.

"I've found something," Maggie said.

"You sound subdued. Not good, I presume?"

"Very bad. And a strange coincidence. I have an Elsie Doughty who died in the Liverpool Workhouse, aged twenty-one. The cause of death was due to consumption and degeneration of the brain."

"Which was often another way of saying venereal disease, probably syphilis," Nick said. "Are there any others of about the same age?"

Maggie checked the list. "No, not around that age. There's no other of the name born in 1865 or thereabouts. I want to see the actual records, if there's any more information about her, but there doesn't seem to be anything online. Might mean a trip back to the Liverpool archives."

"Give them a call. See if they can look it up for you. It's a long journey for just one piece of information."

"It is, but if this Elsie is our girl and she did die of disease related to VD then it's likely she would have been working as a prostitute. Which means she might have been arrested."

"And it's still a strange coincidence. I'd call first," Nick replied.

"I'll do it now."

As she walked up and down in the kitchen, she was put through to the archives staff. Having explained what she was looking for they gave her a rate for two hours research, copying and conditions of use, all of which Maggie accepted. The deal done, the archivist agreed to call her back by the end of the day.

"I agreed to pay for a premium service to get the information today," she told Nick back in the office. "She suggested I try the local newspapers, too, see if there are any reports of an arrest for Elsie."

"Good idea," he replied. "I've found the descendants of Michael Doughty on the 1939 War Register. Fortunately, the spelling stayed constant into the twentieth century and they didn't move far from their original home in Liverpool. I'm about to check the electoral registers once they started again after the War, to see how far I can trace the family."

As midday approached Nick called a halt.

"I have two possibilities, both in roughly the same area of Liverpool. I have a phone number for one and a Facebook page for another. I've sent a message request to the Facebook page owner and I'm about to call the number."

Maggie nodded and Nick dialled. The call was answered. She waited as Nick calmly and patiently explained who he was and why he was calling. She laughed as a voice down the phone screamed "grandad!" and Nick had to pull the mobile away from his ear. A few seconds later another voice came on the call and Nick went through the details again. This time there was a different reaction.

She became impatient as Nick nodded vehemently, at one point giving her a thumbs up, all the time taking notes. Then he said, "Thank you so much, Mr Doughty – OK, Sean. This has been invaluable. And of course I'll inform you if the person we've found is the same lady."

He turned to Maggie. "That was Sean Doughty. He's the great great grandson of Michael Doughty. A story has been handed down in the family, of a little girl called Elsie, daughter of Margaret, who was taken away by 'bad men', told to him by his grandmother. The story has reached mythical status in the Doughty family of the little girl who went out to play one day and never came home. She was the most beautiful child anyone had ever seen, saint-like character, a little angel and so on. The family searched far and wide, but she was never found. A warning to future generations to beware of strangers."

"So, the fact her mother sold her to the 'bad men' has been erased from the narrative."

"Seems so. How are you getting on with newspaper reports about Elsie?"

"Nothing yet. I've looked at the time she left Liverpool in 1878 up to the next five years, when she would have been eighteen. Nothing at all. She wasn't on the 1881 census anywhere."

"Keep trying."

"What are you going to do next? Go back to Rosen?"

Nick paused for a moment. "No, I'm going to find a Liverpool historian. This was the work of more than just one man; if there might have been an organised ring going in Liverpool at the time."

Maggie shrugged. "OK. Leave you to it." She turned back to the British Newspaper Archives and loaded the next set of years in her search for any mention of Elsie Doughty.

Over the afternoon Nick made several phone calls. Maggie tried to tune them out as she searched – in vain – for any newspaper articles about criminal behaviour by Elsie. In one way this was a relief, but it was also disappointing there was nothing to learn about her life from her disappearance from Liverpool to this final fatal discovery back in Liverpool.

Camberwell could wait, as Jack wasn't home and he had other matters to take up his time, having been loaded with an avalanche of homework. She didn't believe, from what she knew of Christopher Camberwell, he was the number one contender, anyway. There were matters about him that puzzled her, but not to the extent she felt about Rosen and Wakelin.

She knew from Lady Virginia's diary they had arrived at around the same time on Anglesey and had been together at a meeting in Liverpool, but hadn't found any information on the meeting itself and who was there. Nick was trying to find out, unsuccessfully by the sound of it. She also read Wakelin went back to his house in

Chester to leave something there and collect his wife. Could the 'something' have been Elsie Doughty? Was his bombastic, bullying nature a cover for an interest in young girls? And she was interested to hear what Nick had to say about Rosen. His daughter was accompanied by a 'friend', with whom Lady Wyn Davies was not impressed, the girl being *'pleasing enough, but taciturn in nature. I do not believe she comes from a good family'.* Again, a possibility for Elsie, but in this case the wife and daughter would have been part of the deception, which seemed unlikely. There was nothing in the diary to suggest whether the girls were close friends or not.

"I've had another idea," Maggie said. "What about the servants hired for the party? The other book Trys gave us, the one with the details of the costs, I remember it mentioned additional servants. Did it name them, or give any other information about them?"

"I'll check," Nick replied. "But I can't see how or why a girl who was bought from her mother in Liverpool would then be hired as a casual temporary servant on Anglesey. I expect those who were hired for the occasion were local, but I will check."

"How's your search going for a historian?"

"Good," Nick replied. "I've found a Liverpool University professor who's going to talk to me tomorrow. She has expertise in nineteenth-century trade and professional practices in Liverpool."

"Excellent," Maggie replied as her phone rang. It was the Liverpool archives. She listened and scribbled notes for ten minutes then said, "Thanks, and yes, please send me what you've found and told me about."

She turned to Nick. "We have our girl. It seems she did go home, after all."

Chapter 26

Nick swung his chair around, but as Maggie went to speak, the front door opened and banged shut. She glanced at her watch, saw it was six already and waited for a moment for Jack to appear. It wasn't Jack. Zelah marched into the room, looking thunderous and without looking directly at either of them, said, "What are you up to? Fill me in, please."

"No," Maggie replied. She picked up her phone and typed in a text with two words: '*she's here*'.

Zelah looked at her, then at Nick. She turned on the spot and went to make for the door, but Maggie jumped out of her chair and blocked the doorway.

"You aren't going anywhere. Bob was already on his way; he'll be here in a few minutes. Then you are going to tell us what you've been up to."

"Get out of my way," Zelah shouted. "Now!"

Nick leapt up and stood next to Maggie.

"Watershed moment, Zelah." He spoke quietly, not rising to Zelah's expectation of someone shouting back. "I hope you realise what I mean."

Zelah stared keenly at him for a few seconds, nodded briefly then turned around and sat on the settee.

"You can take your coat off if you want," Maggie said, returning to her seat. Zelah didn't move.

After an incredibly long five minutes, Maggie let out an audible sigh of relief when the front door opened and closed. Bob marched into the office, followed by Jack.

"I met him at the bus stop," he said to Maggie, not looking yet at Zelah. "Can we please sit around the table?" He paused. "Should Jack be included in this?"

"Of course," Maggie replied. "In these circumstances he's part of Maze."

A goggle-eyed Jack took off his coat, put his school bag on the floor and sat in the nearest seat. Bob took the head of the table. Zelah went to sit at the other end. Maggie and Nick took a chair on each side.

The five-minute wait had given Zelah time to think about what she could, and could not say.

Bob glanced around, then began. "Zelah, Gerard Quinn left the country yesterday, for Australia. You paid his fare. I want a full explanation of why, what led to it and what agreement you have with him. This is informal. If I'm not satisfied with what you have to say, I will arrest you and we will continue at the station."

Maggie was watching Zelah. She saw a brief flaring of her nostrils, but also a flash of fear, so rapid she suspected no-one else would have noticed. *At last,* she thought, *something has got through.*

She watched Zelah take a deep breath and put her hands on the table. She sent a silent wave of beseeching to her colleague and friend not to accuse, prevaricate or lie. Just explain.

Zelah began. "On Friday night, when I arrived home, he forced his way into my flat, threatening me with violence if I didn't tell him where he could find his mother..."

For a further fifteen minutes, without any interruption, she told the story. Maggie desperately wanted to ask questions, but at one point when she lifted her shoulders and went to speak, two words from Bob silenced her. "Not yet." It was the tone as much as the words that ensured her silence throughout the remainder of Zelah's speech.

Zelah explained how she calmed Gerry down, put him in touch with his mother and got as much information as she could from him about Kennet Quinn's actions and plans.

"I told him it was a quid pro quo. He and Michelle talked for two hours."

She then explained how Stephen Dawes sat outside her flat, which terrified the boy, and was the point at which she believed he truly wanted to get away from his father. She then bought the ticket and took him to the airport before going to Ireland to explain to Mischa what had happened. Then she sat back.

"That's not all of it," Bob said, his head still in his notebook.

"Ask away," Zelah said. "And comment. If any of you believe I did wrong, say so."

"Why did his father send him away?" Bob asked.

"He did something wrong. I don't know what. I asked, but he wouldn't tell me. He was particularly tight-lipped, and I thought if I pushed he might clam up completely. Perhaps it was about his failure to shoot you."

"Rubbish," Bob snapped. "That was a year ago. Kennet doesn't wait. Did the boy tell you he injured Kostov so severely the man is still in hospital in France?"

Zelah closed her eyes for a moment. "Yes," she replied. "Like I care what happens to that thug."

"The French police want to question Gerry." He thought her answering smile held an element of relief.

"Has Kostov said it was him?"

"No," Bob replied. "Kostov says it was an intruder and the boy ran away."

"So the French police are just verifying his statement? Is that why you wanted him?"

"What else would I want him for?" Bob asked, raising his eyebrows.

"Nothing I care about," she replied, meeting his gaze. "He's in Australia for six months with Michelle. Then they both have to come back. No visas."

"What happens to them when they do?" Maggie asked.

"Again, I don't care."

"Is that all of it?" Nick asked.

Again, Zelah took a deep breath. "No. Three things more, and you aren't going to like any of them. They will hurt people. They are not illegal," she spoke directly to Bob, "but none of you is going to like any of it."

"Then you'd better get it out, so I can make a judgement call," Bob replied.

"Right. First, Kennet Quinn has a new business venture. Whatever it is, it's lucrative. So much so he's looking to divest his company of most of the property. Before you ask, I don't know it nature. He apparently talks about 'the merchandise' and 'shiploads' and 'consignments'. Kostov was tasked with bringing it into the country, whatever it is. He'll be even angrier now Kostov is unavailable, thanks to Gerry."

"Drugs?" Maggie asked.

"Maybe," Bob replied. "But unlikely to be Kennet's thing. Too many others already at it. There'd be a turf war. I'll think about it." He turned back to Zelah. "Next?"

"This one I found out about on Sunday, no, Saturday evening, and I didn't want to speak about it at the dinner. I don't know how this is going to land, so I'm just going to speak about as much as I know, which is not much. Kennet has a new 'property manager', to replace Timothy Redland. A young man." She stopped and looked at Nick. "His name is Max. He's eighteen. It might be your son."

For a millisecond it seemed as if the world stood still. A pin dropping would have been akin to a gunshot. Nick stared at Zelah, looking as if he had stopped breathing.

"Are you sure it's him?" Bob asked.

"Not entirely, but he's a young man who hasn't been long in the country and took the job when he heard about Kennet's feud with Maze. As I said, he's eighteen. Quiet, apparently. Willing to do whatever Kennet wants of him."

Nick stood and left the room. Maggie went to follow but Bob stopped her. "Leave him be for a few minutes. Let him process this."

He turned back to Zelah. "The third thing?"

"Gerry accosted me in a shopping centre a while ago. Asked about his mother. Threatened me if I didn't tell him. I laughed. I Said something similar to 'What are you going to do, you stupid boy, shoot me in the middle of a shopping mall?' He laughed and said, 'I had a knife that night, not a gun, you stupid cow.' On Saturday he told me there was someone else there. A woman, who ran past him, laughing. A woman with long fair hair. I'm thinking it was..."

"Emer McCarthy Miller," Maggie interrupted. "Just what we needed."

Bob stood up. "If you told me this when it happened it would have changed our whole investigation. My God, Zelah, you have screwed up this time." He stood up. "I have to go back to work. You realise this could constitute perverting the course of justice?"

"Why the hell do you think I came back?" Zelah shouted at his departing back. "I was going to stay in

203

Ireland until tomorrow, but I knew this couldn't wait. Don't I get some credit?"

"No," Maggie replied. "I'm going to find Nick. Jack, up to you if you come with me or stay here. Zelah, I suggest you make yourself scarce."

"She should stay." Nick's voice came from the door. He walked into the room. "What's done is done. What matters is what we do next." He returned to his seat. "I want everything you know," he said to Zelah.

"That's all I know," she replied, somewhat mollified. "Look, I should have told Bob about what Gerry said, but I thought at the time he was lying." She put her hands up to her brow, placing her elbows on the table. "I'm sorry. More than I can say."

"Contrition, from you," Maggie said. "Well, I suppose it's something to be grateful for."

Jack sat up. "Just stop it, mum. Zelah was wrong, she's apologised. Nick is right. What will you do now?"

"Bob's just been told the person who shot him is on the loose, could be close by. And I'm just supposed to shrug and move on?" Maggie barked.

"We make a plan," Nick said. "It's a shock for all of us. However, Ms McCarthy Miller hasn't tried anything since. Maybe she's not around and close by. But..." He held up his palm to stop Maggie's retort. "We must assume she's here, somewhere, biding her time. This means I need to protect Stella. I'm going to see her now, explain what's happened. I won't be back tonight. Let's reconvene in the morning, after we've had some thinking time." In the following silence he picked up his bag and left the house.

"Do you want me to go?" Zelah asked Maggie.

"Yes," she replied. "But I want you to come back in the morning. I'm guessing you went to Cork to tell

204

Mischa about her brother. Can I assume it didn't go well?"

"You can. I'll see you tomorrow."

Chapter 27

"Will she get into trouble?" Jack asked Maggie after dinner, which had been a mostly silent meal.

"She's been foolish," Maggie replied. "She thinks she's always in control of everything and knows best, better than anyone else, including us. She doesn't. Maybe this will make her reconsider how she respects us. Yes, she may be in trouble. We'll have to wait for Bob to tell us."

"I'll go and do some research," he said. "This is what you so-called grown-ups call 'way above my pay grade', far as I'm concerned."

Maggie didn't call him back. She sat alone at the table, trying to banish the unpleasant thoughts of what she wanted to say to Zelah. As much as Zelah had always been her loyal friend, supporter and, to some extent, saviour, there was always an atom of annoyance at Zelah's high-handed judgement of her friends' abilities. Now, the boot had permanently moved itself onto the other foot, and Zelah was going to need their support. In addition to contrition, she needed to develop humility, fast.

She tried Bob's phone, but it went straight to voicemail. This situation wasn't going to improve his standing in the eyes of his bosses, either. She knew he had hopes of reaching the rank of Chief Inspector before he retired. Would this scupper his chance or would his ambition lead him to throw Zelah under a bus? The fact she couldn't easily answer the question was more than disturbing.

She joined Jack in the office, deciding distraction was the immediate necessity. He was engrossed in his screen.

"What about the homework you've been complaining about?"

"Couldn't concentrate. This is better."

"Where have you got to?"

"There's something off about 'The Clown'. That's how I've been thinking about Camberwell."

"In what way?"

"He went to more than one school from when he was eight to eighteen. He would have changed schools when he was eleven, but there were a few more changes."

"How many?"

"I've found six so far. All public schools. He ended up at Allbery. He'd already been at Eton and moved on."

"That's a lot," Maggie replied. "Any information about why he left so many?"

"Nothing, yet. I'll keep looking. What are you working on?"

"I'm finding out as much as I can about Wakelin. He had no children after the two he had died, so there's no direct descendant. He had one brother, whose single child - a boy - inherited the fortune. I'm tracing him now. I want to see where the line went and if there are any living descendants. Nick's doing the same for Rosen."

"Why does it matter?"

"A few reasons," Maggie replied. "A living descendant may have something about the individual's history, if they are willing to share it with us. If it's their ancestor who turns out to be the person who bought Elsie Doughty, and brought about her eventual death, they may want to know. Or not. We can give them the option. It depends on what we find out about the culpable man and the wider circumstances."

"Do you know what happened to her, mum?"

"I have some information. I was going to share it this evening, but can you wait until tomorrow? I'd want everyone to hear it at the same time."

"Fine with me." He turned back to his laptop.

* * *

"He was expelled," Jack said half an hour later.

"Was he, indeed? From where?"

"From a prep school, then from Eton."

"Is there any explanation of why?"

"From the prep school for bullying. From Eton, not exactly. Unacceptable conduct, whatever that means. Could be bullying."

"Could be any number of things. But it develops what we're learning about his character, doesn't it?" She paused, then added, "He went up to Oxford; but did he stay the course there?"

"Yes," Jack replied. "But not with honours."

"I'm starting to see a pattern," Maggie said. "Bullying, unacceptable conduct sufficiently appalling to get him expelled from one of the country's top public schools and a poor degree from one of the country's top universities. Perhaps not 'The Clown'."

"No. What should I look for next?"

"Makes you wonder how he made his way in life. His father must have paid out a lot of money during Camberwell's youth to get him into a new school each time he messed up, and to keep the reasons hidden. Maybe he was the wild child, or even the 'black sheep' of the family. See if you can find out what happened to him when he left university. Remind me how old he was when he attended the party at Fallough Hill?"

Jack checked back through the file notes. "He was born in 1852, so twenty-six."

"Five years out of university with an unremarkable law degree. See if you can find any mention of him during university and the following five years. And check on the fiancée and the niece, too. Lady Wyn Davies thought they didn't gel." She glanced over at him. "Now, pack it in and go to bed. You look tired. School tomorrow."

He nodded. "I'll put my notes on the log."

As he left the room he turned back to Maggie and said, "Text me with whatever happens tomorrow, please, mum. I can't wait until I get home. Especially if it's bad."

Although she also wanted to sleep Maggie knew she would wait until Bob came home. He texted her to say he would be back, but couldn't say what time.

She didn't want to think about Zelah and the problem she caused. There needed to be a reckoning, but that was for tomorrow. In the meantime, this was a window of opportunity to concentrate on developing her idea of specialising in 'brick wall' cases. Having thought about how to present this to her colleagues and not coming up with any ideas, subtle or otherwise, Maggie wondered if she was overthinking. Maybe she should just tell them this was what she wanted to do. She had enough experience; Nick had created an amazing online catalogue of resources. Her children no longer needed her presence every day so she could travel whenever necessary. Each thought about this 'project' was an exciting one. Yes, it would be challenging; yes, there were going to be more failures than they were used to. Maze's reputation was for solving cases, never letting go. Well, this current McRoberts case was proving her point. So the information that re-started the case had come from a somewhat – unusual – source. So what?

Maggie had already closed her eyes to work through more detail when the sound of a key opening the front door jumped her out of a gentle doze.

Because the lights were on Bob Pugh put his head around the office door as Maggie tried to stand up.

"I nodded off. What's happening?"

"Zelah will have to come into the station tomorrow to be questioned about Gerard Quinn. Not by me. She'll have to make a formal statement about the shooting. After that, I don't know. It'll be up to the Super to decide if there's to be a formal charge."

He sank onto the settee. "I've been told to take a few days off."

"Is it bad?" Maggie asked, sitting next to him. "Will this affect your career? If it does, I won't forgive her."

"I don't know yet. The Super isn't pleased, of course. But he knows I've acted as soon as I knew. I don't think there'll be a problem." He put his arm around her shoulders. "If she gets a caution, I won't be sorry. About time she got pulled up."

"What about Sherry?"

His gaze focussed rapidly. "What about her?"

"Is she carrying on without you?"

He rubbed his chin, then his head. "No. I agreed to take a few days, but said I want to go back to aspects of Malky Thomas' suicide when I get back. The Super agreed. Sherry will be reassigned until I'm back."

He banged his fist on his leg. "Bloody Zelah! She's got me suspicious."

"No, Bob. You already were. You just didn't recognise it until Zelah put it into words."

He grimaced at her, then laughed. "You around the next few days?"

"Yes. We have a lot of work to do."

"Fair enough. Come on, let's go up. Zelah won't be here in the morning, so you can have a lie in. We can have a lie in." He grinned at her.

"No we can't. Jack has to get up and off by seven."

"You can see him off, then come back to bed."

"What will you be doing for the next few days? Apart from sleeping in?"

"No idea. Take it as it comes." He paused as he reached the stairs. "Jack has a girlfriend problem. I can take some more time to talk to him."

"Is it serious?"

"Not sure. Zelah's been talking to him too. She noticed how he's been a bit quiet lately."

"Me, too. But he hasn't said anything to me. Why did he speak to Zelah?"

"He didn't," Bob replied. "She asked him. He told her a bit about it. Do you want to know?"

"Why doesn't he speak to me?"

"Because he thinks if he tells you, you'll go all warrior mother on him and go for the girl in a face-off."

"I would never do that!"

"Huh. Of course you would. It's who you are. Leave it, Maggie, I'm dealing with it OK."

"Sorry. But you have to keep me informed."

He didn't reply and she didn't push it. She trusted him. And he was right; if this girl did anything bad to Jack, Maggie knew she would rip her apart with her teeth, regardless of any embarrassment to her son. Warrior mother, eh? Not a bad thing to be.

Chapter 28

Anglesey 1903

Sir Richard Wyn Davies wriggled himself comfortably into his armchair, put his feet out to catch the warmth of the fire and opened his newspaper. He was feeling at peace with the world, until the door opened.

Lady Virginia lowered herself into the chair opposite his and put her hands in her lap. A glance over the top of his paper told him she was thinking. Not a good sign, these days.

He ignored the lashing of rain at the library window, waiting for whatever she had come to say. After five minutes of silence, he couldn't bear it any longer and lowered the paper.

"Virginia, what do you want? I like to read my paper in peace."

"Yes, Richard, but I have something to say. I'm thinking."

"About anything in particular, my dear?"

"Yes, Richard. Something happened yesterday."

"Can you remember what it was?" He knew this was unlikely. Her memory was failing a little more each day.

"Of course I can remember. A man came here. He was asking about the party in seventy-eight. I wrote about it. But I can't find my diary."

Sir Richard rested the newspaper on his lap and gave her his full attention. "What did he want to know, Virginia?"

"He said his father, a detective, came here, looking for a street child, who had been kidnapped. His father never went home after his visit."

"Hmm. Strange story. Most unlikely, I think. Did you ask Evans?"

"Yes, Richard. He doesn't recall it."

He picked up his paper again. "Then it didn't happen. Chap's got the wrong house."

Virginia Wyn Davies sat for a further few minutes, then stood and left the room. She went to her bedroom, to the little desk where she kept her private papers and her diaries. She remembered she had gone there... when was it? Yesterday, perhaps. Yes, yesterday, after the man left. She found the diary and put it somewhere else so she could read it later. But then, she forgot. And now she couldn't remember where she put it. She must have been anxious to read it, because the papers were in such a mess, too. Not her usual way. She liked tidiness and order. She tutted at herself and began to tidy the papers, putting the diaries back in their box. She didn't remember leaving them untidy. But how else could they have become so disordered? Back in the box with them. She would sort them out later. Now, where was the diary? Oh yes, of course. She retrieved it from under her bed and sat to read through what she had said. How amusing it was, back then.

An hour later, after she put the diary back in its box, she went back to the library.

"What now, Virginia?" Sir Richard said as she sat again.

"I found my diary and I remembered. I didn't like any of them."

"Any of who, my dear?"

"Those men and their families you invited back then. The Jew and his wife, and the London man and the other one."

"I received good investment advice, the profit from which allowed me to invest in the estate. And some good connections. They weren't so bad."

"Yes, but it wasn't right. I see it now. I heard, you see. I wasn't supposed to hear. But I heard her say it. It should have been impossible."

Realising he wasn't going to be able to get back to his paper until she had her say, Sir Richard laid the paper on his lap and turned in his seat towards her. "What did you hear, Virginia?"

She was shaking her head. "It was wrong, I see it now."

"Are you going to explain in any more detail," he said, knowing she couldn't keep her train of thought running to any kind of detail.

"I can... I think... no. I shall have to write it down. Now, where's my diary?" She looked around, puzzled. "I remember. It's in the bedroom." And she left the room.

Sir Richard shook his head, rang the bell and retrieved his paper. In seconds Evans appeared.

"You need something, My Lord?"

"That was quick, Evans. Were you listening at the keyhole?"

For a second the butler blanched, but realised Sir Richard was talking about the ringing of the bell, not about the preceding conversation. He laughed.

"I was on my way, My Lord, to ask if you are ready for luncheon."

"Yes, yes. Five minutes."

"Will her ladyship be joining you?"

"She's wandering around somewhere. Send a maid to find her, will you?"

"Of course, My Lord." He paused in the doorway. "Is her ladyship quite well? I had the impression something has disturbed her."

"Oh, some man who came here yesterday. I told her he had come to the wrong house."

"Which was my thought also, My Lord."

* * *

After lunch Lady Virginia retired to her room for her afternoon nap. Before she slept, she decided to write in her diary. It was no longer fashionable to do so, but she had been writing for so long she couldn't stop. Richard thought she had stopped years before.

She sat at her desk, thinking with as fierce concentration as she could muster, what she remembered. Strange, how she struggled to remember yesterday, yet the events of that weekend twenty-five years ago were still clear in her mind. And the conversation she overhead. Best to get it down whilst she still remembered in such detail.

* * *

The following day, as Evans served them mid-morning coffee, Sir Richard asked, "What about the man who came here the other day, old girl. Did you remember anything?"

"What man was that?" Virginia asked.

"You don't remember?"

"I didn't meet anyone, Richard. Why would you say I did?"

"No need to be agitated, my dear. No need. Just settle yourself down. Archie and Sophia and the grandchildren

215

will be here tomorrow. You're looking forward to seeing them, aren't you?"

"Of course I am."

He turned to Evans, nodded briefly and dismissed him. Evans understood Lady Virginia was not to be disturbed again by any discussion of the visitor. He left the room with a satisfied smile.

Two days later he passed on the message that, although he had not been able to find the diary, the 'old girl' had forgotten the visitor. He received back the message the other matter would be taken care of and the visitor would not be returning. Their arrangement would continue.

Two days later, as John McRoberts fell under a tram in Liverpool, the body of Ebenezer Evans was found not far from The Black Bull public house in Bangor. He appeared to have fallen down a flight of stairs and broken his neck whilst leaving the public house in a state of drunkenness. A verdict of accidental death was returned.

His assets turned out to be considerable. He died unmarried, therefore his sister, to her surprise, inherited the sum of seven hundred pounds and a small hotel Evans had purchased, to run after his upcoming retirement.

Chapter 29

The following morning Nick didn't appear, either. As Maggie saw Jack off just after seven a text arrived from Nick telling her the professor he had tracked down in Liverpool was travelling to Cardiff and had agreed to meet with him at lunchtime.

Bob hadn't even noticed she was up.

The information about the death of Elsie Doughty gouged deep feelings of anger and disgust, about the girl's early death, about how she was treated during her life. Maggie wanted justice for her, acknowledgement she had been abused and destroyed, by evil men. This meant finding out who these evil men were. It had to be possible.

One of the first issues she, Nick and Zelah agreed they should deal with was to find out if there were living descendants of the three men who attended the Anglesey party. If one of them was going to find out his ancestor was a Victorian paedophile and sex trafficker, they had the right to be told. She could begin with George Wakelin.

Wakelin, Maggie knew, had had no more children after the death of the first two. So where did his fortune go when he died? A recheck of probate records confirmed the recipient was his brother, Edgar. By the time Edgar inherited he was over seventy years old. It was a respectable fortune, just under two hundred and fifty thousand pounds. A quick internet check of the value showed today it would have been worth a little over two million pounds, enough for Edgar to live a good life. It was mainly invested in property. Sir George guarded his fortune well. From Edgar Wakelin the inheritance went to his one son, then to the last family inheritor, the son's daughter. Her name was Laura Wakelin and she died unmarried and childless in 2010. The remains of her estate had been left to charity. There were no more Wakelin family members descending from Sir George.

Maggie was having difficulty believing Sir George Wakelin was Elsie's abductor. Every account of him she could find pointed to a blustering boastful man, trying to enter the upper echelons of local society. He could have left the girl at his home before attending the party, but that would have been complicated. Suppose she escaped, or called for help and been found by one of Sir George's servants?

"I'll have to leave this one, for now," she muttered.

"Leave which one?"

Bob's voice made her jump.

"Talking to myself again. Sorry."

"Sign of madness." He grinned. "So, what's making you mad? I have time to listen."

She talked him through the three suspects and the Wakelin case, ending with, "What do you think? From your experience, would a personality such as Wakelin's be capable of such deception?"

He pulled up a chair next to her, put on his glasses and read the notes on the laptop. "Well, I'd be surprised if he could be so duplicitous. I mean, he was a pompous man, wasn't he? He liked his publicity. He made a fortune from nothing, so he must have had some cunning ways, but if the reports saying he enjoyed a good public row are true, then if he were hiding something on this scale, I'd say it would have been difficult to maintain two such different facades. Mind you, I'm not saying he wasn't capable of it, but I'm thinking something would have leaked out."

"So, on the whole, no?"

"That would be my opinion. Who's next?"

"Nick is looking at Rosen and Jack's got Camberwell."

"Want me to take a look at their notes?"

"Yes, please. Valuable detective insight."

Bob tapped his nose. "Copper's instinct," he said and switched on the main computer and screen.

Half an hour later he sat back. "Couple of questions. First – is this Nathan Rosen any relation to Oliver Rosen QC, the barrister? He has chambers in Manchester."

"I don't know," Maggie replied. "Nick's working on it. We can ask him when he gets here. Who is this Rosen?"

"You haven't heard of him?"

"Obviously not."

"Human rights specialist. Prosecutes at a global level. And defends international cases."

"Sounds a good guy," she replied.

He laughed. "Your kind of barrister."

"You don't approve?"

"Been around too many barristers. Can't understand anyone who'll just take a case for money. Seen too many get off because of their barrister, who should have been put away."

"Mr Cynical," she replied. "There are good ones."

"Well, if it was Nathan Rosen in this sex trafficking ring, because it's looking fifty/fifty that's what it is, the news won't please the barrister."

Maggie shrugged. "If it is, we'll have to tell him."

"This is the one who interests me," Bob said. "Camberwell. What was he doing there?"

"We think he was invited to the party to add a high-societal tone, although he seems to have been brainless."

"I don't mean the party. What was he doing in Liverpool with his fiancée and his niece?"

"Jack's looking at him. We don't have much information yet. We'd more or less dismissed him, based on Lady Virginia's opinion. Although..." she paused, "Jack found Camberwell was expelled from more than one public school before ending up in a minor one, then came out with a poor degree from an Oxford college. Not that any degree from Oxford is poor. He just doesn't sound a serious character."

"Well, if I were looking for a candidate, he'd be my man. Do you have any pictures of him?"

"A few, later in his life." She pulled up three photographs onto the white board. The first was taken around 1890, when Christopher Camberwell would have been in his mid-thirties. He was with his wife, both seated and serious. Trying to decide on his expression, Maggie considered 'smug' then 'superior'. The second and third were from the post-World War One period, the early 1920s when Camberwell would have been in his early sixties. Bob sat and stared at all three.

"A confident man," he said after a couple of minutes. "Nothing vacuous about him."

"Which is at odds with Lady Virginia's impression," Maggie replied.

"Then maybe he was the one who was putting on a façade."

"OK, thanks. Useful. I'm going to switch to concentrating on Camberwell. I'll let Jack know."

She grabbed her mobile phone as the front doorbell rang.

"Damn, who's forgotten their key now?"

The answer was: no-one. As Maggie opened the door, Sherry Martin strode past her with a nod. "Bob's in the office," she said to Sherry's departing back. She stood for a moment to get a control on her mounting irritation, then followed the woman in.

Bob swivelled around on his computer chair. "Take a seat, Sherry. Coffee?"

"No, thanks. I just came to inform you Mrs Trevear has given a statement but isn't being detained or charged." She glanced at Maggie. "Yet."

And I bet that's pissed you off, Maggie thought, standing in the doorway.

"Thank you," Bob replied in a monotone. "Anything else?"

"No, Guv."

"You don't need to check on me. Unless you've been asked to?"

"No-one asked me, Guv. I was just concerned. Thought you'd want to know."

"Well, thanks."

He turned his chair back to the computer screen in an obvious signal of dismissal. Sherry didn't move.

"Who's he?" she said, looking over at the screen where the photographs of Christopher Camberwell were still on display.

"A person of interest from a case we're investigating," Maggie replied.

Sherry sniggered. "I've never understood: what's interesting about dead people?"

"Well in this case, this person may have been involved in murder." Maggie pulled in a deep breath, trying not to rise to the bait. "The murder of a police detective. Surely of interest in any age?"

Sherry shrugged. "Not to me. But we all have our oddities, don't we?"

221

Before Maggie could say anything more Bob swung around again. "As you say, of no interest to you. I'll be back on Saturday or Sunday." He turned back to the computer and Maggie saw the colour rise on Sherry's cheeks. Accepting the dismissal this time, she turned around.

"Maggie, let's get back to Camberwell," Bob said.

Sherry stopped in the door, turned around to look at the photographs. "That his name?"

Maggie picked up the signal and answered, reluctantly. "Yes. Is it a name you know?"

"Never heard of him," Sherry replied. "I'll let myself out." Maggie left her to it.

"Sorry," Bob said when Sherry slammed the door behind her. "Didn't mean to give it away. She knew the name. I'm wondering why."

"Me, too," Maggie replied, sitting at her laptop. "Something's not right there. Anyway, Zelah's done what she has to do for now. I expect she'll be here later. Do you think your boss asked Sherry to come here?" Maggie asked.

He shrugged. "I hope not. I thought he trusted me better. But he does believe I'm too close to Graeme's case."

They both settled back to work. Neither of them heard the soft opening and closing of the front door, as Sherry Martin tiptoed along the path to her car. She drove a few hundred yards away from the house, then stopped to make a phone call.

Chapter 30

Maggie sent Jack a text to tell him Zelah had made a statement but wasn't being charged. She felt obliged to add 'yet'. She also let him know she and Bob were going to start a closer review of Christopher Camberwell, to which he replied '*goodx2. no classes this af. back soon*'.

"I hope he's not skiving off," she said to Bob.

"He's got a good attendance record," Bob replied, fixed on the screen. "Won't do him any harm if he is."

"What are you so engrossed in?"

"I'm reading the notes on Camberwell. He was the fourth son, yeh?"

"Yes," Maggie replied.

"What evidence of him practising as a lawyer?"

"We haven't got that far yet. We've concentrated on the other two."

"Shall I take a look?"

She smiled. "Knock yourself out. There's no word from Nick yet. I wonder what he's up to?"

* * *

Nick was ensconced in a deep armchair in a trendy café in one of the Arcades in Cardiff, with Professor Sonia Suri. She had agreed to meet him before her lectures at the university and Nick was enjoying himself enormously. Professor Suri, or Sonia as she insisted he call her, had been fascinated by the story he told her about the party at Fallough Hill and demanded to hear the 'sordid details'.

Her accent was as strong as John and Jacka's. "That's amazing, Nick. So, one of these three guests shot your detective, you think?"

"Yes, we think so," he replied, sipping at a cup of hot chocolate.

"Well, this is different from my usual line of work. I like it. Right, there were several trade groups and associations in Liverpool at the time, working together. I don't recognise two of the names but there were a lot of members. I can check it out for you when I get back tomorrow."

"You recognise one of them?"

"Of course. One of the MPs for Liverpool was Sir Joseph Camberwell, Baron Percyford. He won it for the Conservatives in a by-election in 1875. Christopher Camberwell was one of his sons. And not one of the better ones, by all accounts."

"Now it sounds as if you have some interesting gossip to give me, Sonia."

"Buy me another one of these divine hot choccies and I'll tell you everything I know."

"Done."

* * *

Maggie stopped to get a late lunch for herself and Bob. They were just finishing as Nick, Zelah and Jack arrived within minutes of each other.

"Puts me in mind of number 99 buses," Maggie said. "We each have something to say, so let's get on with it, shall we," she continued, deliberately not looking at Zelah. "If anyone wants a drink, get it now."

It took ten minutes for everyone to discard wet clothes, remove shoes and sit at the table in the office. The room was silent, the atmosphere heavy.

"Who wants to go first?" Maggie said.

"If you will allow me," Nick said, getting in ahead of Zelah. "I have something to say, first of all, on a personal level, before I share what I learned this morning about our three suspects."

Zelah closed her mouth and no-one else disagreed.

"When I heard yesterday my son Max was working for Kennet Quinn I was horrified. I wanted to go to his house, call Max out. I wanted to ask him why he hated me so much. It has been a long time since my feelings were so hurt, so offended. I set off from here intent on confrontation. Then I decided I would stop off to tell Stella, to ask if she would accompany me. She refused, then asked me to sit with her a while to consider what I was going to say when I got there. She gave me the time and space I needed to go through many conflicting emotions. I am not naturally an emotional man. I am rational; I consider before I act. I weigh up the rights and wrongs, the potential outcomes of any situation I am about to encounter. Well, yesterday, my inner psychopath took over. Yes, I do have one," he said to Maggie, who was smiling.

"Never doubted it," she said.

"I have kept it suppressed, but yesterday it got out of the fortress prison I have worked so hard to create. Stella saw this. After a period of silence, she began to speak, about me, about Max and how he might be feeling. And she made me see, if I want to create a relationship with him, I must leave him to come to me." He had, as usual, been fixing his gaze on the ceiling as he spoke, but now he looked around the room.

"How can you be sure he will?" Maggie asked.

"I can't," he replied. "I must rely on fate."

"Sod that," Zelah muttered.

Nick twisted his head towards her. "I am not like you, Zelah. I don't bulldoze into any situation where I might have an interest, to turn it to my advantage, to bring about the desired effect. I will wait, but if I see an opportunity, however small, to have my son look more favourably on me, I will not hesitate to use it."

"I'll keep an eye on him, now I know who he is," Bob said. "If he's a decent lad at heart, he won't be fooled by Kennet Quinn for too long."

"That's a skyscraper of hope with no foundations," Zelah said.

"No visible foundations, Zelah," Nick replied. "You don't know they aren't there, just because you can't see them. Thank you for listening."

"You're welcome," Maggie said. "Zelah, you're next."

All eyes zoomed in like lasers. Zelah didn't flinch.

"My statement didn't contain anything you don't already know. Gerard Quinn and his mother are in Australia, no idea where. Your lot," she nodded at Bob, "will be contacting the Australian forces to find out where they are, so they can talk to Gerry. He'll need to give a statement about the night you were shot. I guess he'll have to come back, unless he can convince them being in the same country as his father is life-threatening and he's just touring Australia for six months with his mother."

"Are you sure you don't know where he is?" Bob asked. "Because if you do and you're withholding information, you'll be charged."

She tapped her fingers on the table. "As I said, I have no clue where they are. Once he left the country I lost interest. I suspect they've gone off travelling, somewhere. It's a big country."

She wasn't going to tell even these, closest and best friends, she texted Michelle and Gerry to tell them to buy a camper van for cash and get lost in the outback, or risk being found by the police and sent back to the UK. It was a risk, but she felt responsible. She knew Gerry couldn't tell them any more about Emer McCarthy Miller's attempt on Bob's life other than a vague description, but he could give them information about why he was there with a knife. He could implicate his father in an intended serious assault on a police officer. Would Gerry have done that? She didn't know. In most cases, people's fear of Kennet's reprisals was greater than their belief the police could protect them and that included his son. It had certainly been so for his wife.

No, she decided she had done the right thing. The main sizeable nagging worry was how much Gerry knew about Graeme Robertson's death, and whether he knew Malky Thomas. She hadn't asked if this was the reason for Kennet being angry with Gerry and sending him to France, and she didn't want to know. Zelah didn't believe in fate, but she decided this was one time when she could leave it in charge.

"That's it. I don't have anything else to tell you. I have to wait to find out if I'm to be charged."

"What's the chances?" Jack asked Bob.

"I can't discuss it, OK?" It was a harshly given answer, which he hadn't intended, but he didn't want to tell anyone in the room about his ongoing enquiry into Malky Thomas, and his suspicion there was a third person in the car on the night of Graeme's death.

Jack shrugged and looked down at the table.

In the seconds following, Nick looked between Zelah and Bob and saw enough to understand neither was being entirely honest. He decided not to question either of them. What would be, would be.

"How about we talk about the case and what we've learned. I had an interesting meeting in Cardiff this morning."

"Fine with me," Maggie said. "Everyone in agreement?" Silence.

"I'll take that as a 'yes, go ahead'. I'll start," she added.

She leaned back to her computer and put up on the screen the information she'd earlier discussed with Bob.

"I called the Liverpool Record Office yesterday and they came back to me last night with information about the Elsie Doughty who died in the city workhouse. This is it. I've used it to create a timeline of her life."

The list began in 1865 with Elsie's birth. It then moved through the 1871 census, where she was recorded as a 'scholar', her father's death in 1877 to the removal from her family home in 1878 and the party at Fallough Hill when she was twelve years old.

The next recorded event was the years 1878–1885 with the remark '*Belgium/France*'.

This was followed by a record of an admission at the Lock Hospital in Liverpool in December 1885, when she was twenty years old. Then her death in February 1886 at the Brownlow Hill Workhouse Hospital when she was twenty-one from, according to the workhouse, consumption and degeneration of the brain.

"I've sent for the death certificate," Maggie said. "I've made it priority, so it should be here by Friday or Saturday. And here's the full report from Liverpool. It isn't much, but there is something of significance in it."

She handed around a set of papers, each of two pages. They read in silence.

Nick looked up first. "She came back to Liverpool," he half whispered.

"Yes," Maggie replied. "It also means you were right?"

"What was he right about?" Zelah asked.

"I didn't have much confidence in Mrs Doughty," Nick replied. "She sold Elsie. Then said she wanted her back, but the police turned her away. That seemed feasible. But Mrs Doughty was a drunk and continued to be so. When I spoke to a member of the Doughty family – I tracked one down, although the spelling has changed over the years – he told me Elsie became a legend in the family, as a child who went missing and was searched for over many years by her loving mother."

"More likely Mrs Doughty dined out, or drank freely, on the story for years but when Elsie did get away from Belgium or France she went home," Maggie added. "I suspect her mother turned her away. I'm making this fit as I go along, but if Elsie got back to Liverpool around the end of 1885, she would have had nowhere else to go but the streets. She was badly diseased enough to be admitted to the Lock Hospital, but died six weeks later, so she must have been beyond treatment."

"So she discharged herself, went to the workhouse and died there," Nick added.

"How long was she in the workhouse infirmary before she died?" Zelah asked.

"Four days," Maggie replied.

"Why are you so sure she came back from France or Belgium?" Bob asked.

"It's in the report from the Lock Hospital. Just a sentence, but it confirms she was 'working' at a

229

'European establishment', before she returned to England. We know from the history of abductions and enticement of British girls that some were taken to Paris and many to Brussels where they were held captive and charged a fee for their clothes, rooms, etcetera, which was far greater than any of them earned from their services. They were subject to vile sexual practices; I don't have much of the details and I don't want to know. There are some descriptions in one of the biographies of Josephine Butler. Basically, those girls were destroyed, physically and mentally. If Elsie had been there for six years, she would have been in a terrible state." Maggie paused. "Every time I think about the girl I am upset and angry. It's too late to bring the perpetrators to justice, but I want to know who they are, and at least shame their names."

"Be careful," Zelah said. "They may have living descendants, who could be shamed by association."

"I know. We can make them aware, though, can't we?" Maggie replied. "We already believe Oliver Rosen, the barrister, might be a living descendant. Nick, I was going to tell you about him. But I'm not sure it was Nathan Rosen, although we should still finish the check on the daughter's friend."

"I will, in both cases," Nick replied. "However, after my meeting this morning, my mind is tending towards another direction."

"I have an idea, too," Bob added. "Are we looking in the same direction?"

"You first," Nick replied.

"Well, I'd be looking at Christopher Camberwell. A lot about him doesn't add up."

"Copper's nose," Maggie said, grinning at the puzzled looks around the table.

"That's what I was thinking, too," Nick said. "Although I will be waiting on information from Professor Suri. She's going to look into the two commercial men, but she told me Camberwell was the son of one of the Liverpool MPs and had a reputation in the City."

"For what?" Maggie asked.

"For moving in circles close to certain establishments run by high-class madams and featured well-known local figures."

"Such as?"

"Such as the boss of your Chief Inspector Monaghan. The Chief Superintendent of Police. And the local coroner. Another Monaghan. I'm going to check, but I suspect the Monaghans were brothers."

"Now we're getting somewhere," Zelah said.

Chapter 31

"My mind is boggling," Maggie said. "Where do we go next?"

"I suggest we go back to the beginning with Christopher Camberwell," Zelah said. "Make no assumptions, take no notice of what Lady Virginia said about him. Construct a family tree, with every bit of information we can find to put on it."

"Jack and I can do it," Maggie replied. "I want – need – some space here, now, so perhaps you and Nick wouldn't mind making yourselves scarce. We can get back together tomorrow."

"Fine with me," Zelah said. "I'm meeting Mischa from the train in an hour or so, anyway. She's the next person I need to talk to."

"I thought things weren't good there," Maggie said.

"She's calmed down a bit since yesterday. She wants to hear the whole story."

"I'm going back to talk to Stella again. I'll collect the info from Sonia Suri and have it ready to discuss tomorrow," Nick said, picking up his bag and walking into the hall to retrieve his coat. "And I have an email from John McRoberts. I'll let you know if he has anything significant to add."

When they had gone, Maggie turned to Bob and Jack. "Sorry, that was abrupt, but I've had enough. There's so much information and so much to think about now, I want some quiet time to consider it. Jack, if you want to get on with the Camberwell research, go ahead. But, schoolwork first, if you have any."

"Just an hour or so, and some reading," he replied. "I'll put together a plan for Camberwell, shall I?"

"Good idea. Talk to Bob about what his nose is telling him. May help you find some additional threads to consider."

"Where are you going?" he asked.

"For a walk along the canal. Alone," she replied.

"Just get back before it gets dark," Bob remarked, back at the computer screen. "I'll be in even more trouble if I have to call out a search team and drag the canal."

She poked out her tongue at his back.

"I saw that."

* * *

Twenty minutes later Maggie walked back into the office, shivering.

"It's bloody freezing out there. I went the other way, towards the chapel. There's no-one else out," she said as she rubbed her hands together. "I'm going to put on some warm socks and slippers and make a hot chocolate. Anyone else want one?"

Bob said, "Yes." Jack, "No." But neither looked up. She stood for a few minutes, then shrugged and walked out of the room.

Ten minutes later she put a steaming mug next to Bob and went to sit on the settee. "Anything interesting, chaps?"

Bob turned to her.

"Elsie is buried in an unmarked communal grave, in the cemetery in Toxteth. I thought you'd want to know," Bob said.

"Yes, thank you. When I was walking I was wondering..."

"If we could get her into her own grave?" Bob said. She nodded. "I don't know. I'll make some enquiries."

"I was also thinking about her family. Should we tell them?"

"I would say yes," Bob replied. "Depends on how much they want to know, though, doesn't it? They have a handed down tale that's way off. But should you tell them what you think happened? I mean, you don't know, do you? You've made some guesses from a pretty basic piece of information."

"True, but it's still more accurate than their tale. I'll talk to Nick and Zelah tomorrow. Jack, what do you think?"

He didn't answer.

"Jack," she shouted.

His head whipped around. "Sorry, what did you say?"

"Never mind. If you didn't hear the whole thing I'm not going over it again. We can talk about it at dinner. How are you getting on?"

"I'm doing a timeline for Christopher Camberwell. What was his fiancée's name, in the diary?"

Maggie got up. "I can't remember. I wasn't thinking too much about him. I'll check the notes for you." Nick had printed out the relevant sections of the diary and she found the page. "Lavinia Duggan. In case you need to know, the niece was..." she rummaged through the pages, "Miranda Elise Camberwell."

"OK. Well, she's not who he married."

Maggie leaned over his shoulder. "Who did he marry?"

"Lady Susan Montgomery."

"Check her out, too, or put her on the list to be checked. You're not going to have time tonight. We'll

234

pack up soon and I'll get onto this tomorrow. Right, I'm going to make some dinner."

"No, I'll order a take-away," Bob said. "I suggest we eat in front of the fire with a film on Netflix and forget this stuff for a couple of hours. OK with you two?"

Jack gave him an immediate thumbs up, and Maggie sighed and nodded. It had been a long and emotional day.

* * *

Having gone to bed at nine the previous evening, Maggie slept for twelve hours and was horrified to find when she woke Jack had already gone to college. She joined Bob in the kitchen.

"I feel guilty. I hope he was OK."

"Come September, if he doesn't take a gap year and goes to Uni, he's going to have to get himself up every day. It's good practice."

"I suppose. Right, I'm going to carry on with the Camberwell research today. You have any plans?"

"I am going to take a day off from everything. I shall go for a walk. I shall read a book. I shall ignore all of you; therefore I shall avoid the office."

"Good plan," she said, swiping him on the head as she walked past. "I expect our paths will cross from time to time. See you later."

Maggie wasn't sure what time to expect Nick or Zelah, but as soon as she opened her laptop she heard Nick letting himself in. She decided to begin the day with an exploration of Christopher Camberwell's marriage and told Nick what she was doing.

"Can you hold on for a moment? I have some news from John."

"Should we wait for Zelah?" Maggie asked.

Sitting down he said, "Honestly? No. She hasn't been part of this case. She doesn't see why we're doing it, apart from the publicity. Plus she has so much going on right now we can't rely on her turning up at any given point."

"OK. But I will tell her when she does get here."

"Sure. Now, John texted me yesterday afternoon, as you know. A couple of things. First, he's been able to arrange the burial of William McRoberts' skeleton in Liverpool. It's in just over a week's time, next Friday. He said we're welcome to attend, but otherwise it's just going to be him and his wife, and his brother, and Jacka, of course. They wanted to keep it quiet and within the family. I said we'd talk it through, but I was sure one of us – you or me – would want to be there. And he's invited Trys and Helen."

"It should be you," Maggie said. "The second thing?"

"John and Jacka are going back to North Wales on Saturday to have lunch with Trys and Helen. Helen has been diving back into their old papers and she's found another diary entry written by Virginia Wyn Davies, this time in 1903."

"The year John McRoberts died under the tram."

"Exactly," Nick said. "She's told them it's going to shed more light on whatever was going on, both then and at the party."

"That's excellent news. Anything else?"

"Well, this morning I should be getting some information about the three suspects from Sonia Suri. She was going to check when she got back to see what she could find, and send it through. Plus she'll look up where she found the information about Christopher Camberwell's peccadilloes. And... I'm wondering if I should contact Oliver Rosen. To let him know."

Maggie turned around. "Let him know what? Look, why don't you wait until you get the information from Sonia Suri, see if she has anything about Nathan Rosen that warrants it. If there isn't, then best to leave him alone."

"Once we get the solution we will have to inform him. Zelah's going to write it up and I can't see how we can leave Nathan Rosen's name out. I agree, though. I'll wait until Sonia comes through."

"I'm going to carry on where Jack left off yesterday, with Camberwell. The deeper we get into this character, the more I'm thinking he's our main suspect, although I'm not yet sure what of."

She picked up the family tree Jack had started work on the previous evening. Christopher Camberwell was one of seven children, the fourth son with one older sister and two younger. The girls would have been married off. The eldest son would inherit, so he would have been OK and something juicy would have been reserved for the second son. The third might have had to work harder. When it came to the fourth, well, hardly anything left for him. In this case his parents tried to give him a good education, but the results were disappointing, to say the least. A good marriage would help.

Maggie looked up Lavinia Duggan. It was likely their engagement would have been announced somewhere noticeable, such as *The Times*. Nothing in the five years before the party. Nothing again in *Debrett's* or *Burke's Peerage*, which was odd, as it was unlikely even a fourth son would have married beneath his social class. Nothing in *The London Gazette*, either.

The most puzzling thing was, three months after the party at Fallough Hill, Christopher Camberwell's engagement to Lady Susan Montgomery was announced in *The Times*, with due ceremony, by her family. What happened to Lavinia? It was possible she died, but even so... three months? *Undue haste*, Maggie thought. Or was there another explanation?

She opened the Free BMD website and looked for a death between the end of 1878 and the first quarter of 1879. Nothing. The same on the General Register Office website. She allowed an age range of ten years either side of Christopher Camberwell's. Lavinia Duggan would not have been ten years younger, but she might have been older. But there was no reported death of any woman with that name between sixteen and thirty-six anywhere in the country. She also tried The British Newspaper Archives and *The Gazette*. Again, nothing. There was one report in a Lancashire paper of a woman called Mary Ellen Lavinia Duggan who had been charged with disorderly conduct in the running of a brothel. The woman had been fined, but that was in 1880.

Well, if she were going to prove to her colleagues she was able to attack 'brick wall' cases with everything she'd got, this was as good a time as any. Having already decided Lavinia Duggan would have been aged twenty to thirty-five, which would mean a birth from 1843 to 1858, at least the range fell within the boundary of civil registration. Then again, the surname 'Duggan' suggested possible Irish descent, so there was the chance Lavinia was not born on the UK mainland. But whatever, she would have to see what she could find.

Beginning again with the Free BMD website she put in the age range and hit the 'results' button.

"What!" she shouted at the screen, shaking her head as Bob walked into the room. "This cannot be happening."

"What's going on?" he asked as Nick spun around.

238

"The fiancée, Lavinia Duggan. There's no-one of that name registered as a birth across a more than sufficient range of years. I expected to find a few, at least, but there aren't any."

"Could she have been Irish?" Nick asked. "It's an Irish name, isn't it?"

"I'm going to try Roots Ireland and the national website now."

A few minutes passed as Bob and Nick waited silently, watching her back.

Then Maggie sat back and folded her arms. "Nothing, not a single one. It would have been a baptism in Ireland. Give me ten minutes, please. I'm going to check every site we have worldwide."

Again they waited, watching Maggie thumping buttons on the laptop with increasing severity, punctuated with frequent sighs.

"Nothing," she said as she sat back and folded her arms. "I don't know what to think right now."

"I have a suggestion," Bob said. "I've just spoken to a friend, Miles Cooper, a former coroner. He knows a bit about burials and if he can't answer questions he knows who to ask. He's suggested I meet him for a pint at The Boat Inn. I thought you might like to come to ask him about Elsie."

The Boat was Bob's favourite pub, where he was on good terms with the landlord and landlady. It sat on the edge of the Monmouthshire and Brecon canal, in beautiful woodland. It was one of the few working stretches of the old canal and Maggie had visited with Bob many times. This time of year it would have a blazing fire and excellent food, which was more than tempting.

"Good idea. I need to think about this. Nick, you want to join us?"

"No, thanks. I'm still working on Rosen and I'm waiting for Sonia to send me her information. You can fill me in when you get back."

"Any more about Max?" Maggie asked.

Nick shook his head. "I've decided to wait for him to come to me. But it's hard. I'll get on with this work."

* * *

"Perfect timing," Maggie said to Bob as they drove along the road between Pontypool and Abergavenny, turning off into a narrow, wooded lane at the sign for the canal. For much of the journey she had been pondering on what the search results had told her. The remaining option was Lavinia Duggan being a widow. She texted Nick to ask him to run a check to find out.

"What is the genealogical outcome of your pondering?" Bob asked as they reached the pub and parked the car.

"Fishy," she replied, grinning back at his snorted laugh. "I know, not a technical term, but I can't come up with a better one right now."

Maggie pulled on gloves and a scarf to make the short walk across a stone footbridge from the carpark to the pub. Glancing down at the canal water she saw ice.

"It's colder. I'm going to run," she said and took off, leaving him shaking his head.

The pub, as expected was comfortable and cheerful. Logs were sending up a roaring, crackling blaze in the enormous hearth on one wall. The landlord had retained the eighteenth-century originality with most of the walls and beams but added modern touches of electric light and comfortable armchairs and sofas without spoiling the atmosphere. They were spotted by a slim, tall man, Maggie guessed over six feet, with a mane of wild, thick silver hair, giving him a rakish look.

He shook hands with Maggie when Bob introduced her. "Told me about you, he has," Miles said once they were settled with drinks and ordered lunch. Maggie smiled half-heartedly. She found this type of statement mildly threatening, as if some life secret had been unwittingly revealed.

"Whereas I know nothing about you, Miles," she replied.

"Well, let's put that right. I was the coroner in these parts for ten years until I retired a year ago. Before that I was a pathologist. I am the husband of the delightful Iris under whose feet I regularly find myself and who encourages me to go out fishing, but not in this weather. She's not so sadistic, or sick of me."

"How did you and Bob become friends?"

Miles looked over at Bob and winked. "He's one of the good, honest ones. And I was also a friend of old Jeremy before he died. Did you meet him?"

"Before my time," Maggie said. "Bob and I met when he asked me to help find out if Jeremy had a living child. We went to Spain together, as you may also know."

"Indeed, indeed. I help out young Lola Vilaro at the animal sanctuary now and then. Strange to think she's Jeremy's great granddaughter. Sad, too, she never got to meet him."

"She's doing well," Maggie replied. "She's got her own vet practice in Abergavenny now."

Their food arrived, interrupting the conversation.

"So, Bob tells me you want to dig up a body," Miles said as the plates were put onto the table, with a moment of hesitation from the waitress.

"Not personally, Miles. I do want to find out how to go about organising the removal of a corpse from one grave to another."

"Can I get you anything else, folks?" the waitress asked, trying to hover.

"No, thank you," Bob replied. His tone was firm enough to remove her from the vicinity, albeit slowly.

"Bob's given me the basics," Miles went on, between mouthfuls of steaming shepherd's pie. "I have to say I admire what you're doing. First thing is, though, you aren't family. It has to be the family who applies, or gives permission for it to be done. Have you spoken to them?"

"My colleague has. Problem will be the story they have handed down has travelled a long way from the truth and I can't say how they'll react to the truth when they hear it. Is there anything else we need to know?"

"Practicalities. You'll get those from the superintendent's office. Your girl was buried in a communal grave – a pauper's grave, I believe?"

Maggie nodded.

"Depends on how many others are in there, and what number she is. You should give them a ring and tell them the story. They'll tell you how far down she is."

"You mean... oh, I see what you mean. Would it make any difference if she died of an infectious disease – two infectious diseases, actually?"

"Remind me of the date of death."

"It was 1886."

He looked up at the ceiling as he calculated. "Almost a hundred and thirty-five years. No, shouldn't matter at all. But again, inform the site staff. They're likely to have their own protocols. Anything else I can help with?"

"I can't think of anything," Maggie said. "We're involved in the reburial of another body, a man who was shot and buried in the grounds of a stately home. He's been identified now and is being buried with his family next Friday."

"What an exciting life you lead," he said, smiling. "Tell you what, here's my card. If you ever need any more info about bodies you dig up, or whatever, give me a call. Cut out the middleman," he said, cocking his head at Bob.

Maggie took the card and put it in her handbag. "I most certainly will do, Miles. And thank you."

"Not at all, not at all, my dear." He went back to shovelling in his shepherd's pie.

* * *

"So what's Iris like?" Maggie asked Bob as they drove away an hour later and she unwrapped the layers of woollen scarf she had curled around her neck and covered her nose.

"She's a sweetie but don't mistake it for lack of strength," he replied. "She's the archetypal Shakespearean Hermia. '*Though she be but little, she is fierce*'. He towers over her in height, but not in temperament."

Maggie's phone pinged. "Text from Nick. He wants to know when we're coming back. He's got information from Sonia Suri. I'll tell him we'll be there in twenty minutes."

Chapter 32

Back at the office, Nick was waiting with an unusual degree of impatience.

"A lot to tell you," he said, ushering them into seats. "I'll start with Sonia's information. She says there was a commercial group of businessmen, established for mutual help which included both of our potential suspects plus the MP Sir Joseph Camberwell. She doesn't believe there was anything suspect about it, but it starts a link to Christopher Camberwell. The group met in a hotel in Liverpool three days before the party. Now, here's the clincher. There was a dinner in the evening, attended by both Rosen and Wakelin, plus Sir Joseph Camberwell. Also on the guest list – Sir Richard Wyn Davies."

"So the invitation to the party was last minute," Maggie said. "That wouldn't have pleased Lady Virginia. How do you think it links to Christopher Camberwell?"

"Well," he replied, "this is surmise on my part, but we learned from Lady Virginia's diary Sir Richard was looking for investment advice and good contacts. If he was talking to Rosen and Wakelin and invited them to the party, perhaps he also invited Sir Joseph. But if Sir Joseph couldn't attend, perhaps he mentioned his son was in town and perhaps he could attend in his place. What do you think?"

"Are you sure his son was in town?" Bob asked.

"Sorry, yes, we are. She found a reference on a society news page to a group of young gentlemen who caused an 'altercation' after a lively evening's entertainment. It refers to the son of one of the city's Members of Parliament. I checked out each of the other

244

MPs. Neither had a son of the right age to be out carousing in Liverpool."

"It doesn't name him, though, does it?" Bob said.

"No, but given the context, there's a good chance it was him."

"I agree," Maggie said. "It's the best reason we have so far as to why Christopher Camberwell was invited. For me, it also adds to the growing concerns about the so-called family he took to the party at Fallough Hill. If he was carousing with a group of young men, where did the fiancée and the niece come from?"

"If there's uncertainty about the fiancée, then I'd check out the niece, too," Bob added.

The sound of a key opening the front door gave Maggie a sudden knot in her stomach and she realised no-one had mentioned Zelah, but it turned out to be Jack.

"Early finish again?" Maggie asked.

"No, teacher's off sick, so they said we could use the time for personal study. I thought I could get on with some research, before I go out later."

"Where are you going?"

"Just out to a bar in Newport with a couple of the guys. A few beers. Nothing wild."

"Get used to it," Bob muttered under his breath to Maggie.

"Well, we have a particular topic for you to go on," she said. "Christopher Camberwell has become the main suspect. The fiancée looks suspicious and we need to check out the niece."

"Wow, that's moved in a weird direction. OK, let me get changed and I'll get on it."

When he had gone Nick said, "There's more."

"Sorry, I thought you'd finished."

245

"Not yet. I contacted Oliver Rosen. He was OK about it, before you ask. Quite interested, actually."

"Well, what's done is done," Maggie replied. "Is there any follow-up action?"

"Yes. He has his great grandfather's private papers. He's read them all. He vaguely remembers something about a party in North Wales. He's going to check tonight and give me a call if it turns out to be Fallough Hill."

"It's time to check out Christopher Camberwell's descendants," Maggie said. "I'll try this afternoon. Bob?"

"I am going to take a book into the sitting room and I expect to fall asleep in front of the fire. Good luck."

* * *

After Jack made himself a sandwich about three inches deep with filling Maggie didn't recognise as coming from her kitchen, they each got down to their research. Nick moved on to reviewing the Liverpool newspapers.

"Well, this is interesting, mum," Jack said, as the light began to fade outside and a sharp wind rattled the plants beyond the office windows.

"What is?"

"Miranda Elise Camberwell does not appear to have ever existed."

"Show me," Maggie said.

He transferred his notes to the white board. Nick stopped, too, and pulled his chair over to get a better view.

"Here's the family chart, of Sir Joseph Camberwell and his four sons. I've added their wives and the dates of their marriages, and the death of the second son, Hugh

246

in 1876. He was the one who had died by 1878. Christopher Camberwell and the third son weren't married. Miranda Elise should have been Hugh's daughter. As you can see, he had two sons and one daughter. She was called Miranda, but she was only four years old in 1878." He flipped to a second page. "Here's my list of sources I've used to check." The screen showed the major genealogy online research sites, plus others he had checked. He also found newspaper announcements of the births of each of Hugh Camberwell's children alive in 1878.

"Good job," Maggie said, staring at the screen.

"These are UK sources," Nick pointed out. "Could she have been born abroad? If the girl at the party was about twelve years old, how does it tie in with Hugh Camberwell's marriage? Can we check the date?"

Jack pulled up the previous page. "It was in 1863. You can see, his first two sons were born in 1864 and 1866. There weren't any more until Miranda was born in 1874."

"Elsie Doughty was twelve in 1878, according to Lizzy McRoberts' letter, which means she was born in 1865 to 1866. Do we have the actual dates for the birth of the second son in 1866, and Elsie's date of birth? Just to be absolutely sure it wasn't possible for the girl at the party to be another of Hugh's children?"

"I'm on it. Where's the best place to look?"

"Start with the quarters on the Free BMD site."

It took just a few minutes. "Elsie was born in Q1 in 1866. The second Camberwell son was in Q3. Is it a possibility?"

"Maybe, just, but hardly possible."

As they waited for Jack and then talked, Nick returned to his computer.

"No, not possible," Nick said. "Look, here's the birth announcement in *The Times*. The boy, Timothy Hugh Camberwell, was born on 1st of September 1866. Even if Elsie was born on 1st of January, which she wasn't because I've found her baptism record. She was baptised on 28th of March 1866. We don't have her exact birth date yet; I've just ordered her birth certificate on special delivery. The maximum forty-two-day period to register a birth didn't come in until 1874, but nevertheless, it's rare for the birth registration to take more than six weeks. So, it's ninety-nine per cent certain she could not have been Hugh Camberwell's child."

"Which means," Maggie said, "Miranda Elise Camberwell of the weekend party could have been Elsie Doughty?"

"I'd say it's beginning to seem likely," Nick replied. "Although we're a long way off actual proof."

"How the hell did he believe he could get away with it?"

"He did get away with it, didn't he," Jack said. "Why would he have done it, though?"

"Why did he need to do it?" Maggie said. "Why risk taking her with him. Plus Lavinia Duggan. Why couldn't he have left her in Liverpool with Lavinia for the weekend?"

"Hmm. Perhaps it was too close to her family; he thought she might get cold feet. Or he didn't trust Lavinia; better to have them both where he could see them," Nick replied.

"Perhaps, if she had been told she was going to be a ladies' maid, or whatever, it would let her see the kind of place she would be working," Jack said.

"Possible," Maggie mused. "For my part it was more likely about trust, in the sense that neither of them trusted the other an inch. He was forced to go to the party, so he took Elsie along, with Lavinia posing as his fiancée, appropriately paid off, to make them appear a normal family. Poor little Elsie would have been told to keep her mouth shut. And what does that say about Lavinia. Who the hell was she?" She paused for a moment. "His degree of arrogance must have been immense, to believe he could get away with it, but as you say Jack, he did. Whatever though, we are just speculating, aren't we? We'll never get all the pieces of this puzzle, but we can get closer to the main picture. I'd like to stop now, give us time to think this through.

"In the meantime, Christopher Camberwell has one descendant. He and Lady Susan had one child, a boy called Joseph, born in 1880. By 1881 they're living at different addresses. The boy, who's one year old, is with his father and Susan is in a different house in London."

"Could just have been a night away from home, with other family," Nick said. "That happened."

"Yes, but I don't think so. On Susan's record she's the head of the establishment and she has a small staff. It's the same address for 1891 and 1901. I haven't checked 1911 yet."

"Where's young Joseph on each of those?"

"Still with his father. The marriage seems to have lasted less than three years," Maggie said. "I wonder if they divorced?"

"Probably not," Nick replied. "Unless she wanted to get remarried. But if she hadn't done so for twenty years, she must have found a way of living that suited her. Do you know when she died?"

"Not yet, give me chance! I'll check it out over the weekend."

He smiled. "Sorry, I'm getting carried away. Oh." His phone pinged an incoming message, which he scanned. "It's from Oliver Rosen. He's checked out the family papers and there is a reference to Fallough Hill. He says I can see it. I'm going to see if I can go Saturday." He left the room, passing Bob in the hallway.

"He's unusually animated," Bob remarked. "What's going on?"

"A lot," Maggie replied. "I'll tell you about it over dinner. Jack, are you joining us before you go out?"

"Yes, please."

"Good idea," Bob said. "Drinking on an empty stomach – bad idea. How are you getting back?"

Jack grinned, raising an eyebrow at Bob.

"What time?"

"Eleven at the latest. Maybe earlier. Depends..."

"On what?" Maggie asked. "How drunk any of you are by then?"

"Maybe," he said, turning away from her.

Nick's return stopped her probing further. "Rosen says Saturday is fine. I've spoken to Stella. She's up for the trip. I'll get off, after I've written my log. I've held off asking all afternoon, but have you heard from Zelah?"

"No, nothing," Maggie replied. "I'm going to text her later to say we're not around this weekend, either. Alice is back Saturday morning. There's a cinema night tomorrow she's staying on for, then she'll be here until Monday morning first thing. We're having some family time. Although, having said that, call me if anything useful comes out of your meeting with Oliver Rosen, please?"

"Will do. Have a good weekend."

Maggie's text to Zelah received '*OK*' in return. Nothing more. She was tempted to ask what was going

250

on, but decided against it. Zelah had not been in touch since meeting Mischa the day before and Maggie guessed the conversation hadn't gone well. Whatever, not her business. There was enough to be thinking about without whatever was consuming Zelah's time. Whatever it was, it could wait.

Chapter 33

For Zelah, the weekend was looming, and not in a good way. When she met Mischa at the station on Wednesday afternoon it was obvious from the frosty, "Hello," relations had not improved over the last couple of days. She was going to have to work hard to return to anything close to their previous easy-going chatty ways.

As soon as they got back to the flat Mischa went straight to her room, to unpack she said, and still hadn't come out two hours later. This was the point at which Zelah decided to intervene. Cards had to be put on the table, ugly as they might be. Make or break, as it might even turn out.

"Can I come in?"

There was no answer so she turned the handle, relieved to find it unlocked. Mischa was sitting on the armchair in front of the window looking out over the Channel, which today was covered by a heavy gloom and a mist shrouding the water.

"Now you're here, I want to give you a full explanation of what happened, with your mother and brother. You can ask me whatever you like. Then, it's up to you if you want to stay or go back to Ireland."

"Why don't Stephen and Niall hate you? You caused their father to die, but they don't hate you." Mischa didn't look away from the window.

"I've often wondered myself. It's because I was brutally honest with them, about their father and their aunt and grandfather, what they did. Maybe, too, because I didn't take their home away from them. They weren't involved in what their family did to mine, nor did they show anything but disgust when I told them. Those are my guesses. I haven't probed any further."

Mischa turned her head. "I thought you were someone special."

"I'm not special," Zelah said with a frisson of annoyance. "I saw what was happening to you. I wanted to help. To me you were a good person in a bad place." She paused for a moment. "Do you think I shouldn't have helped your brother?"

"He didn't just watch when Pa beat me. He laughed." Her hands were twitching in her lap. "I could still hear him, before I blacked out, chatting away to Grandpa."

"Yes. Then the rug got pulled from under his feet when Rufus died. He began to reassess. He knows the way he treated you was unforgiveable and has accepted you won't forgive him."

"My mother ran away from me, but has made up with him. How does that me feel?"

"I don't know. Unloved, rejected, bitter, angry, shall I go on?" She paused and moved to sit on the bed in front of the girl. "Maybe you think I'm helping you out of a sense of guilt? Well, I'm not. I have nothing to be guilty about. That applies to the boys, too. I'm helping you because you deserve the help. I did the same for your brother, not as much, but on the lower end of the same scale. Tell me, Mischa, would you have preferred it if I'd sent him on his way and left him to deal with your father, who'd have hurt him, too?"

"He'd never hurt Saint Gerry."

"Don't you believe it. He's got baby James Rufus now, another child he can mould after his own image. And let's face it, Gerry's not bright, is he? Not the best contender for your father's legacy."

Mischa smiled. "No, he's not the sharpest knife in the box. But he's still a brute."

"Well, maybe your mother can knock some sense into him. She has to be useful for something."

This time Mischa laughed.

"I have no time for family sentiment," Zelah went on. "Respect has to be earned, for me. I loved my husband, better than I can or will ever feel the need to explain. We were what I suppose is called soulmates. I never knew my parents. The other family members I have are the boys. I like them because of who they are, not because of some DNA." She took one of Mischa's hands. "You may never come to like your mother or your brother but it doesn't matter, as far as I'm concerned. Make the best and most of the people you have around you who you care about, and who care about you. That's the kind of family worth having."

"I want to hear the full story, your story and what happened with Gerry."

"Good, let's get some coffee and sit in the armchairs. Sitting on this bed is killing my back already and the whole story is going to take some time, especially if you keep interrupting me."

Throughout Friday, Saturday and Sunday the atmosphere settled down. The outstanding question was whether Mischa could bring herself to speak to her mother or brother. When Zelah took her back to Bristol airport on Sunday afternoon for her flight to Cork, Mischa decided she needed more time. Zelah didn't argue.

Back at her flat she breathed a sigh of relief. Now she thought she could get on with and give her undivided attention to the latest Maze project. First, though, she wanted to check on Sherry Martin's history.

Later in the evening she texted Maggie to say she'd be over first thing in the morning. What she found so far she did not like. Not at all.

* * *

On Saturday afternoon, after a thorough analysis of Oliver Rosen's handwritten memoirs from his three times great grandfather and a gourmet lunch at the luxurious high-rise apartment in the centre of Manchester, Nick stood on the wrap-around balcony looking out towards the moors. The day was cold and clear. Stella remained inside, chatting to Oliver's partner Ben about Llanyrafon Manor, where Nick had introduced Stella to his fellow Maze investigators on a previous case set within the ancient building, which she managed for a local Trust. She chatted to Ben about the challenges of maintaining an important historical building with diminishing support and funding, and Nick left them to it, to join Oliver on the balcony.

"Fantastic view, isn't it?" Oliver said.

"On a day like this, yes. How much does pollution affect the view in the summer, when it gets muggy?"

"Good point. But I'm a Manchester boy, born and bred. So's Ben. We couldn't live anywhere else." He pulled one hand out of a pocket and took a quick draw on a vape. "Interesting work you do. The memoir has helped?"

"Yes, inasmuch as it confirms Nathan Rosen gave Sir Richard valuable investment advice. Why do you think he went there? Just for the party? He could have given the advice anywhere at any time."

"Social prestige. Jews weren't welcome in many such establishments. I suspect he exchanged the advice for a mention in the society pages of the papers."

"Does it make you angry?"

Oliver thought for a moment. "I was about to say no, but deep down, yes. Many things have not changed."

"Does it affect you? Your ability to do your job?"

"No. But there are still some areas... I don't discuss this with many people. But I have good instincts and you're trustworthy."

"Thank you. We are."

"But you personally have more than good instincts?"

Nick smiled. "Perceptive. Can I take another look at the memoir? I understand why you don't want to give me a copy, so I must commit as much to memory as I can. I'll send you a draft of the final report, too. You can fix whatever amendments you consider necessary."

"Thank you. You mentioned the man you believe might have taken the girl. Camberwell. What do you know about his descendants?"

"Nothing yet," Nick replied. "Is there something I should know?"

Oliver Rosen gazed into the distance and pulled another long drag on his vape. "He may be related to Sir Henry Camberwell. He's a dealer in artefacts and curios, amongst other things. An old family business, of sorts. Lives in London. Check it out."

"We will be doing so. Any particular reason you're telling me?"

"Instinct. Anything else you want to ask me about Nathan Rosen?"

"Yes. Some of his business dealings looked a bit suspect when I began to look at him. A couple of his associates were fraudsters. Does it bother you?"

Oliver replied, smiling. "He did what he had to do to get on. I expect he... sailed close to the wind, shall we say. But you've read the whole book of memoirs. Did anything in there give you any idea he could have been involved in something as repulsive as what you've described to me?"

"No, but I doubt he would have committed anything to writing. However, I agree I found his writing amusing and not the tone of a man involved in such an ugly business. He may have been a bit of a chancer when he needed to be, but ultimately no more than that and his investment advice was sound."

Oliver nodded. "I agree. Not that I would have hesitated to accept it if he had been your man, but from what knowledge I have of his history, he wasn't the sort. He loved his family. In other parts of the journal he speaks fondly of them. By the way, the girl who accompanied his daughter Rachel that weekend married his son Julius. She was Esther, my two times great grandmother, not the Elsie you're looking for. Right, let's go back in. It's bloody freezing out here. Fascinating stuff you do. Makes a change for me, the misdeeds of dead people. I like Stella, by the way. She's something special."

* * *

The first part of their journey back home was spent in silence. Stella knew when Nick was deep in thought processing and didn't interrupt. They decided to travel first-class. There were few other first-class travellers, which gave them each some quiet time to think about the day and what they had learned.

After an hour when they had been served coffee and biscuits, she took the opportunity to start the conversation. "Nice guys. Ben says we should keep in touch."

"What did you two talk about?"

"The Manor. He wants to come to visit. He's trying to persuade Oliver to move out of the city centre, buy an old property and renovate, perhaps in North Wales."

"Oliver would struggle with it, from what he said to me."

"Ben knows. We talked about his work. He's modest. You'd never guess he's a professor and one of the country's leading specialist oncologists."

"Something Oliver said suggested a warning. About Christopher Camberwell's possible descendant. A man called Sir Henry Camberwell. At least, it I think it was a warning. I'll do the research tomorrow." He yawned. "A long day but worthwhile. The memoir was an excellent insight into Nathan Rosen."

"In what way?"

"The issues he had to deal with to maintain a place in society, being a successful Jewish entrepreneur in the nineteenth century. He would have encountered a lot of resentment. My main impression was of a good man who wanted to give good advice; not just for the sake of his reputation, but to help people he liked and he seemed to have liked Sir Richard Wyn Davies. Didn't think much of Wakelin, though. Wrote some pretty damning comments about him."

He related to her the information about the Rosen family history that hadn't been in the memoir, ending with, "The girl, whose name didn't get a mention in Lady Virginia's diary, was called Esther. She married Nathan Rosen's son, so she wasn't Elsie."

"Anything about Christopher Camberwell?"

"Interesting. The account of the weekend doesn't mention him at all, although Nathan gave two pages to his impressions of the party and his fellow guests over the two days."

"Puzzling," Stella replied.

* * *

Maggie's weekend started with collecting Alice early Saturday morning and bringing her back to the house, together with her friend Matthew. She had met Matthew the previous summer when Alice had gone to the Dordogne area of France with Matthew's family and a few school friends. He was still a socially awkward Harry Potter look-alike boy, but had grown several inches since the summer and was now the same height as Alice, and both now were as tall as Maggie.

As soon as they were settled with their computers set up to their exacting standards in the attic room Maggie had converted into a teenage den, they didn't appear again until dinner.

Alice had clearly decided to be polite in front of her friend, so asked Maggie about the cases Maze were working on. The information about the murdered policeman received a half-hearted nod from Alice, but Matthew was fascinated, particularly by the part played by DNA in the identification of the skeleton.

"Is science a particular interest?" Maggie asked.

He nodded enthusiastically. "I'd like to do research. I'm not sure what, not yet."

"Good enough for now. If you have a passion, you must follow it. Jack is going to study history at Cardiff in

259

September. He likes research, too, but the historical kind."

Alice went to say something, but changed her mind, which Maggie guessed would have been something rude. She was puzzled Jack hadn't got his retaliation in first, but he still looked tired after his night out and, she noticed, spent much of the day gazing out of the kitchen window. She asked Bob what he thought, should she delve further, but his advice was to leave it alone. She went along with it, although events would later show this was not one of his better pieces of advice.

In the meantime, before they left on Sunday afternoon, Alice and Matthew held court on the issue of the now identified Coronavirus having spread from the Far East into Italy where, a few days earlier, a case was identified in Rome, and Italy had declared a national emergency and suspended flights from China.

"It's going to get here, you know," Matthew said, somewhat gloomily, over Sunday lunch. "We're supposed to be going skiing at half term. My dad thinks we shouldn't go."

"You shouldn't go," Alice said, pushing her plate away. "It's not the flu. It's much worse. We could die. Lots of people in China have died."

"Well, thank you, Mrs Doom and Gloom," Jack said, standing up. "So glad you shared with us."

"You'll see. We'll all see; not too long now. Do you want to hear how I know?"

"No," Maggie, Bob and Jack said in unison.

She shrugged. "Suit yourselves. Time to go," she said to Matthew. He jumped from the table, thanking Maggie for her hospitality. "It's been great, Mrs Gilbert."

When they got to Matthew's house, where Alice was now going to spend the night before being taken back to school the following morning, Maggie gave her a big hug and whispered, "Don't worry too much about a pandemic. It may never happen, but if it does we'll all be sensible and do whatever we have to do, OK?"

Alice's eyes misted up. "I have been worrying no-one seems to be taking it seriously."

"Whatever it is, we'll be in it together. But let's hope it'll come to nothing. Now, off you go. It's too cold to keep Matthew's mum waiting."

She spent the drive home from Cheltenham thinking through the information they had learned about Christopher Camberwell and Elsie Doughty, and wondering how Nick had got on speaking to Oliver Rosen.

As she pulled up to the house and into the driveway, she felt a shiver. This coming week was going to bring something foreboding, that was for sure. But what, and for whom, she couldn't pinpoint. With a strong sense of worrying premonition she couldn't shake off, Maggie ran from the car through the freezing cold darkness and into the house.

Chapter 34

Maggie spent some time on Sunday night talking through with Bob how she was going to react to Zelah the following morning, but in the end decided to play it by ear. Zelah was unpredictable. She might act as if nothing had happened, or take offence, or just shrug it off.

Bob went back at work early on Monday, having taken Jack to the bus stop, leaving Maggie to prepare for her day.

Nick and Zelah arrived together, but their attitudes were as dissimilar as it was possible to be, Zelah having decided on taciturn and Nick full of enthusiasm, bouncingly ready to share his news and hear theirs.

Most weeks they held a Monday morning conference to summarise the previous week, discuss their ongoing projects and set the targets and divvy up the tasks for the coming week.

"I've got nothing to say," Zelah said, "so you two might as well fill me in on what's been going on." She sat back and folded her arms.

Maggie was tempted to give her a short, sharp response, but held it in. She wasn't sure if this was a deep worry on Zelah's part, or a tantrum. Whichever, she wasn't going to rise to it and got on with the updates. What she wasn't going to do was bring Zelah up to speed. She could read the notes.

"Do you want ten minutes to read last week's notes?" Maggie asked.

"No, just crack on."

"OK." She turned to Nick. "From what you've said in your texts over the weekend, I am thinking we're now agreed our main suspect for William McRoberts' murder was Christopher Camberwell?"

"Agreed," he replied. "I have the Rosen information and I had a call from John in Liverpool last night. His and Jacka's visit to Helen and Trys on Saturday has turned up enough to change suspicion into fact. Plus, of course, the information from Sonia Suri."

Zelah shuffled in her seat but didn't speak.

"Shall I go first with the Camberwell info?" Maggie asked him, not bothering to look at Zelah.

"Yes, a quick summary would be useful," he replied, staring back at her.

"Oh alright, enough. I'm out of touch with what's been happening. Give me ten minutes to read through the notes and find out who the hell these people are."

Keeping a straight face, Maggie said to Nick, "Coffee?" He nodded and they left the room.

When they returned with a mug each, and one for Zelah, she took it, slurped a quick sip and said, "Pax. For what it's worth, I'm sorry. OK?"

"Yes, OK," Nick replied. "Can we get on now? There's a lot to get through."

"So," Maggie began. "Christopher Camberwell was not engaged to a woman called Lavinia Duggan. Nor did he have a niece called Miranda Elise Camberwell, or at least he did but she was four years old at the time of the party at Fallough Hill. There was no-one born in the UK, or worldwide as I now know, who was christened Lavinia Duggan in the likely age range of his companion. She was most likely a fraud, unless she was married. Nick, did you get to check it out?"

"Did my best, but difficult not knowing what her maiden name might have been. But I couldn't find a marriage for a Lavinia to a man called Duggan. I tried the

263

death of a Duggan in the years prior to the Fallough Hill party, but there were too many to pick anyone out."

"What if her first name wasn't Lavinia?" Zelah interrupted.

"If she were equal to him in class and social status, she would have been in the society pages of at least one paper. There is no mention of any woman called Duggan of her approximate age over a period of fifteen years, let alone engaged to the Honourable Christopher Camberwell. This is now verified fact."

"Almost," Zelah replied. "I can agree we accept it with ninety-nine per cent certainty. Is that it?"

"From me, yes," Maggie said.

"But not from me," Nick replied. "I have a lot to share. As you know," he nodded at Maggie, "Stella and I went to visit Oliver Rosen on Saturday. Maggie didn't think I should involve him yet," he explained to Zelah, "but since we removed Wakelin as a suspect, there was a fifty per cent chance it was Rosen and at the time we weren't sure Camberwell had the brains to pull it off, so that left Nathan Rosen as the more likely suspect. I thought Oliver Rosen should know."

"I agree," Zelah said. "How did it go?"

"Better than I anticipated. He was interested enough to invite us to meet in person with him. He has a file of memoirs written by Nathan Rosen. He has plans at some point to write up and publish and I suspect he sees this situation as a potential catalyst for action, riding on the back of whatever comes out publicly from us. He knew should expect Nathan Rosen might have been the villain of the piece, but his legal training made him think not. And his level of the perception of human behaviour, as a barrister, also made him sure Nathan was innocent, therefore the guilty party must have been Camberwell.

264

However, he took me through the story point by point, person by person." He paused, smiled and rubbed his chin. "I've never been cross-examined. It's like having the inside of your dissected. What it did allow me to see, however, was Camberwell was the more likely suspect. Now, let me show you my notes on the memoirs. He wouldn't let me have a copy. He trusts us, but not that much. After looking at it, I'm certain it's a genuine document, handwritten by Nathan Rosen. Oliver had copies of other documents and signatures by Nathan. Oliver is thorough and anticipative. My notes are a precis of Nathan Rosen's memories about the party at Fallough Hill."

As he was speaking he handed them each a two-page summary of typed notes. They spent a few minutes reading then began to question Nick.

"OK, so he was a successful businessman, but why does it make him innocent of the kidnapping, or at least a part in it?" Maggie began.

"Why doesn't he mention Camberwell, at all? He was with him for at least two days."

"Which was the first thing occurring to me, Zelah."

For the next twenty minutes they asked questions, Nick answering some, jointly finding an answer for others.

"Rosen was there for social gain, that much becomes clear," Zelah said. "The cost of which was his investment advice to Sir Richard, which seems to have paid off."

"Lady Virginia tolerated him," Maggie added. "Thinking back on what she wrote, although she didn't mention it right out, reading between the lines, she knew Nathan Rosen was there for social advantage. And we can remove the daughter's friend as a potential for Elsie."

"All of which brings us back to Christopher Camberwell," Zelah said. "What next?"

"Well, I have more," Nick said.

"Aren't you the gold star boy today," Zelah remarked.

"Double gold star," he said. "As you know – well, Maggie and I knew – John and Jacka went to have lunch with Helen and Trys on Saturday, so Helen could tell them what she found. There's another diary entry. And," here he paused, building up to what was to be a momentous announcement, "a set of photographs."

Maggie sat up in her chair. "Are they in them?"

"Yes, they are," he replied. "There's a family photo and some guest photos. John scanned the information last night. Here it is. Let's start with the additional diary entry." He handed them another set of papers, this time including the diary extracts.

"Virginia's writing had deteriorated by the time this was written in 1903. She was in her eighties and I am speculating here, but maybe she was going senile. You'll see from the way it's written. There was more but it wasn't relevant. I've transcribed the three significant paragraphs."

"Well, this is going to be interesting," Zelah said, and began to read:

" *13ᵗʰ December 1903*

" *A man came to the house today, Mr Mc...*
something, I cannot remember his name now, asking
about one of our Christmas gatherings, a long time ago. I
could not recall it in detail. His story interested me. He
said his father was a detective looking for a missing girl
who was supposedly at this house. Outlandish idea! He
claimed his father did not return to his own home after
this visit. I called for Evans, who was a junior footman at

266

the time. He also did not remember any such visit. I spoke to Richard. He brushed me off, as he does these days. My memory is poor. However, I do recall those last-minute guests. There was a girl, a beautiful girl, but vacant. I shall ask Archie when he arrives this weekend. He said something at the time, which I do recall. Something about London, or not London.

"*17th December 1903*

"*I asked Archie what he remembers about the party and that girl, when he was seventeen. He recollected she was a beautiful girl, with white hair and strong blue eyes and, as he said, the face of an angel, but had no conversation. He heard few words from her and thought she must have been raised in foreign parts, as he couldn't understand what she said when she did utter the few words. I too heard that conversation, I recall. Richard discourages me from pursuing the matter. I explained to him the man would be back in a few days. He said it would be a wasted journey for no reason. I asked Archie about London, that I recalled something he said. He believes it would have been his attempt at a conversation with the girl asking about where she lived in London. He did not think the girl was indeed ever in the city, which might explain her strange foreign accent.*

"*26th December*

"*Dear Archie stayed with us for the organisation of Evans' funeral. He knew Evans all his life and was most sad at his passing. I am much surprised at the nature of it. I thought Evans did not consume alcohol. So strange he should have fallen at the public house in Bangor. His sister will benefit from his passing. He must have been a thrifty man, to have bought a substantial house and have been able to save a respectable sum. Mrs Handy has told me he was not happy in his last weeks. She found him raising his voice in an unpleasant way on the telephone to some person, on two occasions before he asked for a few days' leave to sort out a personal matter. I asked her what was the subject of his anger. She did not know. He was a close man who did not share his personal life with any of the servants, it seems. She did hear him say something about some digging with which he had assisted, which she could not understand. Nor I. The man from Liverpool did not return. Just as well, as we had nothing to relate further to him. I have agreed with Richard the subject is now closed."*

Maggie drew a deep breath. "For me this is just more confirmation the villain was Camberwell and the girl Lady Virginia was describing was Elsie. Of course she wouldn't have known anything about London."

"Although I'm surprised the Wyn Davies boy didn't recognise a Liverpool accent when he heard one. 'Strange foreign accent' indeed." Zelah snorted.

"If he'd never been to Liverpool, and remember he was just seventeen or eighteen when he met Elsie, if she spoke just a few words, why would he have known it was a Scouse accent?" Nick asked.

Zelah nodded. "You say there are photographs?"

"Yes, here." He put them on the board to display. "I've done the best I can, given the degree of fading over the years. They haven't been well curated."

The first picture was of a family scene, with Sir Richard and Lady Virginia with their children, and what might have been the elderly aunt. The second was of younger adults with more children. The brothers and sister. The third was of Sir Richard and Lady Virginia with two pompous-looking men, one with his arm in a sling of some kind. The notable locals.

Which left Sir Richard and Lady Virginia with another group. Three men, three wives and three young girls.

"No difficulty picking out Elsie there," Maggie said. "She was exceptionally beautiful, even in this faded photo." The young girl gazed at the photographer with an expression of concentration so fierce she was frowning.

"This might have been the first time she had had her photograph taken," Nick said. "And look at the dress she was wearing. Camberwell and Duggan must have provided that."

"She must have been so excited," Zelah said. "She'd been promised a huge adventure, a job as a lady's maid, or something similar, in London. It makes me sick, knowing what they were going to do with her."

"Camberwell's easy to spot," Maggie said. "Apart from being the youngest of the men." The photo showed a good-looking young man with fair hair, large eyes and impressive – for Victorian times – long sideburns and moustache. "Does he appear amusedly arrogant, or is it bias in me, given what we believe he was?"

"No," Zelah replied. "It shows. He must have been laughing on the inside. For whatever reason he ended up at the party he had the confidence, as well as the arrogance, to believe he could pull it off."

"Wakelin is easy to spot, too," Nick said. "You can see how he's trying to puff himself up."

Wakelin was easy to pick out. He was a shortish man trying to stand as tall as possible and wearing what he must have believed was a superior expression.

"He looks a pompous ass," Zelah said, "but there's another dose of bias in there, for my part."

"And Nathan Rosen. Nothing to see there."

"I agree," Nick said. "Just a man posing for a photograph. No agenda. I sent a copy to Oliver last night. I hope you're both OK with that."

Maggie and Zelah nodded. "Anything more?" Zelah asked.

"That's it," Nick replied. "Now, where does this leave us and what do we want to do next?"

"I can start writing it up," Zelah said. "I haven't been much involved in this one, I know, but the notes are good and the research is sound."

"Hold on," Maggie interrupted. "Two things. One: we haven't dealt with the issue of Christopher Camberwell's descendants, which might include the man Oliver Rosen told you about, Nick, Sir Henry Camberwell. Two: I want to talk about a project that's been on my mind and this seems the perfect time."

Zelah sat back and folded her arms, a smile playing on her lips. "I'd like to hear about your project," she said. Maggie, knowing the expression, understood anything new not coming from Zelah held an initial element of threat for her friend, but this time she was prepared.

"Brick walls," she began. "I want us to take on the most difficult of 'brick wall' cases. Cases people have been working on for at least ten years and haven't cracked. I want to take them on and I want Maze to publicise this. I suggest we announce this and offer to do the first two cases for free, to show what we can do, but have a contract for us to use the publicity."

She had speeded up as she spoke and had to pause to take a breath. "What do you think?"

Nick nodded slowly.

"What if you can't crack them?" Zelah asked.

"Then we have to admit failure," Maggie said, at which Zelah scowled. "But we can make more progress than the client has made, or at least be able to offer a solid reason why these cases can't be solved."

"Maze doesn't fail," Zelah said. "It's our biggest selling point and why we attract so many clients."

"Yes, I know. But we've had a couple of failures, haven't we? There was my big mistake and the nurse child case?"

"We haven't failed," Zelah said firmly. "We haven't found the answer the client wanted, yet. And you did find the answer, just not one the client liked."

"John's was a 'brick wall' case, and look what we're achieving with it," Maggie answered. "Before you say it, we got help from Claire Lewis, but this is who we are. Look," she glared at both, "We can do this."

"It's tempting," Nick said. "Risky, of course, but why not? We can't have a business without risk and we have to innovate, change, you know."

Zelah squirmed in her chair. "I'll think about it, OK?"

"Which is all I'm asking for now," Maggie replied. "Right, moving swiftly on, next steps in this case. Sir Henry Camberwell. Is he definitely the descendant?"

"Not yet certain," Nick replied. "I'll get onto it next."

"Let me," Maggie said. "Zelah, will you get on with writing this up?"

"I will, but I have some other research to do first. Nothing to do with any case, just something for myself."

She turned away as she spoke and Maggie caught a whiff of furtiveness. Not like Zelah, but whatever. She just hoped it was nothing to do with the Quinn family and she wanted to get on. "What about you, Nick?"

"I have a few things to catch up on and I'm going to phone John and Jacka, to update them. The funeral, the re-interment, for William McRoberts is on Friday. Stella and I will attend." He paused, then added, "I'm waiting on information from Sonia Suri, although it will just be additional detail now we know it was Camberwell. We're also pretty sure this Lavinia Duggan, whoever she was, was an accomplice, and don't forget Lizzy McRoberts' letter suggests there was something going on at a high level regarding the abduction and removal of young poor girls from their families. I can ask Sonia to check this out. If you both agree, of course."

"Another thought," Maggie said. "Are we agreed the Doughty family should hear Elsie's story?"

"Of course," Zelah said.

Nick looked uncertain. "It's going to be shockingly painful for them," he said.

"This time, I'm with Zelah," Maggie replied. "It will be up to them what they do with the information. We can tell them about the prospect of reburial, if that's what they want. Now we know where Elsie's buried, we can ask them if she should be reburied in a family grave, if there is one. Nick, perhaps you could deal with the cemetery, find out which grave she's in and what number she is in the grave. It will be good to have the answers ready for them. The problem is, we can't tell them about Camberwell for now."

"I'll get started with the cemetery," he said, and took his mobile phone out of the room to make the call.

"Let's go, then," Zelah said. "We have a plan."

* * *

"I have some information," Maggie said an hour later.

Zelah had just come into the office with a plate of scones with jam and cream, and mugs of coffee. She put the tray on the table. "Sustenance," she said. Maggie and Nick moved from computer desks to the meeting table.

Maggie broke open a scone and started to add jam then cream.

"Wrong way round," Nick remarked.

"Today we are not going to get into an argument about jam or cream first," Zelah snapped. "I should have brought biscuits."

Maggie giggled and carried on. When she finished her first mouthful and taken a swig of coffee she started.

"Sir Henry Camberwell is the great great grandson of Christopher Camberwell. We've already found Camberwell and Lady Susan separated after two years of marriage and he kept their one child, Joseph. He raised him and sent him to the best schools. Joseph didn't have to join the armed forces for World War One, because he was thirty-five when it started."

"He could have volunteered," Nick said.

"He didn't," Maggie replied. "In fact, he's mentioned in notes about suppliers to the forces and not in a good way."

"Black marketeer?" Zelah asked.

"Not sure. But he was forced to return some cash to the Ministry of Defence. It's written in a way that doesn't sound criminal, but might have been because he was high society and protected."

"When did Christopher die?" Nick asked.

Maggie checked the family tree she had handwritten. "He died in... 1919, of Spanish flu. He was sixty-seven. He had a reasonably long life, unlike Elsie."

"Or any of the other girls he may have taken and sold on," Nick said.

"What's interesting," Maggie went on, "is each son had one son and each marriage didn't last. Christopher's son Joseph had just one son, called Theodore. He was born in 1912 and he died in 1944 in the D-Day landings, when he was thirty-two. He had one son, called Charles, who was brought up, not by his mother, but by his Grandfather Joseph. On the 1939 War register Joseph is living in Chelsea with Charles, who's three years old. Charles' record has been unredacted, so he must have died after the register was released. I checked and Charles died in 2015. He is, or was, Henry Camberwell's father. Henry himself is now fifty-five, single and has never married as far as I can tell, and he's living at the same address in Chelsea as his father and great grandfather were in 1939."

"Women don't seem to figure much in the family history," Nick remarked. "When did Henry Camberwell get his knighthood?"

"Two years ago. He was awarded it for being an 'entrepreneur'. Plus he was a friend and business associate of a high-level government minister."

"Don't be snarky. What does he do now?" Zelah asked.

"Oliver Rosen told me he's something to do with import and export, of antiques, I think. Old family business."

"I don't like the sound of this family," Zelah said. "Too much dodgy business, between Christopher and his son; that's all I have for now. Is there anything else for today? I'm tired and I want to go home."

"I spoke to the cemetery superintendent," Nick said. "He's going to check their records for me. I thought I'd wait until we find out about whether a reburial's possible before I speak to Elsie's family. I also sent some information to Sonia Suri, plus the photo, see what she makes of it."

"OK," Maggie replied. "I'm happy enough to stop for now."

"I'll just write up my notes, then I'll go, too," Nick added. As he turned back to his computer he stopped, peered forward at the screen. "There's a response from Sonia. That was quick. She's asking me to call her."

He punched in the number. The call was answered so fast Maggie thought it must barely have rung.

Nick nodded a few times, then his eyes widened. "What! Indeed? Are you sure?" A pause. Then, "Tell me as much as you can, Sonia. This could be the final proof we needed." He signalled to Maggie who threw him a pen. He scribbled for a few minutes then said, "Thank you, Sonia. When will you let me know? So soon? I'll be waiting to hear from you."

Maggie and Zelah waited and for a few maddening seconds Nick read through his notes before he looked up.

"I know why you couldn't find Lavinia Duggan anywhere. She didn't exist." He put the photograph back on the screen. "This woman is Mary Ellen Lavinia Duggan. She ran a high-class establishment for what were referred to as 'discerning gentlemen' in Liverpool. She kept girls as young as twelve and she was, apparently, utterly ruthless. She had the appearance of a respectable woman, though, and was known in the city as 'Lady Lavvy'. And there's more."

He sat back, his expression grim.

"What?" Zelah demanded. "What more?"

"Sonia is checking through some documents at the archives and in a private collection to which she has access. There was a scandal of immense proportions in Liverpool around 1880. It involved men in senior positions who were believed to be involved in a sex slave ring. It involved the enticing and selling of young girls to European brothels. Hushed up, of course. One of the men involved was the coroner Monaghan. Another was a head constable of one of the police divisions. They were allowed to resign. Another may, and Sonia emphasised the *may*, have been the Member of Parliament, Sir Joseph Camberwell, Baron Percyford."

Chapter 35

"Well, well, well," Zelah said, with a slow handclap. "It was in the family. I still don't understand why Christopher and Lavvy went to Fallough Hill, though."

"Here's some more guess work," Maggie replied. "If they convened at the trade dinner in Liverpool and Camberwell already had the girl when Sir Richard invited them to join him for the party, Christopher was forced to go along."

"Nope," Zelah said. "He could have left Elsie with Lavvy at the brothel."

"How about this," Nick said, sitting back with his hands behind his head. "Elsie's mother was already making a fuss about Elsie. If she had been left behind, Christopher would have been in a panic. Remember, William McRoberts was already investigating. He had the contacts amongst the prostitutes."

"But that would mean it wasn't a last-minute invitation," Maggie argued. "William left home on the Friday, arrived Saturday and was killed Saturday night."

"How are we so sure about that?" Zelah asked.

"From the dates of the letters. So, Camberwell and Lavvy – I can't call her Lavinia now I know who and what she was – arrived on the Friday with Elsie. At least Sir Richard wasn't involved."

"Which will come as a relief to Trys Wyn Davies," Nick said. "He's been concerned about Sir Richard's possible involvement."

"How do we know?" Zelah asked.

"The diary," Maggie replied. "Lady Virginia thought there was something 'off' about Lavvy. From what she wrote they both just accepted her as Camberwell's fiancée. Maybe it was Sir Joseph who invented the story about the fiancée and the niece and—"

Stop right there." Zelah put her palms up. "We can go on speculating for ever. There's no evidence. The fact is Elsie was bought from her mother by Christopher Camberwell with the involvement of other men, which may have included his father, and was in the process of taking her abroad, but got caught out by an invitation to a party at Fallough Hill. That's enough. We have sufficient proof of the basic story."

Maggie and Nick nodded. "And William found out about Camberwell and where he was going and followed him there," Nick added.

"Right, I am now leaving and I'll start writing this up at home tonight. Nick, if anything else of relevance should come from Sonia Suri, please let me know."

"Will do. I'm going to tell John and Trys the full story now."

"What about Henry Camberwell?" Maggie asked. "He has a right to know, too."

Zelah sat again. "How do you propose he's told?"

"Nick and I should contact him with the basic story. See if he'll meet us. It shouldn't be too hard to get hold of him. He has a business, so he must have an email address at least."

"I'm on it," Nick said. "Let's do this as soon as possible."

"This time I'm definitely leaving. Let me know how you get on. Damn, look at the frost. It's going to snow again tonight."

As Maggie closed the curtains against the fading light she saw Jack running along the path and heard him letting himself in. He stuck his head around the office door and Maggie gave him a quick update on their progress. "So, nothing for you to do for now."

"OK. Is Bob here?"

"No, he's back to work today, but he's expecting to be here in the next hour or so."

"Fine. Give me a shout when he gets back, please. I'm going to my room to work on an assignment."

"Anything I can help with?"

"No," he said and pulled back into the hall.

"Man stuff, I suspect," Nick muttered. "Ah, I've got him. His office has a telephone number."

He entered the number, waited a few moments, then shook his head and mouthed 'answerphone' at Maggie. She mouthed back 'leave a message'.

He gave her a thumbs up and began the message with Maze and their investigation, which had uncovered information about his ancestor, Christopher Camberwell. He didn't want to leave details on the phone, but would like to meet in person. Would that be convenient? He then gave and repeated his telephone number.

"If he doesn't reply I'll try again tomorrow," he began, but as he went to say something else his phone rang. He put his hand over the phone and whispered to Maggie, "It's him."

For the next five minutes Maggie listened to Nick's side of the conversation with Henry Camberwell, gaining the impression Camberwell as the call went on that the man was not hostile and would be keen to meet. This proved correct when Nick said, "Just a moment, I'll check with my colleague." He turned to Maggie and said, "He wants to meet tomorrow. He's going to be away on business for a couple of weeks from Wednesday. Can you make it tomorrow?"

She nodded. "What time?"

He asked the question and said, "That's fine, we'll be there. Please let me have the address of your office. Home? No that's OK with us, if you don't mind us coming there. My colleague is Maggie Gilbert and we'll see you tomorrow."

He put the phone down and turned to Maggie. "Tomorrow at eleven, at his family home in Chelsea."

At the other end, Sir Henry Camberwell retrieved the mobile he had thrown onto his designer settee and punched in another number.

"You fucking stupid bastard," he yelled as the call was answered. "You have properly screwed up."

Chapter 36

Bob returned home too late to speak to Jack, who had hovered in the living room until eleven before Maggie insisted he go to bed.

When he did arrive just before midnight Maggie was already asleep, but woke to tell him Jack was anxious to speak to him.

"I'll see him when he gets up. Take him to the bus," he muttered.

"It's OK, I'll do it. I'm going to London tomorrow with Nick. We've tracked Christopher Camberwell's descendant. He's asked us to see him tomorrow as he's going to be away on business after seeing us. We're on the 7.50 train." She yawned loudly. "You're late."

"Busy day," he said, falling into bed.

"Anything you want to talk about?"

"Tomorrow," he replied. "I went to Cardiff to see Malky Thomas' solicitor. Bit of a creep, but insistent the boy wanted to tell him something important. He thinks it was something to do with the accident and who was in the car."

"I thought you knew that already?"

"I already had the feeling there was another one, in the back seat."

She thought for a few seconds. "Any idea of who it might have been? Bob?" The sound of a gentle snore told her he had already fallen asleep. Well, whoever might have been in the car was nothing to do with her, thank God. She was asleep again within minutes.

* * *

The following morning, after she dropped Jack just in time to get his bus and told him Bob would speak to him later, Maggie headed to Newport station, found a parking spot and joined Nick on the platform. They had again elected to travel first-class on two single facing seats, to keep their conversation as private as possible.

Once the train left the station and they had been served breakfast, Nick asked, "Have you thought about what we're going to tell him?"

"Yes. We should confirm the story of William McRoberts' disappearance for how we became involved in the case, researching the story for his descendants, but I don't want to mention John or Jacka by name."

"OK, I agree with that," he replied, smiling at the passing waiter offering more tea and coffee and paused to pour Nick another steaming cup.

"We can go on to talk about the party at Fallough Hill and Christopher Camberwell being there. Plus the disappearance of Elsie Doughty, and our belief she was sold by her mother to a group of traffickers."

"He's bound to ask what this has to do with Christopher."

"Then we tell him we have the proof Christopher was involved; he took the girl from Liverpool, passed her off as his niece at the party, then took her to London where someone else would have taken her abroad."

"At which point he either faints or throws us out?" Nick said, glaring at her over his coffee mug.

"Or both," Maggie replied. "I can't see any point in prevaricating. We know what we know. We just have to tell him."

"And we have to tell him we're going to write about it, as a case that has taken a long time to resolve."

"Zelah has already started. I texted her last night to say not to put anything on the website yet, not until we've finished this meeting today."

"Good idea," Nick replied. "Henry Camberwell may be so outraged, after he has fainted, before he throws us out, he'll threaten to sue us for libel."

"Could be a strong possibility," Maggie conceded. "Is our proof sufficient for that scenario?"

Nick smiled. "I was joking. Christopher Camberwell will be the victim and he can't sue because he's dead. However," his smile faded, "if Henry Camberwell thinks we might damage his reputation by association, he could sue us for something. If it's bad we may need legal advice."

For the remainder of the journey they tossed ideas back and forth about how they might respond, depending on Henry Camberwell's initial reaction. The train arrived in Paddington station at ten fifteen. They decided to travel to Sir Henry's house by taxi from the main station, given it was impossible to anticipate the state of London traffic. The ride should have taken no more than ten minutes. If they were too early, they could find a nearby café on the King's Road to wait it out.

The anticipation of heavy traffic was correct and, by the time they queued for a taxi, they reached the house a few minutes before eleven.

The ride took them through the west of the city. The address was Cheyne Walk, which Maggie hadn't bothered to look up before they left home, so she was surprised, getting out of the taxi, to find they were overlooking the Thames. The house itself was a slim, white four-storey building, with a black front door and three sets of windows on the upper floors leading to a loft conversion. It was on the end of a road leading back towards the Kings Road.

"What must this be worth?" she murmured to Nick as they walked up the steps to the front door.

"Millions and millions and millions..." He stopped as the front door opened before they had chance to knock.

Standing in the doorway, smiling a welcome was a tall man, perhaps a little under six feet, in his fifties, Maggie guessed, with a beautifully coiffured head of jet-black hair, brown eyes, a nose pure Roman patrician and synchronised lips. An exceptionally handsome man. He had no middle-age paunch and was dressed casually in slacks and a shirt and loafers, which she guessed would have cost more than her entire wardrobe.

He held out a manicured hand to greet them and ushered them in. They followed him through a long hallway past a wide staircase to the right bordered by intricate ironwork which turned ninety degrees and out of sight. Straight ahead he opened a door into a small lounge leading onto a surprisingly large garden.

Maggie noticed antiques in the hallway and a passing glimpse through open doors gave a tantalising peek at high-ceiling rooms.

"Thank you for seeing us at such short notice, Sir Henry," she said as they sank into a deep settee. Henry Camberwell took a chair next to an open fire on which a few logs were burning. "What a beautiful house."

He nodded in acknowledgement. "It was built around 1750 and in my family for over two hundred years."

"It has wonderful character," she added.

Again, he smiled. "Thank you. Now, I am quite intrigued by your story. Can you tell me about this girl and my family involvement? I have thoroughly checked your credentials." He sat back, crossed his legs and put

284

his hands on the arms of the chair. Maggie noticed the fingers on his right hand were tapping a slow rhythm.

She ran through their agreed story, watching his expressions throughout. He nodded, smiled, frowned occasionally but didn't interrupt. At the end, he moved forward and jabbed a poker at the logs on the fire, causing sparks to fly out.

"This is quite horrendous, and upsetting of course," he said, putting the poker down and sitting back in the chair. "But I am pleased you decided to share it with me."

Maggie suddenly realised Nick had not spoken yet and turned to him. His expression was intense, staring at Sir Henry who seemed oblivious.

"What happens next?" Henry said.

"We don't want to cause embarrassment or upset, of course," Maggie replied. "We haven't yet decided on how we'll set the story, but we would be happy to let you see it before it's published."

"Thank you, Mrs Gilbert. I suspect there's no way of keeping my ancestor's name out of it. Perhaps, change the names of all involved?"

Nick sat forward before Maggie could reply. "You have a business, Sir Henry?"

"Yes, Mr Howell, I import goods of special quality, for private clients. And sometimes I export, too. Of course, you will not use my name in your story."

"Of course not, Sir Henry," Maggie said. "The story will be about the detective who disappeared."

"But the trafficking will feature and may be of interest to the press," Nick said. "It's unavoidable."

"Then I would be grateful if you could do your best to keep my ancestor's name out of it. Now, if that's all, I have another appointment." He stood and Maggie and Nick followed.

He showed them to the door, bade a polite farewell and closed it softly behind them.

Before Maggie could say anything Nick took her arm, marched her onto the Chelsea Embankment and headed towards Chelsea Bridge. Maggie had to trot to keep up with him and her breathing became laboured, a white mist coming from her mouth as exhaled breath collided with cold air. They passed the Chelsea Physic garden and were at the bridge when she tugged on his arm to slow him down.

"Where are we going, Nick, and why are we running?"

"Sorry." He slowed down, stopped and bent over, letting go of her arm to put his hands on his knees, taking deep shuddering breaths.

"You're scaring me, Nick. What's the matter?"

"We had to get as far away from him as possible. His was the darkest energy I've seen for a long time. It's not just about him and his ancestor or his business. It's about us, too."

He stood up straight again and led her away from the river along Chelsea Bridge Road.

"Where are we going?"

"Sloane Square. There's a tube station can get us back to Paddington." He stopped and turned a fierce gaze on her. "I don't understand what, but there is a connection between us and that man. And not a good one. He's going to damage us."

"What, us personally, or Maze?"

"Both," he replied and started to walk again.

Chapter 37

They had been with Henry Camberwell for less than an hour and were back at Paddington station ahead of their scheduled train. Maggie wanted to wait, find something to eat to give themselves a break, but Nick insisted they get an earlier train and hope they could find similar private seating. She reluctantly agreed and the train wasn't crowded which allowed them to review what they had learned without being overheard.

"I talked too much," Maggie said. "Did I give him too much information?"

"Why would you say so? We went there in good faith. We were prepared. He gave us nothing in return. He was watching us, observing like a lion watching a gazelle."

"You saw that?"

"Yes. For whatever reason, we are a serious threat to Sir Henry Camberwell."

"A bit over the top, Nick. Look at where he lives. Maybe he just values his reputation, his personal reputation as well as his business's good name. Maybe he thinks we're going to damage him, so he wants to put us down first. Not nice, but understandable.

"I get that," he replied. "But no, there was more to it. My impression was he knew more about us than he was letting on. He was on high alert from the moment we arrived. He was giving off exceptionally high energy. He must have been hovering at the door when we arrived. We didn't have to ring or knock."

"OK, he was anxious. So what?"

"Has there ever been any connection on any of our cases that might have previously involved him?"

Maggie shook her head. "No. I did check out the names on our database as we came across them. We've never dealt with any of them before in any capacity."

"There's something," Nick said, drumming his fingers on the table.

For the remainder of the journey they went back over the conversation with Henry Camberwell. Nothing alerted Maggie to any indication of an undeclared agenda, but Nick was adamant.

They reached Newport late-afternoon and each went their separate way, Maggie to write up the interview with as much detail as she could remember. Nick was going to do some further in-depth research into Henry Camberwell's business dealings, where he thought there might be a clue.

Around seven Nick called to say he had found nothing about whatever Henry Camberwell imported or exported. It was antiques and rare antiquities, the latter likely to involve some illegality, but he couldn't be sure.

"There's something else here, Maggie. It's to do with the dark web, but I can't work it out."

"What does it tell us? I know nothing about the dark web except what I see on the occasional TV documentary talking about paedophilia, how to get illegal drugs, conspiracy theories, etcetera and so on. Should we try to find out?"

"Absolutely not," he said. "It's mostly illegal and we can't get caught up in it for no reason other than a vague suspicion."

"Look, Bob's just come home. I'll speak to him, see what he thinks, OK?"

"I hope he can help us here. My feeling is, it's essential."

* * *

"Nick's off on a mission," she remarked later to Bob, when she told him about their visit to London. "He thinks Sir Henry Camberwell may be doing something illegal, on the dark web. Does it sound right? It sounds odd to me."

Jack said, "It's how to get illegal drugs, the worst stuff."

"If he's trading on the dark web, then keep away from it," Bob added. "I can put out some feelers, see if I get any information?"

"Yes, please. I have no idea what this is about and it's come as quite a shock. Help needed, I think."

"I'll make a couple of calls tomorrow."

"Thanks. Are you getting anywhere with your information about Malky Thomas and the 'third man'?"

He grinned. "No. I'm going to speak to the front-seat passenger tomorrow, see if he wants to add anything to his story. What are your plans? Where do you go from here?"

"Not sure. I need to fill Zelah in about Henry Camberwell and discuss how she writes this up. Nick's going to Liverpool on Friday, to the re-interment of William McRoberts. He can update John's family, and Trys and Helen. There's not much more for me to do." She paused. "Actually, I might start looking at the information we got from Claire Lewis, the Spanish phrase. And find out more about Charlie, whoever he was."

"Good idea," he replied. "I'd like to hear what's been happening about the skeleton."

Jack's ears pricked up at the mention of a skeleton and Maggie gave him what little they knew of the story, including the information about the Welsh miners who went out to Catalonia to fight against Franco's fascists.

"I've got some books you can read, if you're interested," she said.

"Got a lot of work to do," he replied, taking his plate and cutlery to the dishwasher. "Maybe over half term?"

"That's quite soon, isn't it?" Maggie asked.

"Week after next," he replied. "Bob, you got time for a chat?"

"Of course," Bob said, standing up, giving Maggie a 'don't ask questions' scowl and a slight shake of his head. "I'll come with you."

Left alone, Maggie cleared up in the kitchen, then went to sit on her computer.

She had no idea what the dark web was, other than something to be avoided by respectable people. She opened the computer and typed in the search engine 'what is the dark web'.

After less than ten minutes of increasing disgust and horror she shut down the information sites. If Henry Camberwell's business was carried out in such repulsive darkness, Nick was right, this was someone from whom they should keep away. However, there was one immediate positive. If it proved to be correct, she felt no concern about what they could write publicly about Christopher Camberwell. If it caused Henry problems, well tough; but she would wait for Bob's information.

After half an hour Bob had not come back downstairs, and having no desire to think further about the case, instead wanting distraction, she went into the lounge and put on the television, selected a box set and started to watch.

When Bob eventually came downstairs he went to get a beer and sat in front of the TV. Maggie, who was intermittently dozing, sat up.

"What was that about? Is he OK?"

"He's fine. He wanted a man-to-man talk."

"Do I need to be concerned?"

"I said, he's fine." He turned away from the TV. "You can leave this one to me, OK?"

She nodded and yawned. "I might go to bed. It's early, but I've had a long day."

He turned back to the TV and picked up his beer. "I won't be long."

She understood something was on his mind, but didn't probe. If he needed to, he'd tell her, she hoped, especially if it concerned her son.

* * *

When Maggie woke the next morning she realised she had fallen asleep at once and had no idea what time Bob eventually slept, but suspected it was late. In the kitchen she pottered around, clearing the dishwasher and found three empty beer cans next to the sink, which she put in the recycling bin. Definitely something on his mind. Whatever it was, he didn't share any of it, leaving at the same time as Jack.

With a temporary lull in the case, Maggie decided to pitch into her idea of 'brick wall' cases and sketch out a first run at what the deal might look like. She had been thinking about it on and off for a few days and had some basic ideas since she had pitched it to Zelah and Nick. She needed a case to continue the discussion with Nick and Zelah, something to convince Zelah this wasn't just a haphazard idea with no substance.

An hour later she had the makings of a business plan, rough but a good start.

What to do next? Nick and Zelah both texted to say they would be there at about eleven, which gave her an hour. She decided to re-examine the Spanish case, to see what further information she could find about 'Charlie'.

An hour later she had found nothing about the skeleton on the internet but discovered dozens of stories about the ongoing work to unearth the many mass graves where opponents of Franco were unceremoniously shot and, in some cases, buried in ditches at the side of a road.

The arrival of Nick and Zelah shortly before eleven brought her back to the current case. Nick pulled papers out of his case and spent a few minutes arranging them on the table, shuffling in his chair and scraping the legs on the floor, unaware of the ear-splitting squeak of each movement. Maggie made a mental note to get a rug.

Pressing her lips together, Zelah crossed her arms and scowled, waiting for him to stop. He didn't notice. Spots of red began to appear on her cheeks.

"Nick," Maggie called when she could no longer bear the screech of the chair legs. "Are you ready?"

His head shot up. "What? Yes, sorry. Just getting my thoughts in order. How shall we approach this?"

Zelah sat forward and opened her mouth. Recognising the signs of an oncoming sarcastic bullet, Maggie said, "How about we go over what we learned yesterday? What you and I discussed on the train and I wrote up which I presume, Zelah, you've read." She glanced over and Zelah gave a nod. "Is there anything else you've thought about overnight?"

"Yes," he replied. "Two main things I didn't think about as I was concentrating on Christopher Camberwell. I'll start there."

"I don't understand," Zelah said.

"You will. My thoughts have been about Henry Camberwell. First – he didn't ask nearly enough questions about Christopher and what he might have been doing with the girl. Maggie gave him the rundown on what we believe happened in Liverpool and the party, and..." he paused here and cleared his throat, "that we believe Elsie was taken 'abroad'." He emphasised the word. "He didn't ask how we knew, or anything about her eventual fate. Then I nearly missed the big clue." He smiled and gave Maggie a quizzical look.

She frowned in concentration for several seconds, before the significance hit her. She slapped her palm to her head. "I did say abroad, like we agreed. But when he mentioned it later he said 'Brussels'. How did he know?"

"My point, exactly. What does it tell us? Either he knows about the export of girls in Victorian times and the associated stories or he could have made an accurate, educated guess. But many of the girls went to Paris. And the report from the Lock Hospital said, 'European establishment'. The next element was his reaction to the false fiancée. I was watching him when you mentioned Madame Lavvy, when you called her Lavinia Duggan. He betrayed himself with the slightest hint of a smirk and an upward flick of an eyebrow. He knew the name."

"I didn't see that," Maggie conceded.

"Then," Nick went on, "I thought about what happened when we arrived and were shown into his

293

comfortable lounge with the crackling fire and the relaxed atmosphere. You and Henry began to make some small talk and he asked about Maze, about what we do, etcetera. Do you remember?"

She nodded, puzzled. "There was nothing in that, was there?"

"Actually, there was. The questions were designed to sound innocuous, but they weren't. Again, he gave himself away, just once. You talked about yourself, Zelah, me and your son, who has recently shown an interest and has been working with us."

"Yes, I remember. He said how lucky it was for a child to have a parent who supports their ambition and their interests, these days. We talked a bit about the pressure of exams. He said he was lucky, too, in that respect; he had a supportive parent who taught him the family business; he and Jack had it in common. What's the problem there?"

"Who told him your son is called Jack?"

Maggie sat for several seconds, going over her memory of the conversation, her face screwed up in concentration of recalling the detail. The expression changed to dawning understanding. "I never spoke Jack's name."

"Exactly."

"Wait, though, Nick. He said he checked us out. Could he have found Jack's name somewhere on the website?"

"No," Zelah intervened. "I've never mentioned he does any work for us. Nor have I spoken to a client about him. I've kept both Jack and Alice well away from Maze."

Maggie took in a deep breath. "What is going on here?"

"There's a connection," Nick replied. "I'm not clear yet what it is, but we have to figure it out. I sense - as strongly as I have ever sensed - it's important. Crucial even."

"Is there somewhere we can learn more about this man?" Zelah asked. "What does he look like? You've had the benefit of being in his company, but can I get a look at him, see if it tells me anything?"

"He's a private person," Nick replied. "He doesn't keep social company; you won't see him in frilly magazines. But, I did find one picture of him, last night. It's a bit blurry, but it's recognisable. Here it is."

The picture, when blown up on the screen, was blurred, but Maggie was able to recognise him. "He's trying to keep his face away from the camera, isn't he."

"Does it help, Zelah?" Nick said.

His question was met by silence, as Zelah stared at the photograph. They waited in increasing concern as she continued to stare. Nick looked at Maggie, who shrugged her shoulders.

"I recognise him. I've seen him somewhere, recently. I need to think." Zelah stood and walked out of the office. Maggie could hear her pacing around the kitchen and garden room. She looked at Nick again. This time he shrugged.

Zelah came back in, her face determination and concern. She sat down.

"He was there, I saw him," she said. "Henry Camberwell was at Rufus Quinn's funeral, and afterwards in the churchyard he spent a few minutes in deep private conversation with Kennet Quinn and Helen Redland."

Chapter 38

After a few seconds of stunned silence Nick said, "This changes everything."

Maggie shook her head. "How can this be happening? I mean... I'm not sure what I mean."

They sat in silence, each staring at a different part of the room. Nick recovered first. "It seems, for the present, our fate remains tied to the Quinn family. Whatever we do, become involved in, it leads back to them. To me, it seems there is some greater force at play."

He spoke in a quiet, considered voice. Maggie nodded.

"Well, how the fuck are we going to untie ourselves from them?" Zelah barked, making them both jump. "You can talk about the universe's plan, if you want to, and wait to see how it plays out. I can't wait. I've had enough of them."

"What do you propose to do, Zelah?" Nick asked, not raising his voice. "This began with the information passed on to us by Claire Lewis. This was always going to happen. I'm not saying," he held up his hand, "we should sit back and do nothing. But I do think we need to be smart, not rush at them like a bull at a red cape. The bull always comes off worse."

"We need more information," Maggie said. "Bob said he would put out some feelers, see if there's any interest in Henry Camberwell. Can we at least agree to wait for his information to come back?"

Zelah's nostrils were flaring. She was about to retort when Maggie's phone pinged. "It's a text from Bob," she said, scanning it. "OK, I'm going to read it to you. It says

'*Info on Henry Camberwell. Dangerous man. You must not have any further interaction with him. Your visit already known. On my way back. Do nothing until I get there*'."

They waited, not speaking, drinking coffee, looking half-heartedly at computer screens, jumping at each small noise, the picture of Henry Camberwell looming down from the white board.

It took Bob fifteen minutes to get back and he arrived accompanied by a stranger in a dark overcoat and a smart scarf, carrying a briefcase, to whom he introduced them one by one. The stranger nodded, unwrapping his scarf and unbuttoning his coat to reveal a dark, exquisitely tailored suit.

"My name is Will Sharpe. I work in London with a special unit associated with the vice squad." He took out photographs from the briefcase and put them on the table. They were of Maggie and Nick, entering and leaving Henry Camberwell's house. Maggie looked away, blanching.

"What is his true business?" Nick asked. "I guess antiques and rare artefacts are a cover?"

"Yes," Will Sharpe said. "His real business is the import of young women and girls into the UK. As well as servicing brothels it includes the use of imported children for pornographic purposes."

Maggie's knees buckled. Bob ran to support her into a chair. Tears ran down her cheeks. "I was in his house. I chatted with him. I discussed my son."

Zelah's flat palm crashing onto the table turned their attention to her. "What do we do about this?" she shouted.

"You? You do nothing," Sharpe replied. He glanced at Bob, who frowned. "We have good information about a group of girls arriving imminently in this area. I need you to keep out of it."

"But..." Zelah began.

Sharpe turned a fierce gaze on her. "If I see the slightest attempt by any of you to interfere, I will not hesitate to lock you up. Do you understand?"

No-one answered.

"Good. I have to go now."

"Just a minute," Nick said, walking to block the doorway. "Does this involve Kennet Quinn? Because, if it does, you'll have to kill me to keep me away from it. My son is working for him."

"I know," Sharpe replied. "It changes nothing. Now, move out of my way, please, Mr Howell."

Nick stood his ground, until Maggie stood and, walking around to him, took him by the elbow. "Let him go, Nick," she whispered. "Nothing to be gained here." She turned to Bob. "Are you going or staying?"

"Staying," he said. Then, in a low voice, "Let him pass, Nick. He knows what he's doing. It will turn out OK, please listen and trust me on this."

Nick's taut arm muscles relaxed and he unclenched his fists. A glistening appeared in one eye. "If anything bad happens to him..." He looked away and moved from the door frame. Sharpe left the room and closed the front door behind him.

"Sit down, please," Bob said to Maggie, Nick and Zelah. "I can give you some information, not a lot, but enough for you to understand why you have to keep away from this."

* * *

Bob's information didn't give them much more than Will Sharpe had already told them, but he did confirm something was going to happen imminently.

"This 'consignment' is a first for Henry Camberwell in Wales," he said. "You've worked out the 'middleman' is Kennet Quinn. He's making the arrangements for receipt before they get moved on to different locations."

"Are there young children involved?" Maggie asked.

"Yes, which is why we have to make sure nothing goes wrong. We need to catch Camberwell as well as Kennet."

"Camberwell must be a clever operator, if he's been at this for some time," Zelah said. "But I am surprised he gets his hands this dirty? Surely that's why he uses someone like Kennet."

"Usually, yes, but this is a first for him. His patch is the North and the Midlands, but not Wales. Will's team are hoping he'll take a personal interest."

"How do you know he isn't having us watched? That he doesn't find out Will Sharpe was here?"

"He isn't having you watched. For the past twenty-four hours, we are. Rather, Will has organised it. They're checking no-one else is watching you." He turned to Nick. "Please don't worry about Max. He'll be OK. He's not involved in this."

Nick's eyes widened. "Are you sure?"

"Yes," Bob replied. "Now I have to get back. Maggie, I need a lift back to the station. Are you OK to drive?"

"Of course. I'll get my coat."

Outside an icy wind slapped at them and for an instant she shuddered. "This isn't how I expected the day to go," she said as they got into her car. "It's going to be hard to do nothing. Can you tell us anything else?"

He shook his head. "I'm not even sure they'd tell me. They play it close."

"What a horrible job," she said. "Yet that man didn't seem traumatised by what he was talking about."

"They focus on their victories. Wouldn't do to think too much about what they see."

Maggie shook her head. "I have an idea for the next day or so. It's the funeral, or rather the re-interment in Liverpool on Friday. For us, this marks the end of the case in relation to William McRoberts. Maybe we can all go, and I'll take Jack, too."

"Good idea, but no need to take Jack. I can stay with him. I have a day off Friday. I can stay close to him for the next few days."

"Are you sure he's OK, about this girl?"

"Quite sure. Here we are. Why don't you go back and organise the trip to Liverpool? You can go tomorrow evening, stay in a hotel." He jumped out of the car, waved briefly and was gone.

* * *

When Maggie, on her return, proposed the idea of the Liverpool trip both Nick and Zelah were all for it. They, too, felt the need to get away.

"It'll be an opportunity to remove ourselves from the scene, gain some perspective on what's happened," Nick said. "We could talk about it tomorrow evening. We also must update John and Jacka on what's developed."

"And Trys and Helen," Maggie added. "They have the right to know, too."

"How about I organise a lunch on Friday, after the ceremony," Zelah suggested. "Will there be any other relatives present?"

"I'll check with John," Nick said. "I'll call him now."

As Nick made the call in the background, Zelah said to Maggie, "What time is Bob back, do you know?"

"No idea, at the moment, Zelah. Why?"

"I have something I want to discuss with him."

"I can text him to see if he has any idea."

Zelah nodded and Maggie typed in a quick text. The response came back in seconds.

"He says '*is it urgent?*'"

"Yes, it is," Zelah replied. Maggie typed again and another quick response followed.

"He says '*OK, it had better be. On my way back now. Five minutes*'. Is this another secret, Zelah?"

Zelah shook her head. "No, no more secrets. I want you and Nick to hear what I've found."

"Fair enough. I just hope you weren't crossing your fingers behind your back when you said it. Ah, Nick's finished his call."

"He says two of his brothers are coming, plus one of Jacka's sisters. He's organised what he called 'a bit of a do' afterwards, at the old house, just tea and sandwiches. He and Jacka are on for lunch, but he says not to invite the others. He and Jacka want to hear the full story, but he hasn't said much to the rest of the family and he doesn't want them to know. He wants to wait until we decide together on how to put the story out."

"Good man," Zelah said. "What about the two from Fallough Hill?"

"He's calling Trys now, make sure he and Helen can stay for lunch. He'll text me. So, eight for lunch."

"I'll book a table at the hotel," Zelah said. "I'll ask for a private table. If we're going to give them the full rundown we want to be sure no-one else is listening."

The text arrived a few minutes later. "Yes, they're both free for lunch, so a table for eight."

"I'll go call the hotel, book the rooms and the lunch table. The eight includes Stella. I'm presuming she wants to see this through, too?"

He nodded. "Of course. She wants to see this through to the end."

Bob arrived as Zelah finished her call. "All booked. We're going to Liverpool, Bob, as per your suggestion."

"Good. You have something I need to hear, Zelah?"

"We should sit," she said. Then to Bob, "You're going to need to."

"Then perhaps I'll stand."

"No, please sit. It's disturbing news, for you."

Twisting his mouth into a sour expression and muttering a few words under his breath, Bob sat down.

"This is not about Gerry Quinn or any of the cases you are investigating," she said. "It's about someone else I've been researching. You knew I was going to look."

He gave a slow single nod, his eyes narrowing.

"Her name is not Sherry Martin. Well, it is but it's part of her name. Her real name is Shirley Louise Redland Martin. She's Helen and Timothy Redland's cousin. A first cousin once removed, but a close family member."

Chapter 39

"What does it mean?" Bob said. "How, exactly, is she related to them."

"They're different generations, but not too far apart in age. Sherry is in her thirties, right?"

Bob nodded.

"Timothy and Helen are, or in his case was, in their mid-twenties. Sherry's mother was Timothy and Helen's grandmother's sister, their great aunt. This great aunt was much younger than her Redland brother, hence the additional generation, but not a great separation in age. Sherry is also the youngest of her own siblings, so the difference in ages is about seven or eight years." She paused. "My information is Helen and Sherry were close. They went to the same schools, and lived close to each other."

Bob reddened as Zelah spoke and his breathing was audible. He stood up. "Where did you get this information? How do I know it's accurate?"

"The family tree was easy enough to trace," she replied, holding steady in front of his blazing gaze, handing him a document. "Here's a copy, with the names and dates. You'll be able to verify with birth certificates. It was the way the surnames were handled that took some time to discover," she went on, speaking now to Nick and Maggie. "The terrible twins took their family name from their mother, not their father. Their given name at birth was Smith, but they changed it to Redland after their father abandoned the family when they were babies. So, their mother and their maternal grandfather were Redland, as was their great grandfather. Now, here's the interesting bit. The great grandfather,

Sherry's grandfather, committed murder and was gaoled for thirty years."

"It doesn't explain how you found out about their current circumstances," Bob said, pulling at his ear, shaking his head. "That's not genealogical information."

"No," Zelah conceded. "It's private investigator information. I hired somebody after I'd found the connection. I have the report for you."

She held out another document and he grabbed it from her, scanning the pages, a sheen of sweat appearing on his forehead.

"Oh God. Oh... fucking hell. I have to go." He paused and looked at Zelah with blazing eyes. "You'd better be right about this." He spun around, grabbing his coat and left them.

Maggie tried to think of something to say, but nothing came. Nick had put his elbows on the table, hands over his ears.

Zelah was sitting straight in her chair, unmoving. "I'm sorry," she said in a quiet voice. "But he had to know."

"Of course he did," Maggie said, wiping her eyes with her sleeve. "You did the right thing. It's still terrible, though. The evil bitch. No wonder she didn't want to be friendly with us." She sensed a pulse increasing in her neck. "Just a minute." She frowned. "She hasn't been around for a couple of days. Does she know about the connection between Henry Camberwell and Kennet Quinn? Could she be trying to sabotage the raid, or whatever they're planning? Is that why she recognised the Camberwell name when she saw the photograph of Christopher Camberwell?"

"That's what will be going through Bob's mind right now," Nick said, looking up. "I agree, Zelah. You've done the right thing, this time." He stood up. "I have to talk to Stella, tell her about Liverpool." He paused. "There's someone else who either knows or suspects Henry Camberwell."

"Who? Not someone associated with us, I hope. Please tell me that at least," Maggie said.

"Sort of," he replied. "Oliver Rosen. He said something to me about Henry Camberwell last weekend, which I didn't understand at the time, although I knew there was significance to it. When I asked him why he was telling me about a possible connection between Christopher and Henry Camberwell he said '*instinct*'. He said '*an old family business*'. I think he knew, or strongly suspected Henry Camberwell was involved in something dangerous."

"Then why didn't he say so?" Zelah said.

"He's a barrister," Maggie replied. "He wouldn't make such an outright claim without proof. He was guiding Nick." She turned to Nick. "You can't tell him, not yet."

"No, but I will when this is wrapped up."

"Yes, you should. But if there's nothing else, can we leave it for now? This has been more upsetting than I can say and I'm worried for Bob."

"I'm going anyway," Nick said.

"Me, too," Zelah added.

* * *

Maggie didn't see Bob or hear from him until late in the evening. In the meantime, she told Jack about the trip to Liverpool and that Bob would be taking care of him until she got back.

"I don't need taking care of," he said.

"We all need it at some point, son." She smiled at him. "Don't sneer at someone caring about you."

He sighed. "Mum, there's something... I... never mind," he said, shaking his head. "I'm going to my room."

Bob arrived back just before midnight, looking as tired and drawn as Maggie had ever seen him.

"You look dreadful."

"Thanks."

"Have you eaten?"

"No. Is there anything?"

"Yes, I saved some cottage pie."

"I'm starving. Come and sit with me. I'll tell you as much as I can."

She watched him eat, deciding not to tell him he'd get indigestion if he continued to cram in food so fast. When he had scraped the last morsels off the plate he said, "Sherry's gone. All hell broke loose when I passed across the info from Zelah. She's left, her flat's empty of personal stuff."

"How did she know?"

"No idea. It came as a hell of a shock to me this morning. She got wind of it somehow, but I can't think how, unless Zelah's PI got too close."

"We wondered if it was the photograph of Christopher Camberwell. Does it matter, now?"

"Don't know," he replied, yawning. "Will Sharpe is still on the case. He says Camberwell isn't moving yet."

"Did he expect movement?"

Bob stood and stretched his neck. "Yes, he did. They're monitoring his phone, but expect he also has a burner. Nothing from Kennet Quinn, either. Also quiet and not moving from his house and no calls."

"What's next?"

"I'm going to bed, is next. I'm back in at six. Unlikely I'll see you before you leave for Liverpool."

"Take care of Jack. He was going to say something to me earlier."

Bob's eyes narrowed. "What? Did he say something?" he asked, staring at her.

"No, as I said, he changed his mind. Look, what is going on I should know about?"

"Nothing. Come on, I need to sleep." She didn't move so he shrugged a shoulder and left her standing in the kitchen.

In the morning he was gone without waking her. Jack seemed more cheerful when Maggie saw him off. She now had the morning to kill before meeting Nick, Stella and Zelah on the train to Liverpool.

It was agreed in advance they would say nothing yet about the situation in Newport and give themselves some space. When they reached the hotel Maggie felt exhausted and decided to take advantage of the swimming pool before having a meal in her room. She couldn't face any more discussions that didn't resolve anything.

The interment was fixed for ten o'clock on Friday morning at the cemetery in Toxteth, not far from the hotel. They arranged to meet John, Jacka, Helen and Trys at the entrance fifteen minutes before the start, to allow them to reach the grave plot in good time.

When they were gathered, they walked together through the pathways, accompanied by a biting wind. A few family members were already there and introductions were made as the cortège appeared at the end of the row and the undertaker's men removed the coffin onto a set of wheels and trundled it towards them. To everyone's surprise, the coffin was followed by two uniformed policemen, who marched in slow step.

On top of the coffin was a single set of white roses. John had already explained this was Lizzy's grave, so she and William would be reunited at last. The ceremony was simple. A priest, informed of the story, said a few prepared words, then Jacka read out a poem. Maggie could see tears in his eyes. The end was marked by John leading the singing of one verse of 'Abide With Me'. He had a beautiful voice that projected through the bitter cold and wind and echoed around the great open space.

Maggie thought it was the most moving funeral she had been to in a long time.

Back at the family house they shrugged out of coats, hats, gloves, boots and shoes, and fell on the mugs of hot tea made by John's wife and daughter. More relatives were gathered in the house, some too elderly to brave the outdoor conditions, including Jacka's brother Norman. They were introduced to the visitors and chatted away over the tea and biscuits for an hour or so.

When Maggie saw an opportunity to approach John she asked, "What was with the two policemen?"

He smiled. "We weren't supposed to tell anyone outside the family and you guys, but I decided to tell Merseyside Police. After all, they did wrong, back then. I gave them a brief outline of the story and told them about the re-interment. It was a token gesture of recognition, I guess. Nice, though."

Nick joined them. "I thought you must have done. Do they understand the story will be public?"

"Yes, I told them. It was a long time ago." He glanced over at Jacka, who was chatting to Helen. "Those two get on like a house on fire. They're going to do some research together, about that servant bloke, Evans.

They've decided he may have been the one who helped bury William and who pushed John McRoberts into the path of the tram."

"They may well be right," Maggie said. "Tell them to look at the probate for Ebenezer Evans. He had more money that he should have had. Suggest they check through the servants' wages books. They should be able to put the story together."

"Great idea, thanks Maggie," John said, leaving her to talk to his father and Helen Wyn Davies.

Zelah was conversing with John's wife and his brother, talking about Maze and the stories of some of the other cases they were dealing with. She detached herself from the group and joined them. "Almost time to go. Lunch will be ready."

The relatives were already dispersing and when they were gone, John left his wife and daughter to clear up and the lunch group departed for the hotel.

Zelah had booked a private room and after they had eaten, Maggie called for silence.

"I guess this is the last time we'll be together," she began. "Which is both good and sad. I think, I hope John and Jacka believe justice has been done for their ancestors." Jacka rapped three times on the table and nodded. She went on, "Helen and Trys can carry on with the redevelopment of their old home. For us at Maze, it's the end of this story, but you don't have the full details. Nick is now going to tell you. Some of it is not pretty. In fact, pretty ugly. We are going to give you everything, even though some of it is currently coming to a head in South Wales. Some of this will not be ours to tell, but may become public via the police. We trust you implicitly not to speak of these details until we're confident it's OK to do so."

She sat and Nick stood up. In the following minutes he recited the full story, from the beginning when they received their first, unrelated yet vital, piece of information from Ada Blackstock, through the discovery of Christopher Camberwell's terrible deeds and actions, the discovery of the fate of Elsie Doughty, to the imminent arrest of Henry Camberwell at some point during the coming weekend.

"Some of this is more than shocking. But, for me, it shows we must always do what is right, not what is easy. John and Jacka, thank you for your hospitality and your enthusiasm. The same for Trys and Helen. Many people would have turned away. You stepped up. There have been unexpected consequences of this dreadful discovery in both the past and the present. But good has come out of it. And we have reached the end of this particular case." He sat down.

There were nods amidst the ensuing silence, then Helen said, "What about Elsie? Does she have to remain buried in a pauper's grave? Can we not do something?"

"It will be up to her family," Nick replied. "I've had an initial conversation with one of them. It's been upsetting for them, not what they'd been led to believe down through the years."

Helen scowled. "Not nearly as upsetting as it was for that poor child." She paused and glanced at Trystan, who nodded. "Please let me have the relatives' details. I will speak to them. She deserves better. We will pay any costs of exhumation and re-interment, if it's a possibility."

"Helen, that's a wonderful gesture," Maggie said. "I wish you luck, we all do."

Jacka took Helen's hand and kissed it.

"Now," Zelah said, "I'm sorry to say it's time for us to leave. We have a train to catch."

A taxi was waiting to take them to Lime Street station. They said their goodbyes, repeated promises of keeping in touch and making sure everyone approved Zelah's story before it went to print.

"If you get press attention you don't want, remember to refer them on to us," Nick said to John.

A few last hugs and they left the hotel to go their separate ways.

* * *

As their train home was just short of Cwmbran station Maggie picked up a text from Bob. "He wants us to come to the house before anyone goes home. Something must have happened."

Nick, Stella and Zelah looked dismayed. "Can't it wait until tomorrow? Ask him, please," Zelah asked Maggie.

"OK, I'm tired, too. I want to put my PJs on and sit in front of the fire before I go to bed." The reply came back in seconds. "He says no. There's a taxi waiting at Cwmbran station. Damn it."

Just after ten, cold and tired, they filed into the house.

"In here," Bob called out from the lounge. Maggie went in first to find Bob and Jack and the back of the head of someone else, a young man who turned around. Nick stopped in his tracks, Stella walking into his back.

"Max," he said. The boy nodded.

They stared at the tall, blond-haired, well-built young man, who remained silent. Maggie was watching Jack, who looked pale and fearful.

"What's going on?" she said to Bob, a crawling feeling in her gut.

He stood up. "Kennet Quinn is dead. He was murdered some time earlier today."

311

Chapter 40

Twenty-four Hours Earlier

Kennet Quinn put his phone down on his desk and raged. No-one had ever spoken to him in such an unacceptable way. No-one should, not if they knew what was good for them.

He stared at it for a few moments then picked it up again and hit a number, which was answered on the first ring.

"Maxwell, get here now." The call ended. He didn't require a response.

As he waited, somewhere in the house the baby was crying. At first it didn't impact on his thoughts except as irritating background noise. Then he realised it wasn't stopping. He stood up, went to the door and shouted, "Helen?" There was no reply. The crying continued, the mewing and squalling of a distressed baby not receiving the attention it needed. Identifying the source as the nursery, he walked up the stairs and into James Rufus' room. As he bent over the baby his nose wrinkled at the smell and grimaced in disgust. Not just a dirty nappy; James had been sick. The child was a mess and Kennet abhorred mess, of any kind. He took the baby over to a changing mat, pulled on a pair of nitrile gloves and began to tend to him. As he was finishing he heard the front door opening and closing. He picked James up and made his way downstairs.

"Mr Quinn?" a voice called from the office.

"Maxwell," he said, walking in and depositing the baby in a crib. He went to his desk and sat, pursing his lips, as Max Howell hovered in front of him, a child expecting to be told off. "Your father has caused a serious problem. The time has come. I need him removed. This is what you wanted."

Kennet expected the young man to respond with enthusiasm. He was puzzled as he watched for the change of expression that did not come.

"Something wrong, Maxwell? Something you should tell me? I presume all is satisfactory at the warehouse. The delivery this morning went smoothly, I think."

"Well enough, Mr Quinn. But..." The boy licked his lips. "I've changed my mind about this job. I'm resigning. I didn't realise..." His voice tailed off and he looked around the room, left and right, away from Kennet.

"You do not resign from my employ." Kennet stood up. "I am disappointed, Maxwell. I didn't think you were squeamish."

"Some of them are just little girls, Mr Quinn." He shook his head. "I don't want to be involved with this." He turned around and began to walk to the door.

"Do not leave this room, Maxwell."

Despite his determination, Max could feel his heart hammering, his palms sweating. He was still a few steps away from the door, too far to get out safely. He glanced around over his shoulder, half expecting to see a weapon but there was none. Kennet was smiling.

"You believe you can leave and that will be the end of it?" Kennet shook his head "It will be the beginning. You will never feel safe again. You will always be in fear of my being somewhere nearby, waiting to harm you." The speech was delivered in a muted tone and Max had to concentrate to hear what Kennet was saying. He gulped but knew he had to stick to the plan. Hit Kennet on his weak spot.

"She'll get you first. She's coming for you. There's a full moon tonight." He saw Kennet hesitate, a tiny backward pull of his head causing a momentary hesitation, and took his chance. He opened the door and begun to step through when Kennet shouted, "Stop there," but before anything could happen the front door opened. Helen Redland walked into the office and stopped dead, staring from one man to the other.

"Something wrong, boys?"

"Maxwell has resigned," Kennet said. "The work does not satisfy him."

She shook her head. "No, no, that won't do. Too late, Max. Tell you what, go now and come back in the morning. We can discuss this further. In the meantime, if you value your own safety, I cannot support you unless you get back to the warehouse. Now."

Max gave her what he hoped was a crushed look, nodded and left.

"That's how you deal with them, Kennet," she said, smiling casually, strolling over to look at the baby. "They need to understand the alternatives are so much worse. This boy understands."

"You do not give orders in this house, Helen."

She smiled at him again and left the room.

* * *

Outside Max jumped down the steps and ran across the road to the waiting car. He got into the passenger seat, put his hands in his head and said, "I'm going to throw up."

"Not in this car you don't. Let's get out of here, quick. We'll get somewhere where you can puke if you need to and you can tell us what just happened. I'm guessing you told him?"

Max managed a nod.

"Right, let's go." Jack gunned Zelah's car into gear and sped off.

* * *

"Of course you can't go back there in the morning. Kennet will kill you. He won't hesitate now he sees you as a threat to him."

"But if I don't go, he'll realise something's seriously wrong and move the girls."

"If he tries we'll have to move in early. It's a risk but we can't lose track of them," Will Sharpe said.

Max folded his arms. "I'm going back there in the morning. Don't try to stop me."

Bob walked over to sit next to him. "We can be there, outside, but we can't guarantee your safety."

Max nodded.

"I'll go in with him," Jack said from the background.

"No, you will not," Bob replied. "You've done a fantastic thing, both of you. But you," he said pointing at Jack, "will keep out of it now."

"OK, let's discuss how this might go. Maxwell, you are going to wear a heavy parka overcoat with a stab vest underneath, don't argue," Will Sharpe said.

"I wasn't going to."

* * *

At eight the following morning, as Maggie, Zelah, Nick and Stella were starting breakfast at the hotel in Liverpool, Zelah's car, driven by Jack, pulled up outside the Quinn house.

They decided Jack should drive, so if anyone in the house saw him arrive he could say a 'mate' had given him a lift.

The street was full of police vehicles, and armed officers were already at the back of the house. Others were waiting close to the front entrance.

"Remember to speak clearly for the microphone," Will Sharpe said in Max's ear.

"Anything even slightly wrong, get out, run," Jack said. Max nodded.

He paused for a moment, closed his eyes, then opened them. "Off I go, then."

He got out of the car and walked to the front step. As he got there the door opened. Helen Redland stood in the doorway, dressed in a coat, scarf, gloves and hat. She opened the door wide.

"In you go," she said. "He's in the living room. You'll need this." She pushed something into his hands, trotted down the steps and set off up the hill at a brisk pace.

Max was now in the hallway. Looking down, he found he was holding a long butcher's knife. Without thinking he glanced at the open living room door and took a couple of steps forward into the room.

Kennet Quinn was lying on the floor in front of the fire, in a pool of blood. Max went over to stand above him. Kennet's eyes were open, staring.

"Oh my God, oh God," Max muttered. Voices shouted in his ear. He didn't say any more and within seconds, it seemed, the room was full of police, shouting, running around the house. He dropped the knife and looked at his hands. They were covered in blood. Someone took him by the shoulder and walked him out of the room.

"Come on, boyo," Bob Pugh said to him. "Let's get out of here, let these guys do their job. Are you hurt?"

Max shook his head.

"I didn't think so. Let's go back to the station. We heard, of course, but you can tell me everything, OK?"

Max nodded.

"Good boy. Come on. Jack's still outside, having a hissy fit, I expect. He can drive us back."

Gently, Bob led him out of the house and into Zelah's car.

From somewhere in the house a baby was screaming at the top of its lungs.

Chapter 41

"She planned it all, of course," Bob said to the stunned group sitting around the fire. "She was the brains behind the scheme, not Kennet, although he never realised he was just the patsy. Fortunately for us, she hadn't figured out Max had come to the police. She planned to make it appear Max was responsible for Kennet's death. She stabbed him multiple times. Max has been exceptionally brave."

"Where is she now?" Maggie asked.

"That's the bad news. There was a car waiting for her, parked a few yards away up the hill. She got in and they drove off."

"Sherry Martin, I guess," Maggie said.

"Yes, she was the driver. There was someone else in the car, though. Another woman. We don't know yet who she was. There's a national search for them. We'll get them, soon enough."

Throughout Bob's recital Nick had been staring at Max, who hadn't yet looked at or acknowledged any of them.

"How are you involved in this, Jack?" Nick asked.

"I'd like to know, too," Maggie said, glaring at Bob.

"Don't give Bob that look," Jack replied. "I started this. Nick, you decided, when you found out Max was working for Kennet Quinn, you would leave it to fate to decide what would happen between you. I thought 'sod that'. Fate needed a kick up the arse. So me and my mates went out to look for him. We found him in a bar in Newport. He was totally pissed. We got him back to his digs. I went back again the next day, told him who I was and he told me about what was going on. He hated it. I told Bob. Max agreed to help the police."

"This is what you and Bob have been talking about this week," Maggie said. "It wasn't about your girlfriend."

"She's history," Jack replied. "We did talk about her, last week. Bob was right. I dumped her. Look," he said, turning to Nick, "you two need to talk. I've told Max you aren't the bad guy, but sometimes you think too much."

"Max," Nick said. "Will you talk to me? We have a great deal to explain to each other."

Max turned to stare at his father. "Yes. A conversation, for now."

"Can we go now?" Nick asked Bob.

"Yes, I don't see why not. Max, we'll need you again tomorrow. Nine sharp at Newport station."

Max nodded and said to Nick, "Let's go."

After Nick, Stella and Max left and Jack asked to be allowed to go to bed, Maggie said to Zelah, "You've been quiet."

"What have I got to add? Am I sorry about Kennet being killed? No, I am not. Good riddance. What's done is done. My mind is several steps ahead. I'm thinking about the remaining Quinns, what this will mean for them."

"Of course. Mischa."

"And Michelle and Gerry. And what about the baby, Bob?"

"Social services have taken him into care."

"She just walked out on him," Maggie said. "What an evil woman."

"The baby was never more than a bargaining chip," Bob replied. "Helen used it – him – to get into Kennet's organisation. She was the one who introduced Henry Camberwell and proposed the sex slavery scheme."

"What about those girls, Bob?"

"Being taken care of. The youngest was twelve." He shuddered. "Will Sharpe is pursuing Henry Camberwell, but when Sherry saw your investigation into Christopher Camberwell she told him to beware if you found him, Henry, which you did. They realised it might go wrong and abandoned the scheme and the girls."

"Is Henry Camberwell off the hook?" Maggie asked.

"Will Sharpe will do his best, but it's not looking good."

Zelah stood up. "Right, I'm going home. What an interesting day this has been. And not all bad. When can I talk to Mischa?"

"As soon as you like."

"I'm going to tell her when I get home. She can decide what she wants to do. Who will formally identify Kennet?"

"Mischa will have to come back to do it. She's his closest living relative."

"Actually, it's Michelle; they haven't divorced," Zelah replied. "Let's leave it now. I'll call you when I've spoken to Mischa."

When it was finally just the two of them, Bob turned to Maggie. "I expect you're angry with me for not telling you what Jack did."

"Actually, no. Surprisingly, I'm not. Mind you, if anything had happened to him..."

"Well, that's a relief. How did it go in Liverpool?"

"Rather well... Let's go to bed. I'll tell you all about it. There's a lot of talking to do this weekend."

Three Months Later

Lockdown

At least it was warm and they could go into the garden for much needed space and distance.

Living with teenagers had, at times, driven Maggie to despair, but she was honest enough to guess sometimes she drove them nuts, too. Her nieces had also made her home their base, as her sister Fiona had decamped to Spain and become stuck there, expressing not a word of gratitude to Maggie for taking care of her daughters.

To help them cope she bought an additional fifty-inch TV screen, set up a Zoom account, and turned the attic into a Zoom room and lounge. Jack and Alice could use their own computers, of course, but when they wanted a big group session, as Alice did with her school friends every couple of days, it worked well. Jade, Lucy and Sophie loved it, too.

Alice's friend Matthew had not gone to Italy and his parents thanked Alice personally for her 'foresight'. To Alice's credit, she hadn't been smug. She was disappointed she would not be allowed to take the early GCSEs she had been looking forward to, but was trying to be philosophical about it, as she explained daily to Maggie and Bob.

Jack, however, was horrified to discover that, in addition to not attending college, he would not be able to take his exams and there was no news yet about his university place, nor how it would be determined. He had been talking lately about taking a gap year and travelling, with Max Howell, who was now a close friend. If that was even going to be possible.

Max and Nick were managing something of a relationship, but not an easy or settled one. It was clear there were many issues to work through and Max would not be comfortable in the relationship for some time yet. He had talked about travelling and Jack responded with enthusiasm, but not Nick and Maggie.

Zelah had caught the last boat to Ireland in March and remained there.

Maze had, to Maggie's amazement, gained more business in the past three months than in the previous year and her 'brick wall' cases were piling up. It was helped by Zelah's exquisitely written story about William McRoberts, which attracted national and international attention. Lockdown had proved a blessing for John and Jacka, neither of whom wanted to be interviewed by the press, claiming neither of them could manage the remote technology. Interest had now waned, but at the time was sensational enough to have clients flooding in.

Henry Camberwell had not been arrested. In the end there was insufficient evidence. Kennet Quinn had been the main contact and with his death there was little of substance. Helen Redland had been the behind-the-scenes organiser and manipulator. She had still not been found. Nor Sherry Martin. Bob hoped, when lockdown was eased, it would be easier to search for them.

Today the temperature was approaching thirty-one degrees and Alice had spent the day talking about global warming. It was now late afternoon and Maggie felt able to venture out into the garden. Bob was already there. As a key worker, he hadn't stopped work during lockdown. She also felt unbelievably lucky none of them had caught the virus. One of her neighbours was seriously ill, in hospital on a ventilator for many weeks, and was still touch-and-go.

"Any news of George?" Bob asked as she put down a cold drink for each of them.

"No, nothing. Mary says he's holding his own, but she looks haggard." She glanced over at the dark canal. "I am tempted to jump over the fence and put my feet in," she said.

Bob laughed. "I wouldn't trust that water. Who knows what's swimming about in there? How's it going?"

"Never been so busy," she said. "The problem is, I have to rely on the internet. It's good, but I need to go out to archives and libraries, etcetera. Frustrating. How much longer will this go on?"

"A long time. Don't expect a quick end. What we knew as 'normal' is gone. Maybe forever." He paused for a moment. "Malky Thomas' mate Jez pleaded guilty on the advice of his solicitor, so no big trial."

"Oh. How long will he be in gaol for?"

"Sentencing is in a few weeks. Case will be officially closed."

"Are you OK with that, Bob?"

He picked up his drink and took a long swig. "No. I still think there was a third one in the car, but Jez won't admit anyone else was there." He banged the bottle back down on the table.

Maggie was about to ask him if he had any idea who it might have been but some deeper instinct told her not to ask.

She sighed. "And still nothing about Helen Redland and Sherry Martin?"

"No, they've disappeared. My guess, as you know, is they got away abroad; we're thinking over to Ireland possibly then on by ferry to France."

"Yes, but I can't understand why you think that."

He tapped the side of his nose.

"Yes, instinct. Copper's nose," she said. "This won't end until they are dealt with."

"We'll get them, in the end. We've still no proof the third woman was Emer McCarthy Miller but I suspect Zelah is right. We do believe she'd been working with them for some time."

"Well, I'm trying to not think about them at all. I did some more research about the Spanish Civil War today. I'm hoping we can still get to Catalonia when the travel embargo is lifted."

"Have you got anywhere?"

"Not much further yet. But... I got an enquiry today. I don't know why, but it made me think about Catalonia. It was a strange feeling. It's from a family in Scotland whose ancestor disappeared suddenly in 1938. There's no suggestion he went to Spain. But something gave me a gut reaction, you know?"

"I know," he said. "And when you get it you should go with it."

"Copper's instinct," she said, holding up her glass and clinking it against his. "Here's to the third of Claire Lewis' three leads."

* * *

As the sun left the evening sky and a darker blue brought out the first stars, twenty miles south of Mont Saint-Michel, three women sat around a fire pit in a garden in the grounds of a traditional Normandy villa.

One of them sat forward and poked the embers with a stick.

"Put some more wood on it," Helen Redland said.

Sherry Martin obliged. "I'm fed up with this," she said, staring into the fire. "I want to get at them, especially the creepy little kid."

"Patience, cuz. It will end. Stay focussed. Then we can get back and carry on. But keep away from the kid when you get back. Stick to the plan." Helen turned to the third woman. "Any more ideas?"

"Our plans are well-laid," said a soft Irish voice. "Nothing more to do but wait this out. I've waited long enough, longer than both of you."

"I'm sorry about your mother," Sherry said.

"Thank you, but she was completely barking by the end. Better off dead," Emer McCarthy Miller replied and flicked back her long, formerly blond, now dark brown hair. She turned to Helen. "Any news of your toy boy?"

"No," Helen said. "He turned out to be a big disappointment. I don't understand why they didn't arrest him after I gave him the knife. I expect he did a deal with them. Sherry's quite sure he wasn't part of any set up, aren't you, cuz?"

"His name never came up, at any point. I would have known."

"Shame," Emer said. "Inside information would have been useful. Would be worth contacting him when you get back? From what you've told us it was pretty steamy and he was well smitten."

Helen put her head on one side. "Depends on what happened to him. But if he got away with it, I might be able to spin him a story. He was pretty stupid."

"Worth a try, maybe. We have time to decide," Emer said. "But, never mind, sisters. We can do what we need to do. Without the help of men."

The three laughed and sat back, watching the fire crackle as the sky darkened.

* * *

To be continued in *The Soldier* – Summer 2021

Historical Information - Josephine Butler

This is a work of fiction and the leading characters and the historical characters are fictional, except for Josephine Butler and her husband.

In researching information for this book about the horrific practices in Victorian times of the enticing away and kidnapping of young women and girls from poor backgrounds and transporting them to brothels in the UK and Europe, I came across Josephine Butler, nee Grey, born in 1828. Within a short time of reading about her, I realised the significance of her contribution to the human and civil rights of women in Victorian Britain and ever since.

She seems to have been a modest woman, small in stature and often poor in health, but in every other way, a giant in the fight for women's liberties.

Josephine Grey came from a well-to-do middle-class Christian family who believed in social reform in practical ways and in her husband Dr George Butler she found shared values and a kindred spirit. George became Head of a school in Liverpool, and it was there Josephine, following the tragic death of her daughter, became involved in women's rights. She supported prostitutes, never judging them. She understood the circumstances of Victorian women abused and abandoned, left with a family to care for with no means of help or support, who took to selling themselves to save their families from starvation. She helped them to escape and move on, and gain access to education and work. She was a champion of women's education and became President of the North of England Council for Promoting the Higher Education of Women.

Josephine's work, not only in Britain but throughout Europe, speaking out against under-age prostitution, led to the founding in London of a committee to suppress 'white slave traffic'.

She also became Secretary of the Ladies' National Association for the Repeal of the Contagious Diseases Act. This vile legislation was introduced in the 1860s to reduce venereal disease and regulate prostitution. It was known to the women as 'steel rape'. Mainly in garrison towns, Police could take in any woman and force her to be examined, sometimes on a weekly basis and it was much abused and subject to corruption. The women reported it as 'agony', but if they did not submit, they would be detained until they did agree to it, often leaving their vulnerable families without food and aid. No action was ever taken against their clients.

A woman of her social class exposing such practices and confronting Victorian sexual taboos was considered at the time shocking and scandalous, but nothing deterred her. Thanks to her persistence the Act was finally repealed in 1886.

She was a mesmerising speaker, by all accounts.

In her later life, following George's death, she increasingly lobbied for Women's suffrage and supported Irish home rule.

I hope the way in which I have portrayed her in this book, although entirely fictional, is both respectful and honest and shines much deserved light on the unique person she was. I remain in awe and admiration of Josephine Butler's achievements.

If you want to read more about this amazing woman, there are two excellent biographies:

Josephine Butler by Jane Jordan

Patron Saint of Prostitutes – Josephine Butler and a Victorian Scandal by Helen Mathers

Thanks and Acknowledgements!

As always, producing a book involves many people, without whose help, expert advice and encouragement I would struggle.

My first readers, Cheryl, Joy and Rose. Plot holes spotted; excellent suggestions made for improvement.

I have worked with a new editor this time, Louise at Refine Fiction, who has done a brilliant job.

Thanks also to Alison Morgan at Ali-Cat Design for the fabulous cover.

As always, my family, especially Stewart and Alice, for unfailing reassurance and support and emergency IT interventions!

Thank You for Reading This Book.

If you enjoyed it, please leave feedback on Amazon and/or Goodreads and if I have missed anything, then please get in touch.
You can leave me feedback by email on:
mary@mkjonesauthor.com

Maze Investigations has its own website:
www.mkjonesauthor.com and its own Facebook page. I have an author page on Goodreads, where you will be able to read my blog about the next book in the Maze series, The Soldier.
And if you can't wait, you can always catch up with the stories of other cases the Maze Investigation team tackle between the books. These are available when you sign up for my newsletter on the website. You will receive two immediately as a thanks for signing up:
"The Missing Air Raid Warden 1941"
and
"Murder in the Family 1840s"

Following these there will be a new one with each monthly newsletter, in the form a report by one of the Maze Investigators.

Happy reading!

* *

Guess What – I Hate Typos Too!
But sometimes they get through. If you find an error, please send it to me at:
mary@mkjonesauthor.com

I will get it fixed ASAP.

I am grateful to the eagle-eyed amongst you who take the time to contact me. I want my work to be the best it can be, and your help is invaluable.

Coming: Summer 2021

The Maze Investigators have reached the final
message from the medium Claire Lewis – about a young
Scot who disappeared in 1938, leaving behind only a
strange, enigmatic message, in Spanish. Maggie must

return to Catalonia, to a story heard on her first trip which now has a significance she didn't understand or appreciate at the time and further revelations lead back to Glasgow and a long-hidden crime. Back in Wales, the final confrontation with the Quinn and McCarthy Miller families is looming. There must be a winner.

Printed in Great Britain
by Amazon